The Last Audit

Barry Lazarus

Inkwater Press

Portland · Oregon
inkwaterpress.com

This is a work of fiction. The events described here are imaginary. The settings and characters are fictitious and do not represent specific places or living or dead people. Any resemblance is entirely coincidental.

Copyright © 2008 by Barry Lazarus

Cover & interior designed by Tricia Sgrignoli/Positive Images

Cover photo © JupiterImages Corporation

All rights reserved. No part of this book may be reproduced or transmitted in any form or by any means whatsoever, including photocopying, recording or by any information storage and retrieval system, without written permission from the publisher and/or author. Contact Inkwater Press at 6750 SW Franklin Street, Suite A, Portland, OR 97223-2542. 503.968.6777

www.inkwaterpress.com

ISBN-10 1-59299-364-8
ISBN-13 978-1-59299-364-2

Publisher: Inkwater Press

Printed in the U.S.A.

All paper is acid free and meets all ANSI standards for archival quality paper.

One

Spending the day in court only served to further his transformation, which was already in an advanced state. Auditing public companies had been his life for fourteen years. Defending them had not. Fortunately, he was not the one on trial. But it made him uncomfortable to think that anything he might say could have a negative consequence on a former client, or anyone for that matter. Jail time and multi million dollar fines were at stake. The defense lawyers had meticulously prepared him, explaining that the jury would have trouble understanding complex accounting treatment. The lawyers told him if the jury was having difficulty following his testimony, they would go back over it a little more slowly the second time. This would not be out of character for a white collar trial where the defendants, officers of a public company, were accused of fraud. The same public company his firm had audited. The same public company that was now the subject of intense and very visible scrutiny.

When his turn came, the lead defense counsel said, "the defense calls Johnny Brandt."

He was sworn in and took a seat on the witness stand. It was his first chance to view the entire court room from the front and he could see the collective look of gravity on the faces staring back at him. He was aware that public accounting firms were linked as one with the companies they audited. On this day, he would officially be aiding the defense of those who were on trial in a court of law. Unofficially, he would be defending those who had signed off on their activities. His firm had been relatively lucky to date, as most of the disputes against them were resolved without going to court. Not so for his all of his clients. Twelve people would likely decide the result of today's proceedings, unless a last minute settlement with the government could be reached. For Johnny and some of his partners, the negotiations, depositions and settlements would continue.

The defense lawyer began, "Mr. Brandt, I'd like to familiarize the court with your professional background. Please tell us where you work."

"Billingsly, Carlton and Craig, or BCC in the industry. We're a public accounting firm."

"Thank you, Mr. Brandt. And can you explain to the court when and how your firm began its relationship with the defendants in this case?"

"Yes. About five years ago Zircon Industries, the defendant's employer, decided to list their stock on a public exchange. They needed an accounting firm that could provide an audit for their SEC required reports. Only certain of the largest public accounting firms are qualified to do that and BCC is one of them. We began our relationship then."

"I see," said defense counsel, "and please give the court some background on yourself, personally."

"I've been in public accounting all my professional Life. I graduated from the University of Illinois in 1986 and received a master's degree from Northwestern University in 1988. I'm a certified public accountant."

The crowd gathered in the federal courtroom in downtown Chicago started to look bored. They didn't come to hear about him, rather what he would tell them regarding the criminal allegations against the defendants. But establishing his qualifications as a witness was a necessity.

"And you've been with BCC since you graduated from Northwestern?"

"That's correct," replied Johnny.

"And what was your involvement regarding the Zircon audit?"

"I was what's known as the review partner."

"Please explain to the court what that means," Counsel lead him.

"It means I didn't supervise the audit, but I reviewed the results before the firm gave an opinion on the financial statements."

"Mr. Brandt we've already heard testimony from Andrew McFarland who was the partner in charge of the 2000 audit of Zircon. Would it be fair to say in your position as audit review partner, you were also familiar with the financial condition of Zircon?"

"Yes."

"Now, sir I want to take you back about a year to the time you reviewed the results of the audit."

The courtroom crowd regained its focus and defense counsel began asking questions concerning specific accounting treatment on Zircon's financial statements. They had heard much of this already when McFarland was on the witness stand. Johnny was there to support his testimony and provide clarification as necessary.

The charges were leveled by the government against the three top Zircon executives, the chief executive officer, the president and the chief financial officer. As with most companies in the technology industry in the 1990's, Zircon was in trouble by 2000. Johnny's area of expertise was technology and he rode the wave of apparent success with his clients. He had become a firm mover and shaker at BCC and made junior partner by the age of thirty two. Now, in 2002 at the age of 38, he was more into damage control. Today was no different.

When the defense counsel had finished with Johnny, the government's lawyer began his cross examination. He stood slowly and looked around the courtroom for effect. He sneered at Johnny as he spoke. "Mr. Brandt, do you expect the jury to believe the defendants followed generally accepted accounting principals by not reporting almost $100 million in debt on their balance sheet?"

The faces in the courtroom wanted an answer as well.

"Yes, under certain conditions a lease is not considered debt and is not reported as such."

"And do tell us, Mr. Brandt what those conditions are?"

The defense lawyers had told Johnny not to stray into specifics, so he repeated the line he had been given, trying not to sound too rehearsed. "The leases entered into by Zircon didn't violate criteria established by the profession allowing for exclusion from their balance sheet. They simply reported the results based on their interpretation of acceptable accounting treatment. We had no basis for disputing their presentation, but we did require them to disclose the nature of the lease transaction in the footnotes." Johnny realized he sounded like an accountant as he finished. Who was he kidding?

The faces didn't like this answer, but it was true.

The government lawyer was all over him. "What does that mean?"

Johnny saw an opening. He paused for a second and looked earnestly at the jury as he spoke. His response was completely unrehearsed and surprised even him. "It means they didn't break any rules, period."

The accounting profession had made a good faith effort to keep financial reporting as transparent as possible. It was never possible to anticipate all of trends in any industry, so some of their pronouncements were reactionary. At times this left gaps and, for some, opportunities. A heady business environment can cover bad judgment. For a while. Besides, it seemed very few people read the small print which was plentiful in the public company reports.

The prosecuting lawyer asked him a few more meaningless questions and then he was done with Johnny. The faces nodded their approval as he walked from the stand and out of the court room. The trial was already going badly for the government and their lawyer was really fishing by the time he got to Johnny.

He didn't have enough time to make it back to his office and get to the train station on time for the commute to his suburban home. He was drained from giving testimony anyway, especially from worrying about saying the wrong thing. He was pretty sure he had done well, but the lawyers would tell him tomorrow.

If the trial served any purpose for him, it was to help keep Johnny's mind off of his other problems. His walk to the train station changed that. The gray sky and light drizzle were appropriate accompaniment on his march with the other commuters who worked in Chicago's 'loop'. The 'loop' as its known, is a few square miles of dense office buildings located inside an ancient circle of elevated train track, defining a dynamic financial district. With the trial over, Johnny would be free to serve his few remaining clients and try to finish up the loose ends related to BCC's former tech company work. If he had ridden the wave up, he was surely in the middle of its crash to earth. A senior partnership seemed far away now. Even a bright man like Johnny was not prepared to deal with the reality of a stalled career as he approached midlife.

"Hey," the voice called, waking him from his sleep walk. Scott Borden, Investech's chief financial officer had spent considerable effort catching up to Johnny and appeared slightly out of breath. Scott's round face and happy blue eyes were moist from the drizzle.

"I didn't get a chance to say thanks for the help on the Intercontinent financials. I've already got one of our analysts putting together a spread sheet."

"Glad I could help," Johnny responded. Investech underwrote or sponsored many high tech firms as they attempted to raise capital on Wall Street. Some of Investech's clients were Johnny's as well. He was happy to help, enjoyed working with Scott and had, at times, been able to expedite the process.

They talked briefly about Intercontinental as they reached the middle of train depot. As they parted to catch their separate trains, Scott said to Johnny, "Let's get together for lunch next week."

Not wanting to sound too available Johnny responded, "OK. If we make it about mid-week it should be doable."

Scott told Johnny he would call him on Tuesday. As soon as the conversation ended Johnny retreated back into his mind. Often Johnny would get one of the last open seats on the train, next to the aisle, and hold his brief case on his lap. Not that he really needed the brief case much these days. But it did complete his wardrobe for the ride to and from the Loop. It was mid April and, judging from the number of completely open seats, a lot of people were on spring vacation with their children. With his choice of where to sit, Johnny put his briefcase down on an aisle seat and settled in next to the window. He didn't even waste the effort to open his brief case before he turned to look out the window at nothing. Suddenly, against the dark backdrop of the terminal, the lights from above illuminated his face so that he was looking at a distorted reflection of himself in the glass. For just a moment Johnny wasn't sure who he was looking at. Was this the hard charging professional still on his way up? Or, as the image seemed to suggest, a man staving off burnout as he struggled to salvage his career? A career that, for better or worse, Johnny had allowed to define him.

Two

It was by no accident that Maria Brandt was known as 'All A' Maria to her friends. It started in High School where she graduated with nothing less than an A minus in any of her classes, was captain of the cheerleading squad and valedictorian of her senior class. Although she was seriously interested in drama, by the mid 1980's it was clear to her that computer science would be the next glamour profession. It was a time when women were rapidly becoming accepted in the business world and, she believed, computer skills were the ladder which she could climb to the top.

When it came time to decide where she would go to college, it was only a matter of which scholarship she would accept. Northwestern University in Evanston, Illinois seemed like a great choice. It was just far enough from her home in Madison Wisconsin, had high academic standards and was a prestigious big ten school.

It was during her senior year that she noticed Johnny in the computer lab. He came occasionally at first, but after a while he seemed to be almost a regular. Maria, of course, was in the lab all the time so she managed to get the desk of her choice. The one with the best view of the door. Their brief glances at each other became more pronounced and then progressed to full fledged smiles. Eventually, he asked her for help in accessing a program and she was able to give him the right answer. He made a point of finding her in the student union at lunch the next day. He bought an extra desert and as he walked by her table said, "I'll trade you that empty seat next to you for an apple pie." She would have told him to take the seat for nothing, so how could she possibly refuse his offer. When she had seen him in the computer lab she thought he was cute and as they had their first real conversation, she was even more attracted to him. The boyish good looks meshed well with his bright, but unassuming mind.

Their first real date happened a couple of weeks later. It was a Saturday night and it started off at an Italian restaurant with Maria offering to make the reservations and Johnny gladly accepting. The meal began with a glass of wine for both and they talked all through dinner, barely taking their eyes off each other. Afterward, they walked along Sheridan Road on the Northwestern campus as it ran next to Lake Michigan. It was well after midnight before they talked themselves out. On the second date they were joined by several friends and ended up at someone's house playing word games. Maria and Johnny complimented each other well, having fun and not taking the games too seriously. After the second date she was sure that she and Johnny were suited for each other intellectually and were at ease together as a couple. Johnny had been a perfect gentleman on both dates, so there was one more level that Maria needed to explore. On the third date she left nothing to chance, wearing an outfit that Johnny would've had to be been blind not to notice and inviting him for dinner, so that he would have every opportunity to make a move. By the end of the third date the important questions had all been answered.

As she thought back over her courtship with Johnny, she remembered their happiest times together had been the summer after she graduated. They rarely left each other's side, except when they were in a prone position together, which was quite often. She and Johnny spent as much time as possible on the Northwestern campus which runs for several miles along Lake Michigan and is a thing of beauty in the summer. They had each achieved their academic goals, had good job offers for the fall, enough money to get them through the summer and not a care in the world. Now, fourteen years later, she loved Johnny as much as she ever had. He had reached his professional potential, gave of himself without hesitation and was a great husband and father. Somewhere over the years they had settled into a life of obligation. Not so much to each other but, it seemed, to everyone and everything else. The obligation extracted its toll. When Johnny's career took a turn for the worse, she could feel him sinking emotionally, but she could do nothing about it. Meanwhile her career was at least temporarily on hold as she raised two young children. At the age of 36, she had become the suburban everywoman. She was comfortable in almost every aspect of her life, but wondered if her happiest years were behind her.

When Johnny arrived home dinner was waiting, but Maria and the kids, five year old Lindsay and three year old Josh were upstairs. Johnny hung up his raincoat and despite his hunger went upstairs to see his family. All three were in the bathroom, where Josh was entering the most unpleasant phase of his bath, the part where he got washed. The timing was perfect. Johnny was greeted with a big hug from Lindsay and a loud "Daddy" from Josh. Maria smiled and gave

Johnny a quick peck on the check. Both were dedicated parents and if they had true emotions that they could share it centered on the kids. Johnny finished washing Josh and capped off the bath by reading his favorite story, *Pinocchio*.

Johnny eventually made it down to a cold dinner while Maria put the kids to bed. He wasn't sure what he would say to her when she came down to join him, but before she did the phone rang and he let her answer it. He couldn't hear what she was saying, but guessed that it was her sister on the phone. If they were planning to shop tomorrow, she could be on for a long time. A reprieve he thought. Any conversation would be a strain on him and it would be better not to say anything.

This would be a long weekend. At work, Johnny's clients had dwindled to a number that kept him busy at less than half the pace he was used to. Then there was the time spent with the lawyers or in negotiations which he filed under the nuisance category. As much as he hated the damage control, at least it helped keep his mind reasonably occupied. Weekends were designed as a mental and physical break from work, but Johnny had never quite mastered the art of the weekend. The demands of public accounting at a big five firm were such that if you didn't come to the office, you took work home. It was not uncommon to be on the phone with clients on a Saturday or even a Sunday. When the technology sector was hot, Johnny would often work twelve hours a day and a good part of the weekend. He got used to it. He relished spending more time with Lindsay and Josh, but had come to the realization that workaholic meant you might not be there physically, but you couldn't get away mentally.

After her call was over, Maria came downstairs and sat next to Johnny who flipped on the TV and was half watching the Cubs. "So how's the auditor today?" she asked.

"Auditing less and enjoying it less" was the response. "I probably spent a total of twenty hours this week doing anything productive. The rest of the time was spent sorting through problems."

"Like what?" Maria tried gently to pull it out of him, if only to help relieve the burden.

"I answered all my questions in court today Mar," Johnny replied gently. "I'm beat and it's late, lets talk tomorrow." 'Mar' had been Johnny's name for Maria since they started dating and she liked the natural way he said it. It made her feel close to him. And more frustrated at her inability to help.

Three

THE OFFICES OF BILLINGSLY Carlton and Craig occupied eight floors in the Gateway Building in the heart of Chicago's most prestigious office district. In the mid 1990's, when BCC's clients seemed to all be doing well, the firm decided it was time to upgrade its rather stogy image by refurbishing its digs. Millions were spent on rich wall treatments, carpet, paint, furniture, state of the art computer equipment and lots of glass so everyone could see the benefits of hard work and success. The senior partners reasoned that successful clients would appreciate being associated with equally competent professionals.

The main reception area was located on the tenth floor and, together with the executive conference room behind it, occupied two floors. You accessed the reception area directly off the elevator and could get to the eleventh floor by walking up a winding stair case. The reception area itself was large and with the volume of two floors felt very open. Comfortable rich looking couches and chairs adjacent to tables with reading material were placed without pattern in the reception room. The receptionist's desk was custom built in the form of a large semi-circle with a raised counter top for resting files which had either been delivered or were waiting to be picked up. Behind the desk on the wall hung a large tapestry with the letters BCC stitched in descending order from top left to lower right.

Monday mornings began with the partners meeting at 8:00 a.m. in the main conference room. Twenty-five partners less anyone who was out of town attended. Bill Lewis, the managing partner of BCC, rarely attended since he found a way to be out of town most of the time. Second in command and one of the three top senior partners was Charles Stein who ran the meetings. To his right sat Andy Van Dyke who had come to the firm through its merger with Carlton and Bennet and, as its senior partner, was given a spot in the brain trust. Charles or "Charlie" Stein was the true professional at the top, the man who probably knew the most about pure accounting, had his pulse on new pronouncements in the industry and was aware of every major audit proceeding at any one time. You called him Charles to his face, but when talking to others in the firm there was only one "Charlie". If Charlie said it, it stuck.

Charlie had been a mentor to Johnny through the early years. When Johnny had reached a certain level of maturity within the profession, their relationship gradually shifted to that of mutual respect. One, the older experienced pro realizing that his protégé had absorbed his lessons well; the younger man grateful for the imparted wisdom. Johnny believed that he could consider himself a success in the industry when, and only when, he reached Charlie's level.

The Monday morning meetings were a forum where the partners discussed the assignments that each was working on. Charlie prepared an agenda and called on each partner to update the group on the progress of the work. Problems were discussed, and if appropriate, partners experienced with similar problems offered their help. If issues needed further attention, they were continued after the meeting in smaller, more focused groups. The Monday morning meetings had become a source of embarrassment for Johnny, since most of the time spent talking about his assignments involved a description of various settlement discussions with former clients' creditors, or attorneys. It was less about accounting and more about survival. Johnny hoped that his partners did not hold him personally responsible for the serious position the firm was in, but he knew there was a certain guilt by association in the air.

After the meeting ended, Charlie caught Johnny by the door and asked him to come to his office in about an hour. This meant more of the same, since Charlie and Andy were with him on all of the important decisions concerning legal matters or settlements. At shortly before 11:00 a.m., Johnny took the elevator to the fifteenth floor and knocked on Charlie's door. Charlie's office measured about 25 by 30 feet and included a conference table where several people could sit comfortably. As he entered, he saw three people look up at him, all with measurable concern on their faces. There were Charlie, Andy Van Dyke and Warner Simmons, BCC's chief counsel.

"Come on in and sit down Johnny" Charlie offered with only a hint of friendliness in his voice. The others watched silently as Johnny moved to the conference table and took the seat across from Warner.

It occurred to Johnny, at that point, the normal procedure for these types of discussions involved Johnny bringing his files on the particular case to be discussed. He had not been asked to do so for this meeting. Something new and different was in the air. The only thing that kept Johnny from feeling panicky was that Bill Lewis was not in the room. He wondered if Bill was really out of town and hoped this meeting was just too unimportant for him to attend.

Charlie continued, "Johnny, Warner here got a call from the lawyers for some of the shareholders at WestPac Industries last week. Seems they want to come here on Wednesday and have a meeting. According to their lawyers, they're saying we knowingly overstated Frontier's earnings on the 2000 year end audit."

WestPac had bought the stock of Frontier Data Systems Corp., in part based on the results of the audit BCC had conducted. Shortly thereafter Frontier disclosed huge losses related to their on-line sales order system. When the system was developed, it was considered a breakthrough for Frontier's clients who were mostly in the heavy manufacturing industry. The system allowed the sales representatives for Frontier's clients to do a rough design of any product in the field. The design could then be emailed simultaneously to different divisions at the home office where specifications were run on-line, and the product priced and scheduled for production in a fraction of the time it had previously taken. For more complex designs, instead of waiting for rough drawings, the emailed design could be submitted to a team who could finish the work and fast track production. For this, WestPac had paid close to five billion dollars in a highly controversial stock for stock acquisition that did not sit well with some of its shareholders. When Frontier ran into major problems with reliability of its software, the stock of WestPac reeled and there were rumors of a possible class action suit by its shareholders. Now, someone was looking for a place to spread the blame.

"That's ridiculous," was all Johnny could muster when Charlie had finished. "They did all their own independent evaluations."

"Yes, of course they did," Warner spoke for the first time, "but their lawyers seem to believe that some people at this firm benefited personally when the merger went through."

"What do you mean?" asked Johnny.

"They believe," Warner went on, "we misused our inside information and violated firm and SEC rules. They're saying members of this firm knew there were problems with Frontier's software and assisted in artificially valuing the company, for their own benefit."

"This looks like another classic case of finding deep pockets to help pay for the mistakes their board and senior management made," was Johnny's almost causal reply.

"We all agreed, at first, Johnny," said Charlie," but West-Pac's lawyers want to come here and show us a small part of their case, so we'll take them seriously."

"Fine," said Johnny, "they're wasting their time."

"By the way, Johnny," Andy spoke for the first time, "you might be interested in knowing who they're they're insinuating might guilty of criminal activity."

"Who?" asked Johnny.

"You."

Four

IN HIS TWELVE YEARS as a member of the group of three executive partners at BCC, Charles Stein had never been threatened with a criminal action against the firm, or one of its partners. He considered the depth of the accusation by the lawyers representing WestPac's shareholders. They were no doubt looking for any and every possible place to lay blame and in the current business environment, auditing firms were becoming an easy target. He had heard of criminal charges being threatened against other firms when the government was involved, but to the best of his knowledge, no one had ever actually been convicted.

Nevertheless, Charles considered the matter serious enough to call Bill Lewis in New York. At the age of 61, Bill was three years Charles' senior and would end up casting the deciding vote if one were needed, regardless of the matter. Bill maintained all of the important relationships necessary to run a global accounting firm of BCC's stature. He believed it was his responsibility to nurture these relationships by personal contact on a regular basis. His list of friends and acquaintances read like a who's who of influential people, not necessarily limited to the profession. While

Bill was pursuing BCC's business on the outside, Charles essentially ran the firm on the inside. Bill was the politician while Charles was the tactician. This arrangement bothered Charles not in the slightest. He took pride in the quality of work produced by the firm. Bill made sure that business kept coming through the door, and Charles saw to it that the work that went out the door measured up to or exceeded industry standards. This was becoming more difficult all the time.

Bill and Charles agreed on several things regarding WestPac. First, all threats of the nature of WestPac's needed to be taken very seriously. Second, when their lawyers came to town, all three of the managing partners would be present at the meeting. They agreed that it would probably be better to keep Johnny out of the first meeting. The fewer people who knew about the specifics of the criminal accusations, the better. Both men had trouble believing that Johnny could be guilty of any form of illegal activity. But WestPac's lawyers had a reputation for being ruthless. And would they really fly in from San Francisco to level an idle threat? Charles believed that business, and the world for that matter, had become a much more dangerous place over the past twelve years. He wasn't convinced that it was purely by coincidence. In many instances, risk was structured so that it could be spread a mile wide and an inch deep. No matter who you were, it was hard not to fall in somewhere along the line.

Johnny left Charles' office in a hurry, his head spinning as he worked his way to the elevator. Rather than go back to his office, he rode down to lobby and stopped at the snack bar. He needed to compose himself before facing anyone. The conversation he had just been involved in left him angry more than anything else. Just when he saw some hope that the worst was over, he was now likely to become the target of a very public controversy. He had done nothing wrong, but might well pay the price simply because BCC and its insurance company had deep pockets. The stakes had just been raised in his battle for normalcy.

When Johnny got back to his office, he had a message from Charlie. He realized Johnny must be upset and asked Johnny to call him back. The two traded phone messages all afternoon. Finally at about five Johnny went back up to see Charlie, who was seated at his desk behind a huge stack of files.

"Johnny, I'm sorry about the earlier discussion. This news has got us all a little upset."

"I understand, Charles. Don't worry about it, I think they're just blowing smoke." replied Johnny.

"Let's go over what you remember about the audit and the buyout of Frontier," Charlie suggested.

"Well," said Johnny, "as you probably remember, Frontier came to us just before the audit started and told us they were approached by a couple of possible suitors for a leveraged buyout or merger. They asked our advice as to how to best position themselves to attract the highest price." Charlie nodded, indicating that he did remember.

Johnny went on "We told them that in our opinion their software hadn't passed some critical tests. But let's face it, with the large high tech firms all flush with cash and looking for places to put it, they weren't paying any attention. We hooked them up with a firm that gave them a fairness opinion regarding the value of their stock. This way it was in place so they could use it in an SEC filing if they actually received a firm buyout offer. The value came back much lower than they expected and cited problems with the reliability of the software. If I remember, it wasn't much more than their debt of about three billion dollars. They then went out and got two more opinions. The first, from some firm that no one had heard of, at about five and a half billion. The other, from a Wall Street firm, at about five billion."

"But," said Charles, "how does the audit figure into all this?"

"The fairness opinions in and of themselves wouldn't have been supportable without a strong financial report," Johnny went on. "The important part of the annual report, which included our audit, centered around the orders that Frontier had for the manufacturing software. Since the software was just coming out of development, Frontier couldn't recognize a lot of profit. But, that didn't matter for the high tech companies, going back a couple of years. It was all about potential. We confirmed all the orders and deposits that Frontier recorded. As we know, a lot of the high tech investment going on at the time was based on perception, not actual operating results. Frontier made a very big deal about the software orders and trumpeted them in their annual report."

"That's exactly the way I remember it." Charles added after Johnny finished, "But how does that make any of us around here guilty of anything?"

"I'm sure that's a matter of who's doing the accusing," Johnny responded. "The one thing that always bothered me about the whole buyout was that the players seemed manipulative in the process. When the first opinion of value came back, the guys at Frontier went right out and got two more before almost anyone found out about it. I know all the numbers because someone at Frontier mentioned it to me, confidentially. Look at it this way, at least one of the two higher opinions came from a New York group and it cost Frontier a small fortune. The other one, I have no idea where it came from. It seemed to me that when the first opinion came in so low, they simply hid it and decided to get two more opinions, instead of one, so they could really cover their asses. Then, WestPac paid an amount just below the lowest value quoted in the two new opinions."

"I see where you're coming from, Johnny, and I think the courts will see through this one as well. I'm not inclined to let these guys push us around in the hope they can get some kind of settlement out of us." Charles tried to sound strong, while the specter of highly public litigation scared him to no end.

With the conversation over, Johnny told Charlie he would see him in the morning and returned to his office. Charlie had a way of sensing when Johnny needed picking up and always seemed to know the right way to get the job done. Today, rather than give Johnny a lecture on keeping his spirits up, he thought it would be better to talk through the facts surrounding the Frontier audit and their possible exposure. He did this, in part, to refresh his memory, but also because he didn't think the firm had done anything wrong and felt that Johnny would feel better coming to the same realization after rehashing the facts. He was right.

Five

Scott Borden called Johnny on Tuesday as promised and lunch was set for Thursday at noon. They would meet at Rosalee's, a favorite Chicago eatery which had been around since before most of the downtown crowd was out of grammar school. The word around the businessmen who worked downtown was that more deals got done at Rosalee's than in the boardrooms. Rosalee had let it be known that if you were a regular, you could write your deal up on the table cloth even though it was linen, and take it with you. If you spilled food on it, that was your tough luck. Pens were provided upon request.

Just before noon, Johnny exited the Gateway building to a beautiful spring day. The rains of the past few days had given way to a sunny Thursday with low humidity. Johnny decided to walk south on Michigan Avenue, then two blocks to Monroe Street, where he would go west a block and a half to Rosalee's. The light breeze off Lake Michigan, the low humidity and the feeling that the latest threat could be contained put a little energy back into him. The walk would be a pleasant fifteen minute hiatus that he looked forward to. He was not in a hurry.

When he entered Rosalee's, he saw Scott about thirty-five feet away next to a very tall, dark-haired man. Johnny recognized the man as one of the principals at Investech, but could not remember his name. As Johnny approached, Scott shook his hand.

"Johnny, you remember Alex Franklin, our president?" Scott asked. Alex reached over and shook Johnny's hand as the introduction was being made. He guessed that Alex was about six foot three, since he appeared to be a good three to four inches taller than Johnny. Alex' hand easily wrapped around Johnny's, and was not connected to a weak man, although he couldn't be sure how solid Alex was in his dark gray suit. Alex looked to Johnny to be in his mid-forties, probably an ex-athlete of some sort, who had done a good job of staying in shape over the years. Johnny appreciated this because he did everything he could with his free time to accomplish the same goal. A goal that was more easily achieved these days. Johnny did remember seeing Alex once in the Investech offices, but did not believe they had ever been introduced. His inclusion at lunch caught Johnny slightly by surprise.

The three were seated at a booth. Scott remarked that the weather had improved quite a bit since he last saw Johnny. They had a discussion about what each of them had done over the past weekend. Alex mentioned that he had gone to his summer home in Michigan City, Indiana, about one hundred miles from Chicago. The southern end of Lake Michigan as you worked your way east from Gary, Indiana had some beautiful beaches and was a favorite place for many Chicagoans to spend their summer weekends. Alex had gone to open his summer home. Johnny assumed that Alex had done well financially, based on his description of the house.

Then they got down to business. Investech was in the middle of underwriting an initial public offering for one of Johnny's clients. It was their obligation to learn as much as they could about each client, so they would pump Johnny for as much advance information as possible before the results of their annual audit was made public. Of course, Johnny was ethically bound to reveal almost nothing, so this would be somewhat of an exercise in futility for all of them. He believed he had been the most help to Investech by interpreting financial statements after they had been made public. Johnny and Scott had been through this a number of times before, so they knew how to play the game. Alex's presence added a new dimension to the meeting, and Johnny was sure that this was not by accident. In the past with Scott, Johnny could say just enough to let him know generally what to expect without being too specific. Scott respected the boundaries and knew when to quit. Alex was a very focused man, and pushed beyond the limits of the norm. At one point, Johnny looked very hard at Alex and told him in a quiet but firm tone that, for him, Johnny, to say too much would be worse for Investech than if nothing was said at all. The inference was that if word got out that Johnny was leaking information, they could all be in trouble. Alex backed off, and Scott changed the subject.

They talked through lunch about other relatively minor points concerning some of Johnny's clients that Investech was moderately interested in. As they were finishing, Alex said, "Johnny, I don't want to catch you off guard, but we're aware that you have some trouble brewing over the Frontier audit."

Despite Alex' attempt to soften the blow, it didn't work. Johnny was left temporarily speechless, and this time Scott said nothing.

Johnny had no idea how to respond, and he realized his silence was an admission that Alex was right. But how the hell could they know?

"First, Alex, you know I can't discuss firm business and even if I could, I really don't know what you're talking about," was the best Johnny could do.

"I didn't come here to embarrass you," Alex spoke softly. "I don't expect you to admit it and I am aware that you will protect BCC anyway possible. Just please listen to what I have to say."

Johnny nodded and Alex continued, "Criminal charges in securities matters are serious and will no doubt disrupt your life if you end up in court. Even if you don't, the word will be out in no time. How will this affect your business and your ability to retain your clients?" Alex was wasting no time and Johnny now realized that Alex had come to lunch for a lot more than small talk. In fact, Johnny doubted that Alex was even familiar with the term.

"Have you ever considered leaving public accounting?" asked Alex.

"No," Johnny was able to respond to that question very quickly.

"I wouldn't have expected you to say yes. Not a man who's been in the profession for years. Right out of college. Illinois wasn't it and then Northwestern for grad school." Alex had done his homework.

"This time the answer is yes," Johnny responded, not wanting to sound intimidated.

"Scott has spoken highly of you for sometime now. You've helped us immensely, without ever violating your professionalism," Alex now lightened up a bit. "We're in the midst of a huge push to underwrite more deals than we can handle with our current manpower. With your knowledge of the high tech industry and unique ability to understand complicated accounting treatment, you'd be a welcome addition to Investech." Alex paused to let the last couple of sentences sink in.

Johnny looked at Alex with a questioning face. "Is this a job offer?"

"I'm putting the matter on the table for you and Scott to discuss," was Alex's response. "But here's what I want you to think about. We have some idea what you've been through the last couple of years. I'm sure its not very different at any of the other big five. The technology industry, the telecommunications industry and the accounting profession are going through this together. At what point do you say enough? You're a young, talented guy. You have a family to support. Do you want to spend more of your time healing wounds from the past, or move forward with your life?" Alex was hitting a bull's eye in Johnny's mind.

Alex could sense he had scored and decided that any more would be overkill. He finished by saying. "I'm guessing that if you're interested we could work out a nice package, including any personal expenses that you might face in the WestPac matter."

At that point, Alex excused himself to go to the men's room, leaving Johnny and Scott looking at each other in silence. Scott's blue eyes seemed particularly earnest when he said, "I really didn't know for sure if I'd be doing you a favor by bringing Alex to lunch. I know everyone at Investech likes and respects you. We see a lot of potential profit in picking up some of the promising small tech firms that are left. They're all undercapitalized because everyone is afraid to invest a dime in tech right now. Who better than you to analyze them? Most of the people we have on staff are looking from the outside in. You've been on the inside of more tech business than any of us. And you can knife through their financials faster and better than any of us. Plus, you have the trust and respect of a lot of the guys that run these companies."

Scott's argument was sound, Johnny admitted to himself. But he was in complete denial about what had just happened. You didn't just throw a job offer out of the blue. Or did you? Was it a job offer, or an offer to discuss a job offer?

Alex returned and the three of them made their way to the door. Nothing had been written on the table cloth, so they left empty-handed. Johnny thanked Alex and Scott for lunch but made no mention of the offer, or the offer to offer they just discussed.

On the way back to work Johnny had a lot to think about. At first he wasn't sure if he should he be mad at Scott for surprising him. Johnny decided that, at least for now, he would give Scott the benefit of the doubt. Scott's explanation seemed genuine. Alex, on the other hand, was not a man to be taken lightly. Johnny felt that Alex had the personality of a man who let very little stand in his way, but was seasoned enough to know when to back off. His last comment bothered Johnny though, at least in part because he had thought of something that Johnny had not. Criminal defenses can cost a lot of money. It hadn't occurred to Johnny that any part of the legal bills, however high they might be, wouldn't be covered by the firm or the firm's insurance carrier. But would this be true if the WestPac litigants could somehow prove criminal activity on Johnny's part? Up until now Johnny hadn't worried about it because he was completely innocent. But no one knew what WestPac had up their sleeve. If Johnny had to pay some of the legal cost himself, it could be disastrous. And, yes, it might be very nice to get the past behind him and move on with his career. He had never imagined that when the dust settled he'd be anywhere else but BCC. Maybe, just maybe, he had found a way out.

Six

AT THE AGE OF 58, and with no less than thirty-four years of work experience behind him, Charles Stein estimated that he had been through literally thousands of meetings in his life. He knew by now which meetings to prepare for, and how to prepare for them. In fact, preparation was a way of life for him; after all he was an accountant. He had graduated from a top private university summa cum laude, passed the CPA exam with the second highest score in the state of Illinois and had three job offers from big eight firms within weeks of graduating. He had the brains and was willing to put in the time and effort. His wife had been a steadying influence in his life since he met her in college. She encouraged him in everything he did and was a confidant as well as partner. When they were first married, Betty Stein taught high school and had a keen mind and sincere interest in the welfare of her students. Charles often wondered how she could know so much about each of the kids in her class and his work as well. Although not trained as an accountant, she could discuss details of his professional life with him. She listened and when he was done, responded with unusual clarity. It didn't matter that she was unfamiliar with a particular engagement or had not previously been exposed to the facts. She could absorb details and offer Charles an enlightened sounding board for anything he wanted to talk about. She took some time off to raise their two children, but then went back to teaching when the youngest started high school.

In 1998, Betty went to the doctor for a routine visit. Her doctor didn't like something he saw in one of her x-rays. She went to a specialist, and began a series of treatments for something she didn't even know existed a few weeks earlier. At first the treatments seemed successful, but the disease overtook her more rapidly than anyone had expected. The last two months were a terrible strain on Charles, as Betty was past the point of understanding what was going on. In the end he was more relieved than anything else, after seeing his wife suffer so much. As time went by, the terrible void of living without her caught up with Charles. Work was his salvation, but even his beloved profession couldn't replace the pillar that he had lost. His stealth-like focus began to wane. He drifted. He was still professional enough to hold the firm together, but what used to be a joy and come almost effortlessly, was now a strain. Add to that the battles that BCC had faced, both public and private over the past couple of years, and Charles was a tired man.

His instinct was to prepare for the meeting with West-Pac's lawyers, but he couldn't muster the energy. Besides how would he prepare to respond to an accusation he knew nothing about? Charles felt a little emasculated. All he and the others could do was wait around to be ambushed without preparing a suitable defense. The only question was would they be ticked off at a meaningless accusation, or embarrassed by a legitimate complaint? Charles was apprehensive either way.

WestPac's lawyers arrived at BCC's office at shortly after noon, having come directly from the airport. They had caught a 6:00 a.m. flight and with the time difference from the West coast, arrived at O'Hare right on time. They would stay at BCC's office no more than an hour, briefly layout out their position and be on the way back to California on a mid afternoon flight. There would be no feel good conversation. Just the facts for BCC to digest after they left; and then decide how to respond. Their lead lawyer was Jonathan Blanchard, a man of about sixty, who wore thick glasses and if you didn't know otherwise, would have thought was a college professor. With him he brought a team of three other lawyers, all quite young, including a stunning woman who looked like she had just graduated from the school he should be teaching at. The three managing partners of BCC and Warner Simmons were present. With eight people in attendance the meeting would have normally been held in the main conference room. But no one at BCC wanted this meeting to be seen, so they all managed to squeeze around Bill Lewis' conference table, making an uncomfortable situation even worse.

After they had shaken hands and been seated, everyone looked at Jonathan. It was his show. He had a deep and confident voice, and from the beginning it was obvious that the studious persona disguised a commanding personality.

"We appreciate your taking the time to meet with us today. We'll be brief and get right to the point. We believe that BCC was negligent in their audit of the Frontier Data Systems Corporation for the year ended 2000. More specifically, the procedures followed in the audit were not as prescribed by the accounting profession and not in compliance with the Securities and Exchange Commission reporting requirements. Rather than make you try and figure out what we're talking about here, the issue concerns the confirmation of the orders for Frontier's manufacturing software. A lot of people lost a lot of money when Frontier imploded. The sale to WestPac was based on values supplied in the fairness opinion, but those values were in part supported by the orders for the software. Your firm oversaw the confirmation process, but did not ensure that the process was not flawed."

At that point Bill Lewis interceded, "You understand, Mr. Blanchard that the partner in charge of that audit is not here today, specifically because neither he, nor we believe there is anything to discuss. We agreed to give you the courtesy of a meeting because we're professionals. But the particulars of that audit were reviewed by Charles, and there was no deviation from the firm's standards."

"On the contrary, Mr. Lewis," responded Jonathan Blanchard, "the stakes of the audit were well known to everyone. The fairness opinion was inextricably linked to the audit confirmations. Some of the companies who returned audit confirmations didn't even exist or were no more than startups. Most could have ill afforded to place deposits or orders with Frontier in the amounts that were reported in the audit. You should have known that."

All three of the senior partners wanted to look at each other, but knew better. They had no idea what to say either. Charlie wondered if his strategy of not having Johnny present was the right one. Only he knew for sure if Jonathan Blanchard could possibly be correct.

Without waiting for a response, Blanchard continued. "My associate will now move on to some other information."

With that, one of the younger men leaned forward and began to speak. "We indicated to you that we believed a member of your firm was guilty of criminal activity. We're not prepared today to reveal all of the evidence we have. But, we're not in the business of making threats that cannot be substantiated. I have here a piece of paper that we'd like to show you. We can't let you keep this, since it may be part of an evidentiary proceeding if we end up in court." He then handed the paper to Warner, as all three partners moved closer to look.

The paper appeared to be a copy of a report of stock trading issued by a firm called IFS Securities. It had the name of the trader at the top. The name was Maria Dann. In the purchase column there were several entries dating back to August of 2000, and continuing through December of that year. In all a total of about 60,000 shares of Frontier had been purchased in a little over four months. Then, beginning in March of 2001, the sales took place. There were four sales between March and April of 2001. The sale prices were much higher than the purchase prices. The purchases corresponded to the time right before the Frontier sale to Westpac was announced, in early February 2001. The sales took place after the audit results were released at the beginning of March. Whoever this Maria Dann was, she had made a lot of money and timed it perfectly. The accusation the WestPac lawyers were making was obvious. Someone had insider information and was passing it on.

"I'll save you the time of doing the math," the young lawyer went on. "Maria Dann made almost one and a half million dollars trading Frontier stock. We don't think she had a crystal ball. And, this represents the tip of the iceberg."

Now, the three partners and their lawyer could not help but look at each other. Jonathan Blanchard and his group had made their point. But, who was Maria Dann?

Bill Lewis spoke, "We can read this statement very well, but frankly it's meaningless to us. We have no idea who this woman is."

The young lawyer responded, "If you don't know, we suggest you ask the partner in charge of the Frontier audit."

The meeting was basically over. The BCC four, through their lawyer Warner Simmons, told the Blanchard group that if they had any response to the accusations, he would call them in a few days. Otherwise he thanked them for coming to Chicago, without trying to make it sound like he really meant it.

After the California lawyers left, Andy Van Dyke said, "Who is Maria Dann?"

"It's Johnny's wife." replied Charlie.

Seven

As much as she loved her children, Maria Brandt was not fulfilled as a housewife. She missed working. Her husband had become as uncommunicative as ever. And she was bored. Her oldest child, Lindsay went to pre-kindergarten all day, while Josh now went to day care every afternoon. The role of suburban housewife simply left too much time for her to contemplate what she was missing.

When the phone rang at 2:00 p.m. on Friday afternoon, Maria assumed it was Johnny calling to tell her if he would be home on time. Hearing Charlie's voice, she was surprised. "Maria, I need to see you." was how the conversation began.

"Sure, Charles, love to. When do you want get together?" She assumed Charles was having a bout of loneliness, with Betty now gone.

"As soon as you can make it." There was sense of urgency in his voice.

Charles and Betty had been nothing but supportive of Johnny's career. This included occasional dinners among all four of them. Maria had the highest regard for Betty and she knew that the feeling was mutual. When Betty died,

Maria tried to do everything she could for Charlie. At times he was receptive and other times not. She understood. Now, she thought that Charles needed someone to talk to and was glad that he had called her. Johnny would be happy to have Maria spend some time with Charlie.

Somehow Charlie's tone indicated to Maria that this might not be purely a social call.

"Charles, are you all right?"

"Yes, yes of course," Charles responded, realizing he might be upsetting Maria.

"I've got a few things I'd like to talk over with you. I'm going to be pretty busy next week, so I was hoping we could get together over the weekend. How about we meet for lunch tomorrow at the Orrington?" The Orrington Hotel was a landmark in Evanston, Illinois. This would be a very short drive for Maria. For Charles, coming from the gold coast just north of downtown Chicago on a Saturday, it would be no more than half an hour.

"Fine," said Maria "Johnny can probably watch the kids or I'll get one of the neighbors."

"OK, great. I'll see you at noon."

Maria had an unsettled feeling after she hung up. It would be like Charlie not to alarm her about anything. She was pretty sure the call had nothing to do with him personally, but she wouldn't tell Johnny that. She would make it sound like he finally decided to accept one of her lunch invitations; almost a father-daughter thing. But for Maria, if getting together with Charlie meant she was finally going to hear some of the inside information about Johnny's problems, she was all for it.

Johnny enthusiastically agreed to watch Lindsay and Josh, saying he would probably take them to a movie. Maria decided that a nice sundress would look casual, but elegant enough for the Orrington. She looked good, and when Charlie saw her, his eyes light up.

"How are you dear?" he asked.

"I'm great," she responded. "A little bored, but otherwise great."

"I know, that's what Johnny's been telling me. Now that the little one is going to daycare, it opens up some free time for you. Have you thought about going back to work part time?"

Maria responded, "Frankly, yes I have."

"There must be plenty of part time jobs in the suburbs, and with your skills you could work almost anywhere." The light part of the conversation continued while they were seated and looked at the menu.

After the waiter took their order, Maria turned to Charlie and said, "Charles I detected some anxiety in your voice yesterday."

"Maria, I don't know how much Johnny has told you. We've been working our way through the collapse of most of our dotcom clients. It hasn't been pleasant, but our heads are still above water. Johnny has taken it particularly hard. Somehow, he feels personally responsible, like he let the firm down. Then there's the loss of prestige that goes with something like this." Charles paused for a moment then went on. "On Wednesday we had a meeting with some lawyers that represent the majority shareholders of a firm called WestPac."

Maria was familiar with the WestPac buyout of Frontier, but knew little more than the names, having heard bits and pieces from Johnny.

"WestPac is accusing the firm of negligence in our performance of Frontier's 2000 audit. In and of itself, it isn't especially alarming, since it's a typical 'deep pockets' fishing expedition on their part. The bad news is they're also accusing Johnny of passing on insider information so that someone or some group of people made a fortune buying and selling Frontier stock."

"No way" said Maria. "Not a possibility."

"Obviously, none of us believe this," said Charlie, "but here's what's so troubling. The lawyers showed us a copy of a transaction summary of stock trades. If you trace the purchases and sales through, you see that the purchases occurred right before the buyout was announced and the sales right after the buyout was made public. The trader made almost a million and a half dollars. And according to the lawyers, there are many more instances of the same thing."

"But what does any of that have to do with Johnny?" Maria asked.

"The name on the transaction statement was Maria Dann."

Maria gasped, almost choking while she ate. As she looked at Charlie in disbelief, he continued.

"I remembered that you told me your family had a building supply business in Wisconsin and that Dann was part of the name."

Maria, now able to speak answered, "That's right. Dann was my maiden name. But I have never been involved in any of the family investment activities."

"Maria, none of us believe for a minute that you or Johnny did anything illegal. But this still leaves us with a problem to solve. Before we decided on a course of action I had to lay this out for you."

Hearing the word "illegal" did nothing to make Maria feel any better. But it was clear that the type of trading that Charlie was talking about would be just that. You may as well call it what it is. "How much does Johnny know about this?" she asked.

"The only thing he doesn't know is that the person accused of doing the trading is you and presumably other members of your family. After the lawyers left our office, I told him everything, except the name on the statement. I told him that they blanked it out on the copy they showed us."

"So he thinks they're really bluffing?" asked Maria.

"To some degree we all do. But if you're the one accused of being a criminal, until you're officially cleared, you can't feel too good about it." Charlie answered.

"Well, at least this explains some things. Just when Johnny started to show signs of becoming himself again, a couple of days ago he slipped back even deeper. I've been trying to get him to talk about it, but he won't open up."

Charlie said, "I know exactly what you mean. There's no way I could have told him about you possibly being involved. I'm afraid he might get irrational with WestPac's lawyers."

Maria's mind started to kick in as she realized the seriousness of the situation. "Before you do anything, Charles, give me a few days to do some digging around. I can't take this lying down, either for me or Johnny. And for now let's keep this between us. It's better if Johnny thinks you're feeling down personally and that's why we're seeing each other."

After thinking for a minute she asked, "What can you tell me about the trading statement? Was there a company name on it?"

"Yes" answered Charlie. "It was a firm called IFS Securities."

"Is there anything else you can remember?"

"Nothing else," responded Charlie.

When lunch was over, they walked to the front door and briefly hugged. The weary old pro looking for answers and the young housewife whose family was now threatened. She would try to provide them.

Maria had made a career of assembling pieces to various technological puzzles and successfully putting the puzzles together. The puzzles got progressively tougher, and the greater the challenge, the more she responded. Her first job after graduation was as a systems analyst for a management consulting company. Although she hadn't realized it at first, the variety of applications she worked on gave her a broad background in problem solving. She honed her skills and focused on complex applications in unique industries. Over time she gained a reputation as a trouble shooter and she was in high demand. One of her clients, Abcon Pharmaceuticals, recognized her outstanding skills and made her a job offer as Assistant Director of Information Systems. Her income increased substantially and she worked with the most state of the art equipment in the industry. She focused on computer aided research and development, which was the backbone of Abcon's profitability. She saved Abcon a small fortune by setting up computerized models of chemical compounds and their likely effects on humans. She left work briefly after Lindsay was born, but when Josh came along she couldn't bear to let someone else raise her children. Although greatly conflicted, she gave up her position, but promised herself that, when the kids were older, she would go back to work.

Charlie had not been able to give Maria much to start off with, but she would approach this as a matter of finding the pieces that were out there and figure out who was framing Johnny. And she would move quickly. Her first thought was to find out more about IFS Securities. It had been quite awhile since she had gone through the various investment files that her family set up for her. These were all in a lock box in a bank in Milwaukee. The trust department oversaw their investments and deposited related documents in a lock box for the family's use. Maria's accountant provided her with summary information twice a year, but she never really paid that much attention to it. All of the investments were in safe, secure assets, so she didn't need to worry. She did remember that to this day the name Maria Dann still appeared on a few of the bank statements, but she had just never gotten around to changing it. Was IFS Securities one of them?

The drive from Maria's house to Sea First Bank, in Milwaukee, took about an hour and twenty minutes. She would need more time than the three and a half hours that Josh was at day care. So, on Sunday night, she called her sister and asked if she could drop Josh off for the day. Normally she would give her sister a full explanation of the day's plans, but all she could tell her was that it involved a quick trip to Sea First and to please not ask a lot of questions. And for sure not to tell Johnny. This was completely out of character for Maria, but her sister was totally reliable.

On Monday, Maria loaded Josh and a few of his most valuable possessions into her Honda Accord and off they went. She would have enjoyed the leisurely ride on this spring day if it wasn't for the accusations hanging over her. She hadn't slept at all well since Saturday and she had a heavy feeling as if a lot of weight had been put upon her. Although she might approach this information gathering expedition in a workman like manner, it was not work. The consequences were too personal and too frightening.

Sea First was located in a tall, modern building in downtown Milwaukee. Maria parked in the bank's garage and took the elevator to the seventh floor. She had made this trip about five times since she and Johnny were married, so she remembered just enough to find the right floor. From there she found the trust department and asked for the family's trust officer. Unfortunately, she was out on vacation, but Maria was directed to her assistant, a short stocky woman who was eager to please. Maria explained that she needed to gain access to her trust lock box and gave the woman the requisite pass code and social security number. She gained access to a room with hundreds of metal boxes and a few tables positioned to allow the owners to view their contents in privacy. Maria unlocked the box and carried it to one of the tables, where she carefully removed a rather large stack of papers, pass books and computer print outs. All of the material had been put in alphabetical order, so she went right to the stack of trading statements and there, to her surprise, she found a rather official looking document marked IFS Securities. The first entry on the statement was made on June 18, 2000. It showed that the account was opened with a deposit of one hundred thousand dollars. A series of purchases with symbols that Maria didn't recognize appeared in one column. Similarly, she could see that some of the securities purchased were sold shortly thereafter at either a small gain or loss. Then, beginning in August, 2000 she could see the first purchase of Frontier stock, with the symbol FTR in the purchase column. The amount purchased was twelve thousand shares at a price of twenty five and one-eighth. Three more purchases of FTR followed from August through December, all at about the same price, but in larger quantities. Then, entries in the column marked sold began in March, 2001. The prices were more than double the purchase prices. The name at the top of the statement was Maria Dann held jointly with Henry Dann, her father.

Maria looked at the computer print outs and found that they were organized by investment type. She located a print out marked "Stock Portfolio," and read down the list. It too was alphabetized and she found IFS Securities right where it should be. The print out listed the carrying value of the IFS holdings each month for the year to date in 2001. During the months from March through May the value of the holdings decreased by well over a million dollars. This corresponded to the sales of FTR stock shown on the IFS statement.

Maria thought for a moment. Was it possible that her father had done this trading and not told her? Not for the kind of money involved here. Why wasn't a profit of a million and a half dollars reported by her accountant on their tax return? She didn't have the answer to that question, but could get it easily enough. Now, what to do with the statement? She didn't want to appear to be covering anything up by removing it from the lock box. Copies of it were already circulating out there somewhere. So she went to a copy machine and made one copy of the IFS statement and the computer print out, placed those in her brief case and returned the originals to the box. She put the box back in its place, locked it and exited the large, sterile room.

The assistant trust officer was seated at her desk, talking on the phone. When she saw Maria, she smiled and placed the phone on the receiver. "Did you find everything all right?" she asked.

"Yes," said Maria. "When will Mrs. Milton be returning?'" she asked.

"She's on vacation until next Monday. Is there anything I can help you with?"

"Are you familiar with my family's account?" was the question.

The stocky woman answered, "Not in any great detail. If you'd like to purchase or sell something, or transfer some funds, I can help you with that."

Maria realized she would not receive much help from the woman, but did ask, "What information is needed to execute a purchase or sale?"

"You can either call a trade in or do it electronically. You need your account code and social security number."

Maria felt awkward now because she had never executed one trade. In the past this had been done for her and, to the best of her knowledge, no trades had been made in years. She really didn't know what else to ask so she turned to leave. As she did this, she asked the woman to have Mrs. Milton call her when she returned from vacation; just her luck another week. But there was no way Maria was going to wait a week for some answers.

....

How do you call your father and ask him if he made a million and a half dollars illegally trading stock? Could Johnny be in this with him? These questions were so surreal to Maria that she realized she would never ask them. Maria knew that her family had established similar trust accounts for her sister and brother. Was this happening to them? And what about her uncle and his children? Someone with knowledge of her access code and social security number had set up the trades, but it wasn't anyone in the family.

On the ride home Maria decided that the next move would be to find someone at IFS who had set up her account. The trading statement listed the address of IFS as a post office box in Las Vegas, Nevada. There was an eight hundred number to call. On Tuesday afternoon, she called the number and a pleasant sounding woman answered the phone. Maria asked to speak to her account representative.

"I'm sorry, I don't know the person's name. My husband set up the account, but he recently passed away and I'm trying to clean up his estate."

"I see," said the woman in a clearly sympathetic voice. "If you have your statement handy, there's a number assigned to each of our representatives. You'll find it in the upper right hand corner of the statement."

Maria looked. She found the number and repeated it to the woman.

"OK, just one minute please." She could hear the woman typing on a computer keyboard. "That representative is Jonas Smith. Unfortunately, Mr. Smith is no longer with the firm."

"Oh," said Maria, "does he have an associate or someone else who might be familiar with the account?"

"If you give me your account number, I'll see whose taken it over." the woman offered.

Maria gave the woman her account number. There was more typing on the other end of the line.

"Is the account still active?" the woman asked.

"No" responded Maria, "it's been closed for about a year."

"We keep the records of accounts on our system for a year after they're closed. Beyond a year the information is stored on disk, but I don't have access to that information here."

Maria thought quickly. It didn't matter if the records were available or not. She needed an explanation from a live human being, not access to some computer records. "Well" she said, "I could use some advice on how to reinvest the estate proceeds. Is there another representative I could talk to?"

"Sure." the woman answered. "George Blair manages this office. Let me connect you with him."

She could hear the phone ring through the handset and it was answered after two rings.

"George Blair here."

"Hello, Mr. Blair, my name is Maria Dann. We recently had an account with IFS. My late husband worked with Jonas Smith, but with his illness and all the complications we sort of lost touch with Jonas. Do you have any idea where we could find him?"

George Blair came back, "You know it's the strangest thing. Jonas worked here until about six months ago. One day he left work and we haven't seen him since. He and I were sort of friendly, so I would have at least expected an explanation."

"I see," said Maria. "Don't you even have an address or phone number?"

"He used to live at the Sonoran Apartments on Twenty-Fifth Street. His phone was disconnected when I tried to call him." answered George. "But, you do have to understand one thing, Mrs. Dann. This is Las Vegas. A lot of people come and go. You get used to it."

As George was talking, Maria took another look at the IFS statement. In the lower right hand corner she saw the word "monarch", without a capital M, written in small fine print.

"One other thing Mr. Blair," Maria said, "your receptionist said your computer records are current only for one year. Does that mean they're stored somewhere that I could access them?"

"We use a central trading system that's shared among a number of small to medium sized securities firms in the West. Its run by a firm called monarch located in San

Francisco. They handle all the money and print out the monthly statements. Let me get their phone number for you." He put her on hold for a minute then came back on the line with the number. She could think of no other questions to ask, so she was about to hang up when one last thought came to her.

"Mr. Blair, I noticed the trading statement shows the commission paid for each trade. If Jonas Smith had commissions due after he left IFS, is it possible that monarch would have a forwarding address for him?"

"Yes, I suppose so," was his response.

Rather than let him wonder why she would ask such a question, she quickly thanked him and hung up.

Maria chose not to immediately think through the information she had just received. She decided to put it out of her mind for a minute and call her family's tax accountant. They had used the same accountant since Maria could remember, although he had changed firms a few times. When the call came through he was not available, but Maria asked his assistant if she could check Maria and Johnny's 2001 tax file, specifically with reference to gains reported by a firm called IFS Securities. This the assistant promised to do and call Maria back. Maria explained that it was rather important and asked if she could hold while the information was obtained. She was on hold for several minutes before the woman returned. She was able to tell Maria that no information whatsoever had been given to them concerning IFS Securities. Again, Maria gave thanks to the woman for her efforts and hung up.

Now it was time to examine what she had learned. Indeed her trust account bore evidence that indicated she could well be guilty of insider trading. The only other person who had access to the account was her father who, she was certain, could not possibly be involved. She could not even ask him about it because that would lead to questions she was not prepared to answer. The family's trust officer might be familiar with the trades if someone had sought her advice, but that information would not be available for several more days. The account representative at IFS had strangely disappeared and no record of the transactions had been picked by her tax accountant. The thought occurred to Maria that whoever had set up the appearance of insider trading could also be setting her and Johnny up for tax evasion.

Four days had passed since she met Charlie for lunch. He would soon be getting anxious to hear from her. Maria had not forgotten for a minute his words about WestPac's lawyers giving them a week to respond to the allegations before they would take some kind of action. For the first time in quite a while, time was not on her side.

Eight

On Wednesday, Warner Simmons called Charlie to remind him that if they were going to prepare a response to Jonathan Blanchard and his crew, they ought to do it soon. As if Charles needed reminding. Warner was sure that Blanchard would call him at least one more time before taking any action, but Warner preferred to make the next call, if only to appear to be on the offensive. A meeting was scheduled for the next day, including Bill Lewis and Andy Van Dyke. Johnny would be at the meeting. Charles had made it a point to tell everyone that Johnny was not to know about Maria's possible involvement in the insider trading matter.

When the five men were together, the first order of business was to talk about the competence of the audit procedures, specifically as they related to the orders for Frontier's software. Johnny had reviewed the audit files and found that BCC mailed forty-six audit confirmations. The auditing firm always mailed the confirmation letters, although they went out on the client's letterhead. The confirmations were sent with return envelopes addressed directly back to the auditors. By mailing to and receiving back the confirmations directly from the client's customers, the auditors could be assured that the process was not flawed. Each confirmation had a brief written statement describing the details of the software package ordered, the amount of the customer's deposit and any future progress payments required. In some instances the total price was not yet determined because the software packages would be customized on an ongoing basis. At the bottom of each confirmation was a signature line to be signed by an official of the customer, acknowledging the correctness of the information. There was also a space for comments where the customer could correct any misinformation. The Frontier audit confirmation process was the same that BCC and every accounting firm used, at least in concept, since the inception of the profession.

As the discussion progressed, Johnny admitted that he was only really familiar with nine of the forty-six customers who received confirmations. He recognized those nine as repeat customers, the rest he did not. Johnny also had to admit that considering the early stage of the system development, the number of confirmed deposits and value of the software orders seemed high. But the deposits had been received and traced to Frontier's bank account!

None of this made the senior partners feel very comfortable. Andy suggested that they conduct some kind of investigation into the validity of Jonathan Blanchard's claim that many of Frontier's customers were bogus. Everyone agreed that this was a good idea, but Warner said he felt Blanchard would see this as a stalling tactic. Warner would press the point that BCC was entitled to do some research into the accusations. He would be vague about the specifics. Certainly this investigation had to be done quickly and it would be handled by professionals outside of BCC. If he wasn't careful, the results might well be used in a lawsuit against BCC. As such, Warner did not want Blanchard to know what BCC was up to in case the investigation substantiated WestPac's claim. He would do his best to contain the work within the realm of attorney-client privilege.

The conversation then turned to the criminal charges which Blanchard felt would be forthcoming if he made his evidence available to the government. Johnny expressed his extreme frustration at not knowing who was supposed to be the inside trader. The others commiserated with him. Eventually they would have to tell him, but Charles had promised to give Maria some time to clear her name as well as Johnny's. Just how much time they had wasn't certain. There were some other issues that needed to be addressed. Bill, of course, was concerned about the effect the accusations, if made public, would have on the firm's business. The threat of a highly publicized lawsuit, civil or criminal, could be as bad as the reality. Either one would be devastating to the firm. BCC and particularly Bill Lewis had done a masterful job of holding on to clients until now. The public was getting tired of seeing large accounting firms dragged through the dirt. Still, Bill knew at some point client defections could occur and shuddered to think of the possible snowball effect.

Then there was the matter of possible discipline by the governing body of certified public accountants, the American Institute of Certified Public Accountants, or AICPA. The five discussed strategy to deal with these problems. The discussions fell under the familiar category of damage control which had become all too prevalent of late. In addition to the investigation proposed by Andy, the usual measures would be taken. Bill Lewis would start talking to the right people as soon as necessary.

The meeting ended, but all agreed the next meeting could be scheduled on a moment's notice.

For a week now, Johnny had been dealing with the stress of the WestPac matter and the unsettled feeling he had after his meeting with Scott Borden and Alex Franklin. Scott had called him on Tuesday to talk more about the "possibilities" offered by Investech. Johnny politely put him off, telling him that he had been too busy to really give it any consideration. When Scott called again on Thursday, he sounded a little anxious. This annoyed Johnny. He hadn't known Scott to be the kind of guy to put undo pressure on other people. The pressure was obviously coming from higher up. Alex Franklin. And why were they so interested in Johnny anyway? Perhaps they sincerely respected Johnny and saw an opportunity to land a valuable man. Or, they wanted to use him to disclose information about his high tech clients, then discard him. Johnny wished he could take a pass on any future conversations with the people at Investech, but he simply couldn't. He sensed he might need a safety net without knowing if there would be any other options. He agreed to meet with Scott and Alex the next afternoon.

Johnny entered the Investech offices at 2:00 p.m., as scheduled. Investech's offices were even more lavish than BCC's, also having been furnished a couple of years earlier during the dotcom boom. Investech had taken several high profile technology firms public, as well as arranged a number of industry mergers and had reaped huge fees in the process. When the bubble burst, many of those firms were sold for pennies on the dollar, or simply filed bankruptcy. By that time, Investech had already pocketed their fees. Johnny wondered though, how Investech seemed to be doing so well now that the high tech feeding frenzy was over.

An attractive receptionist led Johnny to a large conference room with a panoramic view of the Chicago skyline. She asked Johnny if he wanted anything to drink and when he declined she told him that the others would join him in a minute. As he waited, Johnny took in the view. He couldn't help but be impressed with the aura of Investech. Everything visible gave the impression of success, even down to the well dressed, pert looking staff. But, at the same time, he wondered how well he would fit in with the reality behind the Investech image.

The door opened and Scott Borden walked in. He greeted Johnny warmly, as if the two were best friends. "Johnny," Scott said after they had shaken hands, "Alex will be joining us in a minute. We've also asked Brad Warshaw to sit in. He's the CEO and a director of the company and wants to be sure we put our best offer out there for you today."

"Good. I guess if we're going to have a frank discussion, we may as well put all our cards on the table," Johnny responded.

Within a minute or so the door opened again and Alex entered with an older man, who looked to be about sixty, with thinning gray hair and a slender build. Both had on dark business suits with white shirts and ties. The two shook hands with Johnny and then they all took a seat at a conference room table which could have accommodated a meeting five times as large.

"We're very glad you could join us today," Alex took right over. "As I mentioned at lunch last week, we think there's an excellent opportunity for us to work together and we believe the timing may be right. We know you're committed to your career as an auditor, but the events that have plagued the industry of late couldn't have been foreseen, even as recently as a couple of years ago. These are times of change for all of us. What we've elected to do here is go with the flow. By that, I mean we feel there are still some undercapitalized technology firms out there that could benefit from an infusion of funds. Our goal here is to identify those firms, match them up with a suitable merger partner and then fund the deal through a venture capital firm that we'll be forming. You could fill a strategic role in that process."

His little speech finished, Alex paused to check Johnny's reaction.

"Well, Alex, I have to admit you have my interest," was Johnny's response. "Now that I've had a chance to think about it, I'd like to pursue it a little further."

"Good. I've asked Brad to join us today in order to give you some idea of what we have in mind for you."

Now Brad spoke. "Johnny, as Alex explained we're going to go on a large scale due diligence exercise for the tech firms that offer the best opportunity to turn a profit in the shortest amount of time. The landscape has changed, obviously, since the fiasco of the couple of years. Money that is committed for investment in high tech has got to be based on reality. A man in your position could significantly improve our chances of success. You have some clients that probably already fit our profile. Since we don't have a lot of time to waste, we could focus right in on them. The top management at those companies know you and would trust you in any negotiations. With regard to analyzing other firms, your experience would be invaluable." Brad finished and took a sip of water. Johnny understood the silence to mean that he was to acknowledge his agreement with Brad.

"Yes," said Johnny, "I see what you mean. But, since you already know about the problems brewing with WestPac, aren't you worried about whether I would still have credibility with my clients, if the news becomes public?"

Said Brad, "that's another area where we can help you."

"You know, of course," Johnny picked up the conversation, "I'm curious as hell as to how you know anything about WestPac."

This time it was Alex who responded. "We also use the services of Jonathan Blanchard's law firm. The truth is they're not being too closed mouth about this whole thing."

"You mean they don't mind if a little negative publicity builds up before anything official comes out?" asked Johnny.

"That's right" said Alex

"So," continued Johnny," what you're saying is they don't have much of a case. They're willing to let us be tried in the media in the hope of getting a settlement?"

"We really don't know how much of a case they have," Brad smiled at Johnny as he spoke. "In any event we have access to someone at the law firm who's in a position to make sure we know the essential facts. I'm not going to beat around the bush here, Johnny. This is business. There are very substantial fees out there for us to earn. We see you as a key to helping us achieve our goals and we're willing to put a lot of resources in place in order to reach those goals. Those resources include money and influence at the right levels. We think they have some ammunition regarding the way the audit confirmations were handled. We don't think they're going to go away empty handed from this thing But, we do think we're in a position to help mitigate the losses."

Johnny wasn't exactly sure how to react to Brad's comments. He had a pleasant demeanor and didn't seem threatening in any way. Johnny sensed Alex knew that he could appear overbearing and brought Brad in to play the good guy role. And let's face it, this was how business worked. In the past, Investech may have let a few secrets slip to someone properly 'positioned' at Blanchard's firm. Now it was pay back time. Alex and his group seemed to have it all in a neat little package for him.

"Let's talk about money," Brad shifted gears. "We're prepared to offer you a minimum of twenty percent more than you're making now, plus some serious incentives.

"I'm listening," Johnny now returned Brad's smile. They did truly have his interest.

"This isn't quite like public accounting where you're expected to leave a significant portion of your earnings with the firm to pay for your partnership interest. To the extent you're involved in signing a target firm to an advisory agreement that results in the consummation of a merger, you'll receive a portion of the fees we earn. If the deal involves the funding of capital, so much the better. The money could be very significant. I'll let Scott fill you in on the numbers."

Scott took his turn. "Let's assume we fund twenty five million dollars of venture capital. If you add our placement fees and preferential return, altogether we could be looking at close to three million dollars. That doesn't take into account the merger related fees and possible back end profit if the merged firm eventually goes public. You could earn ten percent of the fees as part of an incentive package. And this is just a small example. The merger and acquisition fees are a smaller percentage of a deal, but with company values in the billions, the dollar amounts are much higher"

Johnny was impressed. He knew there was serious money in investment banking, but had never really known the exact numbers. He did some math quickly in his head. The chance of making a million dollars a year didn't seem all that remote.

"What do you think?" Alex asked.

"I think you people are very focused. You've looked at this from all angles. I admit I can't think of anything you haven't covered. And the kind of money you're talking about is too much not to take seriously."

"Good," Alex responded, "we'd love to have you on the team. I'm sure you'll want to give this some thought and talk it over with your wife. But we'd like to move fairly quickly. Why don't you give Scott a call next week and we'll work out all the details. We'll have an employment and confidentiality agreement drafted as soon as you say the word."

An employment agreement would be standard practice for this type of job and so would a confidentiality agreement. After all, if you disclosed information about the firms you were researching, a competitor could swoop in and make a better offer. A lot of hard work and money would go down the drain. Signing this type of agreement didn't bother Johnny. In fact he really liked the idea, because if properly drafted, it would offer him some protection as well.

The heavy part of the conversation over, Brad excused himself as Alex and Scott offered to take Johnny on a tour of the Investech offices. Johnny had been there a few times previously, but had not seen the whole operation. They walked slowly and made a few light comments as they did. The tour ended about a half hour later in the lobby, with handshakes and Johnny's promise to call Scott next week.

Johnny's mind raced as he exited one of the most unique job interviews in his life; and one of the few. By simply saying "yes", he could seemingly put his problems behind him and have a chance to make more money than he had ever dreamed of. What really made his emotions start to take over was that Scott, Alex and Brad had convinced him they had a well thought out plan. Not just a job offer, but a plan. They wouldn't offer him a huge compensation package if there was any risk of his being charged with a felony. They had done they're homework better than Johnny first realized. He would think this through for a few days to see if he could find any holes in their story. But if he couldn't, he would discuss it with Maria. His leaving public accounting would come as a shock to her, but she knew how miserable his life had been the last couple of years. The chance that their marriage could get back to the level it had been on would mean everything to both of them. But before he put her on an emotional roller coaster ride, he had to be sure.

Nine

THE WHEELS BEGAN TURNING in Maria's head by Wednesday morning. By that time, she absorbed the surprises of the past few days and started to formulate her own plan. There was only one lead to pursue, so it wasn't a question of which, but how. Jonas Smith had left IFS unexpectedly and all but disappeared. He left no forwarding address or phone number. He was in the business of serving clients and being paid for his services. No address and no phone number meant no clients. Unless he was independently wealthy, he would need to have his commissions forwarded to him. Apparently he could do this without going through IFS by leaving his forwarding information on the monarch clearing system. The trick would be to get this information from someone at monarch, or find another way to get it out of monarch.

Maria felt she had two possibilities. First she could go to the monarch offices in San Francisco on some pretense and, once there, persuade a sympathetic individual into telling her what she needed to know. Or, she could attempt to hack into monarch's computer system and obtain it that way. Given enough time, she was confidant she could do it through the wonderful world of information technology. She could call her old boss at Abcon and ask for access to their system. State of the art as it was, it would give her all the tools she needed. But it would be a trial and error process and there simply wasn't time. So that option had to be ruled out. She had to find the most fool-proof way of playing on the emotions of the right person at monarch. She also had to find an excuse to be in San Francisco. Finally, she had to call Charlie and let him know enough to keep his hopes up without telling him too much.

By Thursday morning she was ready to put the plan into action. After Johnny had left for work and Lindsay was off to school, she sat Josh down in the chair next to her computer, put his favorite movie on TV and started typing. She prepared an official looking form with the heading STATE OF NEVADA--MARRIAGE LICENSE. She put lines and boxes on the form. The groom's name was Jonas Smith and the bride's name was Gina Polarski from Cheyenne, Wyoming. The marriage had taken place about eight months ago. She had to decide just how much information she would have to put on the form in order to make it appear real. Too much and she might get tripped up. Too little and it would appear fake. She reasoned that she would have to show some identification to prove she was Gina Polarski, so she included her social security number on the fake marriage license. How many people really know what a marriage license looks like in all fifty states anyway? After the marriage license was finished, she took her Illinois drivers license out of her wallet. She prepared a form that fit neatly over the written part of the license, but left the picture visible. She would go to the laminating machine at WalMart and, for all intents and purposes, Gina Polarski would be licensed to drive a car in Nevada.

The rest of the plan would require some lying, but certainly for the best cause she could think of. She would tell Johnny that her ex boss at Abcon had called and asked her to stand in for him at an information technology seminar in San Francisco. She would say he couldn't make it at the last minute and, because he knew how much she wanted to start working again, he thought this would be a great opportunity for her. Johnny knew she had stayed friendly enough with him for this to be believable. Her sister would take the kids again for two days on Monday and Tuesday. This would allow her time to fly out and, hopefully, get the forwarding information. If Jonas Smith was anywhere in the area, she might even be able to get to him.

In order to put the finishing touches in place she would need a little shopping time. This she found on Friday afternoon. At the mall, she bought a long maternity dress and a girdle that was about two sizes too big for her. She found a large foam pillow that she could cut and round to fit into the girdle. The length of the maternity dress would not allow anyone to see that her legs weren't those of a woman who was at least six months pregnant. Gina Polarski would appear at the monarch doorstep, sobbing and visibly pregnant. Her husband of eight months, one Mr. Jonas Smith, had left her with an unborn child and no means of support. She wouldn't be asking for money, just some information about where to find him. She had decided against calling ahead for an appointment. Better to catch them off guard. Maria liked this plan in particular, because she didn't know if she would be dealing with a man or a woman once she got to monarch. Anyone in their right mind would be ready to rat on Mr. Smith.

By the end of the day Friday everything was in order. The plane reservations had been made. Maria's sister would pick the kids up on Sunday night. She called Charlie to tell him that she had one good lead and would need Monday and Tuesday to begin getting some answers. She made herself sound more optimistic than she really was.

....

The plane fight from Chicago to San Francisco would last about three hours. With a time difference of two hours flying from East to West, Maria left at 8:30 a.m., and would arrive at 9:30. On the plane, she had plenty of time to think about what she would say, once she arrived at the monarch offices. She went over a couple of possible scenarios, but decided that it would be better not to sound too rehearsed. Instead, she focused on the craziness that had become her life within the last week. She was flying cross country to pose as a pregnant woman in order to find a man who had set her family up. Why would someone do this to them? Had Johnny made any serious enemies that she didn't know about? She thought that nearly impossible. Johnny was one of those people who was too sincere and forgiving to alienate anyone. No, it had to be part of what Charlie explained to her during lunch, the deep pockets theory. Now, she wished she had thought a little more about what he had said. WestPac's shareholders had taken a big hit and were looking for a way to recover as much of their loss as possible. Did this involve deliberately framing innocent people? She had done absolutely no research on WestPac. She could find out who the major shareholders were and do some checking on them as well as the law firm making the accusations. She knew she was starting to beat herself up mentally. She had done all she could in the short time since she first talked to Charlie.

As the flight dragged on, she felt fatigued and started to drift off to sleep. She thought about the early years of her marriage. Johnny made her feel warm and loved at the same time that their sexual energy was at an all time high. With no kids to take care of, they spent almost all their free time together. A few times they made last minute plans to fly out of town on a Friday night, for the weekend. Maria remembered that one trip they took was to San Francisco. They went to the wine country, sampled a large quantity of delicious wine and made love in one vineyard while the rest of their tour moved on. It probably wouldn't have mattered she thought, everyone was too drunk to notice anyway.

As soon as the plane landed, Maria made her way to the women's restroom to perform her quick change routine. She found an empty stall, closed the door and propped her roll-on suitcase on top of the toilet seat. She opened the suitcase and took out the maternity dress, which she hung on a hook on the back of the door. Next came the girdle and the foam pillow, which had been shaped to resemble more of an oversized football than anything else. The clothes she wore on the plane came off quickly and were placed in the suitcase. She stepped into and pulled the girdle up, stuffing the pillow into it. Once the pillow was in place, she adjusted it so that her shape resembled a woman at least six months into her term. The maternity dress came last. She then zipped up her suitcase and moved out of the stall to a sink. She washed off all of her makeup and then reapplied a small amount of eye shadow, which she smudged slightly with her hand to give the appearance that she had been crying. She then took her more than shoulder length hair and tied it back behind her head with a cheap looking bandana she had purchased at WalMart. She took one last look in the mirror and Gina Polarski Smith was ready to go about her business.

Maria took the airport shuttle bus to the rental car lot and picked up the Ford Taurus she had reserved. She looked at the map she had downloaded from the internet. Monarch's offices were located in Sausalito just north of the city and over the Golden Gate Bridge. She would drive North through San Francisco and, assuming rush hour was over, expected to arrive at monarch by about 10:45 a.m.. So far everything was going according to plan.

Monarch's offices were in an unassuming building located just off the highway. Before leaving her car, Maria opened her purse and removed a baggie she had brought from home. She took out a small piece of onion and squeezed it into her left thumb and forefinger which she then rubbed lightly over both eyes. They instantly turned red and began tearing. Crying would be easy.

The glass door entry to monarch bore the same symbol she had seen on the trading statement printout, the word monarch spelled out in slightly rounded letters without a capital m. Under the symbol the word 'systems' appeared. Maria pushed the right door open and grunted a little to make sure that the effort of a very pregnant woman could be heard. No one was seated behind the receptionist's desk, but she did hear voices off to the side in the next room. She shuffled over and peered around the corner. There she saw two middle aged women having a light conversation and unaware of her presence.

"Excuse me," she said in a half sob, "could either of you help me?"

Both women looked up and the one standing, who Maria assumed was the receptionist replied, "Why yes dear, what can I do for you?"

Maria made sure to place her right hand briefly over her stomach and noticed the woman's eyes follow her hand.

"I, I'm so sorry to bother you with something like this," she said. "I didn't know what else to do."

The woman looked puzzled, so Maria went on.

"My dead beat husband worked for a company called IFS Securities in Vegas. We got married about eight months ago. Then, six months ago, right after he got me pregnant, he disappeared. I don't have no idea where he is and he didn't leave me no money or nothin. The jerk musta freaked when he found out I was pregnant. Anyway, I ain't been able to find out nothing about his whereabouts. The idiots at IFS say he didn't tell them where he was goin. I called the state welfare department in Carson City, but all they could tell me was to fill some stupid forms and they'd get back to me. Great, what am I suppostta live on?"

"But, how can I help you?" the woman asked.

"I know before he left, Jonas useta get envelopes from your company, most times with his commission checks. I figure he ain't stupid enough to leave his money go the way he left me. I'd like you to tell me if he left a forwarding address."

"Oh," said the woman. "I don't know if they'll give you that information. They're pretty confidential about that kind of stuff."

"Please," Maria began to sob, "I don't have nowhere to turn." I lost my job at the casino when I got pregnant. No one in Las Vegas is interested in a pregnant showgirl."

The woman was clearly sympathetic. "Please, have a seat. Let me see what I can do."

Maria shuffled over to a couch in the reception area, as the woman disappeared into a long hallway. She sat down with a small thud. She had done well in round one.

About five minutes passed before the woman reappeared with a rather somber looking middle aged man who wore half glasses that sat well down on his nose. The receptionist introduced the man as a Mr. Davenport who she said would try to help. Mr. Davenport asked her to step back to his office. Rather than stand straight up, she slid forward on the seat she was sitting on as if the weight of her body was too much to bring up in one motion. After sliding forward, she rose with great effort. None of this was lost on Mr. Davenport.

Mr. Davenport had a small, cluttered office with a large computer screen on his otherwise messy desk. He gave the impression of being bored and, she guessed, he spent a lot of time moving papers from one spot to another without getting very much done.

"I'm sorry ma'am, I didn't get your name."

"Gina, Gina Polarski Smith," she replied.

"I understand you would like us to help you find someone," he asked in the form of a half question.

Maria measured her response. She decided against the sympathy routine. Mr. Davenport, she thought, looked like a man who lived in his own little world and didn't want to be hassled. But, probably not a sympathetic man.

"My husband, the bum, knocked me up and left me with no money and no job. You're damn right I want to find someone."

He looked at her over his glasses. "You understand we have rules about giving out confidential information like that. Have you contacted the authorities?"

"Yeah, sure, Mr. Davenville. Do you have any idea how many missing persons reports the Las Vegas police get every day?"

"Davenport, ma'am," then silence as he considered his next move.

"I'm sorry, I really am. But I could lose my job if I violate company policy like that."

"And what am I suppostta do? I got two people to worry about and I already lost my job."

He paused again and then asked, "Do you have any identification ma'am?"

She reached into her purse and pulled out the Nevada driver's license and marriage certificate, which she handed to him. He looked at these briefly and handed them back to her.

"Do you have any idea what your husband's pass code is?" he asked.

"No. I know his representative I. D., but not the pass code."

"OK. What's the rep I. D.?"

Maria had written down the number on a piece of paper which she showed to Mr. Davenport. He turned to his computer and typed in some information. Maria could not see what was on the screen, but he repeated this process a few times. Finally he stopped, obviously having found what he was looking for. He then looked at her. A scene with a pregnant woman was not in Lou Davenport's plans for the day.

"I'm going to step out to the men's room for two minutes. Please be gone when I get back. And Mrs. Smith, remember, you didn't get a thing from me." With that he got up and left the room. She quickly moved to his desk and looked at the computer screen. There she saw a grid with the name Jonas Smith at the top. Her eyes moved quickly through the unimportant data until she saw the address line. There it was, 1245 Redstone Road, Reno Nevada. There was even a telephone number shown. She grabbed a piece of paper and wrote down the address and phone number, then stuffed the paper in her purse.

Now, without the need to shuffle, she walked quickly through the office and back to the reception area. The receptionist looked up and smiled. Maria guessed that, whoever this woman was, she had softened up Mr. Davenport. Maria returned the smile and was gone.

Maria got into her car and drove away without looking back. She turned South on Highway 101 and headed back toward San Francisco. It wasn't until she made it over the Golden Gate Bridge that she thought about her next move. She would drive directly back to the airport and find the first flight to Reno. During the trip she would figure out how to confront Jonas Smith. She stopped at a traffic signal in downtown San Francisco and rolled down her window to let some air in the car. As she did so, a gray sedan pulled up beside her and the passenger, a square jawed man with crew cut looked right at her and said, "Mrs. Brandt, we need to talk with you for a minute."

Maria sat in disbelief. Was she imagining this? She looked at the man for a moment and decided she didn't want to hear anything he might have to say. She rolled up her window and didn't wait for the light to change. She turned right, and worked her way into traffic, assuming that the gray car would have trouble following her. Maria drove quickly and changed lanes in order to put as much distance as possible between herself and the intersection where she had seen the two men. Unfortunately, no matter what time of day, the streets of San Francisco are clogged. There was no way to avoid it. Within a few blocks the gray car was right behind her again. She drove in circles without any idea where she was going, the gray car behind her the whole way. What was worse, now she was lost.

Maria realized that the men in the car were not going to let her get away. She decided that if there was going to be a conversation, it should be in the most public place possible. She drove on until she was in the middle of California Street, where an early lunch crowd was moving about. She pulled over to the curb with the gray car following her all the way. She was going to wait for the men to approach her when it occurred to her that a crowd seeing two men threaten a pregnant woman would have their eyes on any suspicious activity. She opened her door and walked over to the sidewalk, where a growing mass of people was thinking about what they would order for lunch. Only the passenger in the gray car got out. He was about the same size and build as Johnny and walked with an athlete's movement. She stood and waited for him. He came within about two feet of her, wanting his words to be heard by her only.

"Mrs. Brandt, I have to advise you in the strongest way to stop looking for Jonas Smith. There is more at stake here than you realize. Don't get mixed up in something you don't understand." The words came as a mixture of a mild threat and plea.

There was no point in Maria asking how he had found out about her discovery trip. She also didn't believe he intended to cause her physical harm on the spot. So she kept her eyes focused on him and said, "Do you really expect me to ignore the threats against my family and do nothing about it?"

"All of this will work out in the end. But, we are not prepared to let you take matters into your own hands."

"Who is we?" was her quick retort.

"Never mind about that, everything's under control. It may not seem like it now, but you will be taken care of," were his words. "Just remember, stay away from Jonas Smith."

The man walked back to the gray car and as soon as he closed the car door, the car pulled out into traffic and was gone.

Maria stood there in her maternity dress and watched them drive away, clearly shaken. Her plans would now change again. How naive had she been to think that whoever was framing them would simply let her waltz in and solve the crime. The WestPac acquisition of Frontier involved billions of dollars and for everyone who had lost big money, someone had made big money. Maria could guess that the "we" the man referred to were among the winners. She was in no mood to proceed to Reno on her own. It was time to go home and rally the troops. Maria would catch the first flight back to Chicago and have a frank conversation with her real husband. It was both of their lives that might be at risk. It was both of them together that should plan the next move.

For a woman whose family faced accusations of being guilty of high crimes and who might have just been physically threatened, Maria remained surprisingly calm. Along the way it had become obvious that whoever was framing her family had significant knowledge of information technology; enough to determine account numbers and access codes which could only be obtained by manipulating sophisticated electronic equipment. There was big money involved in the WestPac-Frontier merger. The fact that the person or people perpetrating this hoax had some muscle behind them came as no shock to her.

Maria walked back to her car and realized immediately that she didn't know where she was or how to get back to the main route to the airport. She found a map provided by the rental car company and focused in on the insert of downtown San Francisco. She quickly located her position, made two right turns and was on her way. Once at the airport she bought a ticket for the next flight to Chicago. As it turned out, she made it to the airport just in time to board a

2:20 p.m. departure, which meant she had no time to change out of her maternity clothes. The site of a pregnant woman with smeared makeup and red eyes caused some people to stare, but Maria really didn't care. She had more important matters to worry about.

Ten

THE FLIGHT BACK WAS a series of short interludes of sleep punctuated by an attempt to formulate her next step. She would tell Johnny everything that had happened, starting with lunch with Charlie to being threatened by two men on the streets of San Francisco. Any future course of action to be taken would have to be taken by the two of them together. A logical step would be to go to the FBI and tell her story. But what motivation would they have to believe that her family hadn't decided to profit from insider information. At some point, either the FBI, the SEC or both would investigate WestPac's accusations. If Johnny and Maria went to the authorities now it would clearly diminish their ability to move about without being restricted. At a minimum, they would be followed by law enforcement officials, if not the criminals themselves. Worst case, Maria, her husband and, or her father might be placed under arrest. In her mind, it was way too soon to capitulate the investigation to anyone else.

But what about the physical danger to her family? She and Johnny would have to sort that out when she got home.

Maria turned the knob on the door leading into her kitchen from the garage shortly after eleven on Monday night, a day earlier than she was due to arrive home. She wasn't sure if Johnny would be awake so she tried to be as quiet as possible. Johnny had been thinking about the Investech job offer on and off for the past few days, but now it was continually on his mind. On this day, with the house completely empty, he let his mind roam over all the possibilities presented by the Investech offer. More money, interesting work, prestigious environment and extrication from what had become a personal hell. Was it really that tough a decision? He was deep in thought on the living room couch when he heard the door to the garage open. At first he wasn't sure if his mind was playing tricks on him. He rose from the couch and walked into the kitchen where he saw a pregnant woman with his wife's face, smeared make up and very red eyes, entering his house. His jaw dropped at least two inches.

When she saw Johnny she said, "its okay, I'm alright, but we have to talk."

Johnny could only stare at Maria. She walked over to Johnny and hugged him with all her might. "C'mon upstairs with me while I get out of these clothes," she said.

Johnny's brain finally re-engaged, "What's gong on Mar?" he responded.

Maria took his hand and led him upstairs as she recounted her story, starting with her lunch a little over a week earlier with Charlie. As she spoke, Johnny's emotions ran the gamut from concern for her condition to fascination at the intricacy of the apparent plot to frame him, and then to her counter measures to unearth the details. Along the way he was angry at the idea that his wife had been followed. Although Maria remained composed as she filled Johnny in on all the details, at times emotion overcame her and she sobbed briefly.

When she finished, Johnny responded, "I have some news for you too!" It was then Johnny's turn to tell his story.

They spent the rest of the night talking as they had not talked in years. Their quiet suburban lives had been turned upside down in such a short time. There was reason to despair, there was reason to hope. They could be in physical danger as well as the subject of civil and criminal prosecution, public humiliation and left without any means of support or the ability to raise their own children. They could, with the help of Investech, have a new start, more income than they had dreamed of and, if necessary, the best legal defense that money could buy. By dawn, they were exhausted and fell asleep.

They slept until almost noon on Tuesday. After they had eaten, it was time for some decision making. Maria felt she needed to call Charlie and let him know what she learned. Johnny, who uncharacteristically had not shown up for work or called in, decided they should hold off until they could do a little more research. His first impulse was to call Scott Borden, accept the Investech job offer and ask for some protection. But then a thought entered his mind. He asked Maria, "When you found the stock trade postings for the Frontier shares, did you see a bank statement or some evidence of where the cash is being held?"

"No," said Maria. "Our personal banker was off on vacation last week and I never had a chance to ask her. But I didn't see a bank statement in the lock box."

Johnny said, "In most cases the funds are held in the account of an investment firm and are only forwarded to the investor upon request."

"So?" said Maria. "Since none of us knew about this until now, the money is probably still on account with Sea First."

"Maybe," replied Johnny, "or maybe whoever set this scam up also opened up a bank account in your name or your Dad's name and will have the bank statements handy for the next move. "Or," continued Johnny, "maybe there's no cash at all."

"What do you mean?" asked Maria.

"Well, suppose the bad guys simply printed out trading statements and planted them in your lock box without ever really executing their trades."

"I think I follow Johnny," was Maria's response. "You mean they plant just enough evidence to scare BCC into settling with them on a phony accusation? They know the firm doesn't want the negative publicity, so it never goes any further."

"Right" Johnny came back. "We really owe it to everyone at BCC, including ourselves to try and find out if someone actually made a fortune based on insider information, or if this is a thinly veiled attempt at extortion. One thing I found out was that, of the various firms who supplied audit confirmations on the Frontier audit, most of them either didn't exist or were shells with no actual business activity. There's a pattern here of fake paper trails. Whether any serious cash changed hands on the software orders reported by Frontier or the stock trades in your Dad's account, we don't know."

"Do you think anyone at Investech can help?" Didn't you say they could get to someone at the California law firm that represents WestPac?"

"They might" said Johnny. "But now I'm thinking, if this whole thing is simply phony paperwork, I may not need Investech's help as much as I thought."

Silence for a moment, then he continued, "We really need to go back up to Sea First and see if there is any evidence of money being transferred in or out of your family's account. If we leave now, we can make it up and back before dinner."

They were out the door and on the road within a matter of minutes and arrived at Sea First at by mid afternoon. They repeated Maria's routine of a week earlier. This time they went through the entire stack of papers in the lock box, not just the trading statements. Included were money market account statements from Sea First bank. It took a few minutes to find the statements from 2000 to 2001, but it was easy to see that the deposits and withdrawals did not match the trading activity reported through IFS. They each took half of the remaining stack of papers and went through them carefully. It took another twenty minutes, but Johnny finally found what they were looking for. It was a series of statements bearing the name "Oak Bank and Trust". He matched the IFS statements to the Oak Statements and the transfers into and out of Oak corresponded identically to IFS in inverse order. Purchases of stock involved funds going from Oak to IFS and sales of stock involved funds going to Oak from IFS.

Johnnnie examined the Oak statements carefully. The accounts bore the title "Trust Evidenciary Account" and the name Henry Dann and Maria Dann. There was no address for Oak Bank and Trust, but there was an account number under their names and in the lower left hand corner of each page appeared cryptic, almost ancient Egyptian like letters. Johnny showed this to Maria and they looked at each other without saying a word. It was impossible to tell if this was useful or useless information.

They made copies of the Oak statements, put all of the originals back in the lock box and, their business finished, were back on the road within an hour of arriving at Sea First.

The ride home allowed more time for conversation. "I remember," Johnny began, "talking to our tax guys about off shore bank accounts." Maria turned to Johnny as he had her complete attention. "Some Islands are set up with banks to help avoid US taxes, and some are set up to simply safe keep assets ."

"You think that Oak Bank is a real bank on an Island?" Maria asked.

"I don't know," replied Johnny. "If we could find out if its a real bank, and what Island it's located on, it would help determine whether there was really any money transferred. The guys behind this aren't simply going to be concerned about avoiding taxes. Their main goal has got to be to hide the money and let us swing for the crime."

Eleven

As they drove back from Milwaukee, Maria convinced Johnny that a call to Charlie was absolutely necessary. Over a week had passed since their lunch together and he would be anxious to hear from her. She called him from her cell phone and told him that she had found stock trading certificates and bank statements from a bank that neither she nor Johnny had ever heard of. The statements seemed to confirm a large trading volume in Frontier stock, with corresponding cash deposits. She did not tell him about her trip to San Francisco or Johnny's meetings with Investech. She did say "Charles, all we've seen so far is paperwork that looks incriminating, but I'm very concerned about what all of this means. I think there is more to this than a bunch of paper. Johnny and I will call you tomorrow and discuss our next move." Charlie accepted this and asked her to be sure and call him as early as possible.

Maria hung up and immediately began evaluating the possibilities. There were two that she could think of. They could both go to Reno and continue what she had started a few days earlier, or pursue the Oak Bank lead. Going to

Reno included the potential of another confrontation, so they would have to be prepared, Since they were not ready to involve the police, they would have to hire a private form of protection. The Oak Bank matter was more subtle and obviously more complicated. Where to start? The series of letters and symbols on the Oak statement were all they had to go on. She could go on line and find a directory of banks in the United States, hoping it would lead them to Oak. But realistically, if Oak Bank wanted to be found, their address would be on their statements. She would try anyway, but knew it would almost certainly be futile. She could go out to Abcon and attempt to find the bank by using their computer in ways that were not taught in the information technology programs at the finest Universities.

Then an idea started to take shape. While she was at Abcon, a start up pharmaceutical company seemed to beat Abcon to the punch in introducing a handful of the drugs Abcon had been testing for years. At first it seemed like luck but, as time progressed, a pattern emerged that was unmistakable. Everyone was convinced that an insider was passing information to the start up. With all the money to be made by being first to the market with a new drug, someone would no doubt be willing take the chance for the right price. Maria noticed that some files she had been working on with experimental drug compounds periodically seemed out of order on her system. With all the security Abcon had installed, she was not overly concerned or suspicious at first, but as time passed, she reported this irregularity to her boss. Abcon called in a high tech crime investigation team and eventually found that an expert had hacked into their system and duplicated many of their files. In order to avoid negative publicity, Abcon reached an out of court settlement with the start up. The expert had been cooperative during the investigation and had received a lighter than normal prison sentence. Maria was amazed that anyone had been able to breach Abcon's computer security system and had spent time talking to the expert. She learned that he had experienced some personal financial and family medical problems and had only agreed to pass along Abcon's secrets out of desperation. She had persuaded her superiors at Abcon to recommend leniency for the expert. Now, maybe it was payback time. Maria believed she could defeat almost any form of computer security, but there two problems to deal with. She would need to use Abcon's facilities. She would also need more time than she had available. Access to the Abcon system was attainable, but she would have to explain her intended use, which she simply could not do. The expert might be the solution to both of these problems.

As the idea unfolded in her mind, she started to speak. "Johnny," she said slowly, "you remember the incident a few years ago involving the high tech theft of our drug compounds?"

He responded "Right, you mean where that guy, What was his name….found his way into your computer at work?

"I bet he could help us find Oak Bank", She came back.

She explained that the expert had a very detailed knowledge of computers and systems security. His wife and youngest child had contracted a rare blood disease and he had been unable to convince his insurance company to pay for the expensive treatments required so that his child could live a normal life. His savings were drained and his only recourse was to resort to using his expertise to break into his insurance company's computer system and program it to pay the benefits he needed to keep his child going. He learned that Abcon had been working on a drug to reverse the affects of the blood disease and he then set about to crack Abcon's high tech security. He had accomplished this by developing a program that defeated Abcon's security wall.

"It's only been a few years, but I can't remember his name and I have no idea how to contact him, "she said.

"Wouldn't there be police or FBI records?" Johnny asked, realizing immediately after he had spoken that this would not be an option.

"I'm pretty sure someone at Abcon still has that information" she said, "but I don't know how I will explain why I would ask for such information. I'll have to say I've been thinking about his child and wondered how the family is doing. I don't know if that's believable, but we need to take the chance."

With that she took her cell phone back out of her purse and dialed Abcon's main line. When the receptionist answered, she asked for her former boss. He answered after three rings. After brief hellos, she explained that she had been thinking about the family of the man who had breached their security a few years ago and wondered if Abcon had saved any contact information for them. There was a brief pause and Johnny could tell from Maria's expression that her ex boss had given her a positive answer.

"Yes," said Maria, "that's his name, William Palmer," as if he were an old friend. "OK" she went on, "just call me back when you have his number."

She said thanks, mentioned that she'd like to make the call as soon as possible and hung up.

For the remainder of the ride home, Johnny and Maria discussed their potential sequence of moves. They agreed that if they decided to go to Reno, it would be with adequate protection, although neither knew exactly what that meant. They could hire a private investigator to go with them, or even attempt to track Jonas Smith down without either of them present. This meant the circle of people who would know of their situation would grow. Also, for them to move around freely, they would need to rely increasingly on Maria's sister to take their children. They would definitely have to tell her their entire story and perhaps hire security to watch the family.

For the time being, they believed her father was safe since he knew nothing of the bogus stock trades. But they would have to tell him at the right time. As for the two of them, they agreed to take it a step at a time, and if things got too dangerous they would call in the FBI or SEC. They real question was how would they know when they had reached that point?

Twelve

Jonathan Blanchard's voice lost none of its authority, even over the phone from two thousand miles away, Warner Simmons thought. "Mr. Simmons, I agree your firm deserves the right to do some internal research on this matter," he said, "but just how long do you think it will take?"

"About three weeks" was the response.

"We simply don't have that much time," Blanchard retorted, "My clients would like a quick resolution without a lot of publicity, as I know you would. We can only keep this quiet for so long. Too many people know and the word will get out. You need to get back to me in a few days or less."

With that, the call was over and Warner Simmons was left holding the phone in one hand, while the other pressed solidly against his temples. He had contacted one of the best forensic accounting firms in the business, but after he had explained the circumstances surrounding the Frontier audit and the accusations against Johnny and his wife, the firm had told him they needed three weeks, minimum, to have any meaningful results. Warner, together with Bill, Charlie and Andy had agreed that they had no choice but to hire the accounting firm and pay a rather steep retainer to get them to move quickly. Still, they believed that three weeks was probably the best turn around time they could hope for. Warner would take Blanchard's message to the other three, but doubted it would change anything. The results of the forensic investigation would tell them just how real and serious the accusations were. They couldn't take any course of action without it.

Charlie told the other three about his lunch meeting with Maria and had steadfastly maintained his belief in Johnny and Maria's innocence. But, criminal matters aside, there was still the problem of a faulty audit that could cost the firm millions, or worse. Client defections would surely follow the public disclosure of any large settlement. They all agreed that containing any word of Westpac, Frontier or Blanchard's firm was critical.

The stress took its toll on Charlie. Questions arose as to Johnny's whereabouts after a couple of days of unexplained absence from work. He told everyone that Johnny had decided rather quickly to take some vacation time, but rumors circulated that Johnny was suffering from burnout and couldn't face further humiliation within the firm. Charlie decided that rumors about Johnny were just that and he had more important things to worry about. Still his concentration waned and he felt his leadership was no longer as effective as it had been prior to his wife's passing. He believed he had weathered the worst experience of his life just before the meeting with Blanchard's group. But now he was back in Neverland again.

As he left work on the Tuesday of Maria's call, his mind was immersed in sorting through the possible outcomes of the Westpac audit. He didn't notice, as he entered the elevator on the fifteenth floor, that a rather tall man in a dark blue suit walked in right behind him and that they were the only people on the elevator. He was startled when the man spoke.

"Mr. Stein, pardon me for me for being so direct, but I know time is of the essence."

Charles Stein noticed the man for the first time and turned to him with a completely blank look.

The man wasted no time and went on. "I didn't mean to startle you, but if you decide to take matters regarding the Frontier audit into your own hands, I believe I can help you."

He reached into his shirt pocket and produced a business card. It was a card like no other that Charles had seen. The card bore no firm name, but only a phone number and in small print said "former Securities and Exchange investigators." It did not have an individuals name on it either.

Charlie could not think of a single thing to say. He couldn't acknowledge there was an issue with the Frontier audit, but a denial seemed ridiculous. So he said nothing.

"I'm an entrepreneur, Mr. Stein. When Westpac's stock crashed right after the merger, I was rather certain someone would have need of my services. I can't solve all of your problems, but I can tell you what they are so you will be prepared. I can also suggest counter measures if you're inclined to take my advice, but that is entirely up to you."

The man went on," Since I am catching you off guard, I will give you some information so you don't think I'm trying to hustle you. You might want do a background check on Jonathan Blanchard and some of his past associations. I think you'll find some familiar names. Go back about fifteen years to a defunct Palo Alto law firm called Sullivan and Waters. Then work forward to 1995 and his merger work for a company called Berkeley Partners".

With that the elevator door opened, the man said, "Good night, Mr. Stein," and left Charlie standing alone, still not having said a word.

Thirteen

THE CALL CAME EARLY the next morning. Maria answered, and Johnny knew that her ex-boss was on the line. She began writing immediately – a phone number, name of a firm and the words 'Kansas City'. Maria said "thank you very much," with feeling, and the call was over.

"He has his own consulting firm in Kansas City," she said, "Palmer Consultants". They looked at each other and after a brief moment she said, "I'll call him."

Johnny nodded as Maria picked the phone up and dialed. He could tell that a receptionist had answered the call as Maria asked for William Palmer. Palmer was not in so Maria left a message and requested a return call, indicating that it was important business.

Now, there was nothing to do but wait, something that nether of them did particularly well. Johnny didn't like to think of himself or Maria as type A personalities, probably because the negative implications made him uncomfortable. True some the most intense people he served as clients were very successful in business because they simply couldn't wait or take 'no' for an answer. He had seen executives demean or bully subordinates or opposing business people for instantaneous answers, with little concern for whether they were right or wrong. Answers meant that deals got done, which often became more important than whether they were done for the correct reasons or not. Johnny's theory was that a few people were extreme type A's or extreme type B's and that everyone else was randomly populated somewhere in the middle. No one really liked to wait for anything, but some clearly did it better than others.

Maria and Johnny decided that she would give William Palmer the essential facts regarding their situation, but not all the details over the phone. This would best be done in person. Maria also decided that she couldn't ask her sister to watch their kids for another day without feeling guilty, so she would introduce him to Johnny over the phone and he would fly to Kansas City to meet with Palmer, in person. Assuming Palmer would meet with him.

When the phone rang again, Maria answered, but immediately had a surprised look on her face. She said, "Yes, he's here, please hold for a moment".

"It's Scott Borden for you'" she said quietly with her hand over the mouthpiece so Borden couldn't hear.

Johnny immediately wondered how Scott had obtained Johnny's home phone number, but realized the pattern was becoming familiar. Scott, like everyone at Investech, was one step ahead of him and he still hadn't decided if he liked their aggressiveness or not.

"Hi Scott," Johnny answered.

"Hi Johnny," Scott sounded very upbeat, "just checking in to see if you've come to any decisions yet."

"Scott, since you're familiar with my situation then you know I'm under a lot of pressure right now"

"I know Johnny," Scott responded. "Both Alex and Brad wanted me to assure you the firm would stand behind you regarding the investigation. They're confident they can get the worst of this behind you and they're excited to have you as part of the team."

"It's a big decision for me, Scott. I need a little more time and I want to talk it over with my family," was the reply.

"Johnny, some of the mergers and capital market deals we're working on are moving along pretty quickly and your input would be valuable right now." There was a sense of urgency in Scott's voice that Johnny had not heard in any of his past conversations with Scott. This started to irritate Johnny, but he politely held his ground.

"I understand, Scott" he said. "You've made me a generous offer in all respects and you deserve an answer. I have some personal things I need to work out over the next couple of days. How about I get back to you the first of next week?"

Scott persisted, "Is there any way you can get back to me this week?" he asked.

"Realistically, no" Johnny did not hesitate.

An uncomfortable silence ensued and Johnny waited as he knew he had put Scott in a difficult situation. More pressure from Scott would not be the answer, but Johnny realized that when Scott reported back to his superiors, they wouldn't be happy with the outcome of the conversation. Speaking of personality types, Johnny was sure Alex Franklin was an extreme type A, but kept it in the closet as much as possible. It was simmering just below the surface. Johnny wondered what to expect when it boiled over.

"OK Johnny, I understand," was all he could say, in a resigned voice. Will you call me as soon as you know anything?"

"Yes," he replied, "and please express my appreciation to Brad and Alex. I will definitely give the offer serious consideration." He thought about asking Scott how he had found Johnny's home phone number, but didn't. What did it matter?

Johnny and Maria found odds and ends to take care of around the house as they waited for William Palmer's call. At about 1:30 p.m. the phone rang and Maria answered. "Mr. Palmer, good to hear from you. Thanks for calling back so soon," she said.

As the conversation progressed, Johnny could tell that there was apparently a mutual respect between two computer savvy pros. Maria would later reiterate it to Johnny. Palmer was very appreciative of Maria's appeal to her boss at Abcon to be as lenient as possible regarding his sentencing. She had sympathized with his seemingly helpless situation in trying to obtain medication for his son's debilitating condition. She could only imagine how she would cope with something of that magnitude, if it involved one of her children. With her help, he had been sentenced to two years of minimum security prison with time allowed at home on occasion. More importantly, Abcon had been looking for volunteers when the FDA allowed its blood sterilizing drug to be tested and had selected his wife and son among the first recipients. This meant they received regular transfusions for free, which was a godsend for Palmer, given his incarceration.

When Maria indicated that members of her family had been falsely accused of a crime, he was eager to help. She explained only that she wanted to arrange for a meeting between him and her husband, Johnny. At that point she handed the phone to Johnny. The two agreed to meet in Kansas City, the next day.

Johnny's flight took off from O'Hare early on Wednesday and arrived shortly after ten. He took a cab to a nearby restaurant where Palmer had agreed to meet him. He was early so he found a local newspaper to read as he waited. At exactly 12:00 p.m., a man who appeared to be about forty years old, well dressed, slightly stocky with thick dark hair, graying at the temples walked through the door to the restaurant. Johnny approached the man and asked "Mr. Palmer?" Palmer responded by shaking Johnny's hand and saying "Yes, it's a pleasure to meet you Johnny. Your wife is quite a woman."

They made their way back to a table and the conversation began. Johnny decided that he had nothing to lose by telling the whole story to William Palmer. As he did so, Palmer listened intently, occasionally nodding, but obviously more intrigued as Johnny went on. When Johnny got to the part about the Oak Bank statement, he took a copy of one of the statements out of his pocket and handed it to Palmer. Palmer studied the statement and almost immediately took notice of the cryptic symbols that most people would not have focused on.

After a few seconds he looked at Johnny and said, "I have to guess this statement does not come from a bank in the United States. The experts tell me banks or financial institutions who are not interested in being found don't put their addresses on their statements, but they provide their customers with a code to ensure the customers can rely on its accuracy. The coding works both ways, as the customer can use it to tell the bank where to send the statement, or whether or not to even produce a statement at all. If you found this in your lock box, someone planted it there to make sure you know they're for real".

Johnny understood immediately. Certainly most people who want to hide money are not going to be interested in a bank statement appearing in their mail box. But the same banks that don't ask questions no doubt might have customers who want statements. Giving customers an option made sense.

Johnny then spoke up, "Mr. Palmer, would you have any idea how to figure out where Oak Bank is located?"

"I don't know, but I will certainly try. I'm really indebted to your wife." He paused briefly. "You know the FBI is still watching me. They don't follow me or anything like that, but I'm technically still on probation and they send someone out to my office occasionally. I'm also not sure if they tapped my phone. I never checked because I had no reason to". Johnny knew this was leading to somewhere, but let Palmer finish before asking what he was implying.

Palmer went on, "You'll have to give me a couple of days while I do some checking. We should not discuss this on the phone. Let's meet back here the day after tomorrow at the same time. Another thing, what are you doing for security?"

"Maria and I discussed that, but haven't done anything yet."

"I can help you with that" Palmer said. "You'll excuse me if I don't join you for lunch Johnny, but I want to get on this right away."

Johnny assured Palmer that he understood and shook his hand as he left.

Fourteen

What do you do in Kansas City while you're waiting to find out where a foreign bank is located? Nothing, Johnny decided. He would not stay in Kansas City, but returning home would simply waste two days and that was not in Johnny's nature. He decided he would make the trip to Reno that Maria never got to. Most likely it would produce no results, but simply taking some kind of action would provide temporary mental salvation. Johnny finished lunch and was able to find a cab which took him to the airport. There were no non stop flights to Reno, so he settled for a connecting flight through Las Vegas. While he waited for the flight, he called Maria and relayed his conversation with Bill Palmer. When he told her he was flying to Reno, her tone clearly indicated to Johnny that she was concerned. "Be careful," were her words. He assured her he would, after she gave him the address for Jonas Smith she had obtained while in San Francisco.

Johnny arrived in Reno at 7:45 p.m., just as twilight was giving way to an exceptionally pleasant late April evening. In his auditing life, he had frequently traveled to different parts of the United States. No matter what his destination in the Western half of the country, Johnny was always struck by the immediate difference in humidity levels that were evident the minute he exited the airplane door. Johnny felt a rush of energy as the light air seemed to invigorate him. In the summer, in the desert, the day time heat would set in and sap that energy. But this was spring in the high plains and the rush he felt as he walked outside the terminal seemed to lift his burden, if only temporarily.

He decided to rent a car and, without a hotel reservation, headed for the few tall buildings that dotted the darkening sky line. He decided on Harrah's Hotel and Casino where he checked in and rode the elevator to his room. With the time difference between Chicago and Reno, it was nearing the time he would have been getting ready for bed. But Johnny wasn't tired, having slept on the plane. He decided to go down to the casino and try his luck at the tables. Although he rarely gambled, he seemed to have a sixth sense about games involving cards, so he settled in at one of the blackjack tables.

It was Thursday night, but Johnny was amazed at the activity level that seemed to pervade the casino. This was not the high fashion crowd that you would expect to see in some of the glitzy Las Vegas hotel casinos. This group had a decidedly Western flavor, with the majority dressed in some form of denim, although Johnny guessed at least a few of the patrons had paid in the hundreds for theirs. Within a few hands, Johnny had settled in and was sipping one of the free drinks that would be his for the asking. There were five other people at Johnny's table. Some had large stacks of chips in front of them and others only a few. As the hands progressed and those with the few chips lost what they had, they gave way to new players who, no doubt, would be the next victims. It was only a matter of time. Johnny had always regarded gambling as a short form of entertainment. He felt sorry for the people who were convinced that the next hand would turn up a winner and were actually in it for the money.

As the night progressed, Johnny slowly built up the stack of chips in front of him. At midnight, after three drinks, he counted the chips and was up $580. Enough, he decided. He gathered the chips, handed the dealer a $50 chip and headed for the cashiers booth. Between the drinks and concentration level he applied to the game, he hadn't noticed the man watching him from across the room. Tomorrow, he would.

....

Johnny awoke slightly groggy from the previous night's activities. He decided to skip the workout he had planned, showered and went downstairs where he had breakfast and then walked to his rented car. He checked the map and the directions he had been given and found the entrance to Interstate 395 which would lead to the Redstone Avenue address of Jonas Smith. The ride lasted about 20 minutes and took Johnny through some of the prettiest scenery he had seen in some time. He exited the highway, made a couple of turns and found himself leaving the pavement and heading uphill on an improved gravel road, with fewer and fewer houses along the way. He arrived at a slightly more than modest looking Western style home with extensive wood trim on a large wooded lot. There were no visible signs of life either outside or inside the home. No cars in front, the garage doors were closed and all the shades were drawn. The nearest house was barely within eyesight and Johnny had not seen another person since his last right turn. Johnny realized he was clearly in harms way and had a decision to make. He could retreat and attack the problem from a different angle. Or, he could hope that Jonas Smith had made enough money investing his clients funds that he had decided to retire and live a quiet life in his getaway in the mountains outside Reno. Oh yes, and he also had to be home, have no large dogs and be willing to talk.

Johnny had come too far to head back down the hill without at least a try. He exited the car, rang the door bell and waited. Nothing. He decided to walk around the house and see if he could find any sign of life. He made his way around the side of the house to the rear and walked up a large wooden deck which matched the exterior trim of the house. Every window and sliding glass door was shut and locked with shades or blinds drawn. As he started to walk down the stairs of the wooden deck, he heard a car pull into the driveway in front of the house. One car door opened and closed.

Johnny walked slowly around the far side of the house and stayed close to the building. His rental car was parked in front of the house, so pretending he was not there was useless. He reached the corner and slowly peered around the edge. There he saw a blond haired man, about his own age looking straight at him. The man smiled and held his hands out to his side, palms up, in a gesture intended to show that he meant no harm.

"Hi Johnny," he said, "I'd like to talk to you, if you don't mind".

An interesting statement, Johnny thought. It wasn't like he had a choice and it wasn't posed as a question. The blond man could easily have come around the house with a weapon and either threatened or actually harmed Johnny if he had wanted to. Strangely, Johnny didn't feel threatened, but didn't feel particularly at ease either. He stood there without saying anything.

The man walked slowly toward the front door and reached into his front pocket, producing set of keys. "Please come in and sit down for a minute. I promise you won't be bored with what I have to say and you can leave any time you want". Johnny quickly looked to see that the man had parked his car well off to the side and that Johnny's car was not blocked in any way.

The man opened the door and held it for Johnny who slowly walked in to the house. It was simply, but tastefully furnished. It was no doubt a man's house, clean, but without the touch of a woman and it had the feel of a home which had only occasional use. After Johnny looked around for a minute, the man said, "I'm Jonas Smith," without offering to shake hands. "Please sit down." He pointed in the general direction of a small dark leather couch. Johnny, still not having said a word, took a seat, keeping his eyes on Smith as he did so. Smith, he decided, and the house went together well. Simple, but there was something rugged below the otherwise pleasant demeanor.

"I'm sure you've been through a great deal of stress Johnny and I am in a position to provide you with some answer's to the questions you have."

Now, he really had Johnny's attention and Johnny finally spoke up, "I'm listening" he said.

"This story starts pretty much with the inception of Frontier Data Systems Corporation. Frontier was the brain child of Frank Bishop, who founded the company ten years ago in Silicon Valley. At first, Frontier developed fairly unsophisticated software which allowed people in the field to transmit sales orders electronically to their home office or other points of origination. Over the years, the applications became more sophisticated and about three years ago Frank and a couple of his engineers began working on an application which would allow for the complete design of heavy industrial equipment in the field. Only slight modification was required after the data had been entered. The benefits were obvious. Little or no down time and you didn't have to fly designers around the world for specifications. It meant you could provide the customer with a price quote almost on the spot. The gain in productivity and time could easily mean the difference in orders won or lost.

The first test results of the software were very promising but, as time went on, some of the bugs proved to be tougher to work out than originally thought. Plus, one of Frontiers competitors started working on a similar system and caught up with Frontier, almost overnight. When word of Frontier's fast track order system first leaked out, Westpac approached Frank about a merger. The stakes were high as you well know. "

The pieces of at least part of the puzzle Maria had begun to work on were starting to fit. As Smith paused, Johnny began to fill in some blanks. "So seeing that his huge pay day was in jeopardy, Frank Bishop rigged a scheme to ensure that the merger went through".

"That's basically it. You know about the first fairness opinion and the audit confirmations. Frank was convinced that the few remaining modifications to the system were right around the corner and that they would be in place shortly after the merger was scheduled to close. He simply couldn't let the deal slip away. He had the competition breathing down his neck."

"I want to come back to the audit," said Johnny, "but how did my family get implicated in this?"

"Since Frank couldn't be completely sure when Frontier's software would be operational, he was concerned about a short term collapse in the value of Westpac's stock after the merger. He was looking for a way to pass the blame on to someone else, just in case. BCC and its audit partner were prime targets. A highly visible legal proceeding involving a major accounting firm would shift the focus away from him and buy some time."

Johnny asked skeptically, "And how did you get involved?

"I was the exclusive trader at IFS for Frontier stock. My name was associated with all the Frontier trades. When the truth about Frank Bishop came out, and I'm not sure it's all out yet, I obviously had a lot of angry people looking for me. I just dropped out of sight for a while. I've known Alex Franklin for some time. When he contacted me to try and help recover some of the losses to the Westpac shareholder's, I agreed to help."

Smith continued, "You know Investech was the investment banker in the Westpac/Frontier deal. Although Brad Worshaw wasn't personally responsible for the problems, the results have been very bad for business. He wants to find a way to repay at least some of what was lost in order to sleep at night. That, or he has to see that Bishop does it. Especially with the amount of money involved. Don't be naïve Johnny. And I'm not going to go into a lot of detail. I'm not saying any direct threats have been made, but there is definite pressure on Investech to take care of business."

The dialogue continued back and forth.

"So, are you saying Worshaw has some sort of plan?" asked Johnny.

"Yes, this is in part where you come in. Alex and Brad are pursuing you for a reason. They're right on the edge of being able to underwrite at least two more mergers that involve companies which were audited by BCC. And you were the partner in charge of those audits. Not only do you have irreplaceable knowledge, but both target companies know you and their top brass trust you. With the damage to Investech's reputation, you could bring some credibility back to the firm. They believe you could be the key to a very profitable year for Investech. They're only asking that you join them and give it a try. They have ties to Jonathan Blanchard's firm with all their high tech connections. They probably won't be able to get BCC off the hook entirely but, if you can help them, for their part, they're willing to facilitate the best outcome for everyone. If it all works out, BCC's insurance company won't get into it, so there should be little or no publicity. They would use their influence to persuade the Westpac shareholders to go along with the plan. It would be handled as a negotiation among the businessmen with little or no government involvement. They're not unreasonable people. They have confidence that you can pull off the new mergers and with the BCC settlement they'll come out about whole."

"One question I've been meaning to ask," said Johnny. "How did those audit confirmation come back so strong if the software didn't work?"

"The software worked to a point. About twenty percent of the confirmations were real. For the rest, we think Bishop bought or started shell companies and spent almost nothing in the process. You sent audit confirmations to a lot of companies that existed on paper only and I must say no one is that impressed with the quality of the audit. You and BCC aren't without some culpability here, Johnny."

Johnny didn't dismiss this out of hand, but he wanted to come back to the plan to frame his family. He asked Jonas Smith if he knew any more about that.

"I don't have all the details but, remember, Frank Bishop was a top software guy even with his problems. He had information that an individual in Wisconsin had a taken a significant buy position in Frontier stock just before the merger was announced. He suspected inside information and did a little research. At first he had no idea who Henry Dann was but eventually discovered it was your father in law. Maybe your wife's father was using the small amount of information you casually mentioned to him on a gamble that the merger would go through. We believe Bishop contrived paperwork that inflated the volume of the trades about tenfold over what Henry did on his own. But think about it. Bishop most likely assumed before you went to the police about the trades, you would go to your father in law and discuss it. If you combine the appearance of insider trading with the sloppy audit, he knew there would be no problem with some sort of settlement out of BCC. There's no way they would let any of this go public."

"Then lets cover the matter of threats to my wife while she was in San Francisco," demanded Johnny.

"I really wasn't sure who she was and why she was looking for me. We made contact with her in broad daylight in downtown San Francisco, during mid day. There were no weapons and no threats to anyone's life. There's too much at stake though to let her, or anyone else, start asking too many questions. If the authorities get involved now, everyone loses. No harm was intended to her, but we really can't let control of this matter get out of hand. I'm sorry if we frightened her.

When I was tipped off that someone was looking for me, I called Alex. He guessed it might be your wife, which is why I knew her name. Alex told me you might be dropping by here as well."

Johnny sat in silence. He, of course, didn't trust Smith or anyone involved with the Westpac merger. But, Smith knew too much to be a total fraud. There were a lot of facts to digest and it was just starting to hit him. He had a feeling what he had heard was, at least, mostly true.

Smith continued, "Johnny, if you accept Investech's offer you can help BCC, possibly your father in law and yourself at once. Do you really want to go back to a dead end job in public accounting? I'm sorry for being so frank, but based on everything I've been told by Alex, your star has faded. You have a chance to use the skills and contacts you've acquired to make a lot of things right and some serious money at the same time. It could be exhilarating. There's nothing wrong with that."

The unscheduled meeting with Jonas Smith over, Johnny walked back to his car and began driving without having any idea where he was going. Oddly, he wasn't sure if his trip to see Smith was a success or not. He had come away with a lot more information than he expected and without having to coax it out of Smith. The last thing he expected, though, was another sales pitch for him to join Investech. Although Smith hadn't said it, Johnny might be in a position to help him with his clients as well. Smith was obviously taking his cues from Alex Franklin and the unsettling part was they were getting to him.

Fifteen

JOHNNY REALIZED HE HAD been driving for about ten minutes and needed to get his bearings. He wanted to head back to the airport, but there was no one around to ask directions. He reached a summit on the gravel road he was driving on and saw an Interstate in the distance. He worked his way toward the Interstate by making a series of turns and eventually recognized that he was on the road he had exited on his way to Smith's house. From there he drove back toward Reno and found his way to the airport. He would again have to connect to Kansas City through Las Vegas.

After he booked the flight he decided he would call Maria and update her on the activities of the day. But how much would he tell her? He would leave out the details of her father's trades for now, but cover everything else. As soon as he said "Hi Mar," he could hear relief in her voice. He spoke slowly and deliberately, as he felt he could only go through the story once. She stopped him a couple of times but otherwise let him talk. Regarding the phony trades, he said that Bishop and maybe Smith had contrived them to set up BCC and Johnny as insurance that there would be some money coming back to the Westpac's shareholders. He mentioned nothing about Henry Dann. That would involve a separate conversation between Henry and himself.

When he finished, Maria asked, "What are you going to do?" meaning, "Are you going to take the job at Investech?"

"I really don't know. I have a lot to think about. I might be lucky that I even have a choice. First, I'm going back to Kansas City to meet with Bill Palmer. I'll be home tomorrow night".

The flights to Las Vegas and then on to Kansas City took a total of four hours, but they might have lasted ten minutes for all Johnny knew. He didn't stop thinking about the events of the past few weeks for a second. How did all this happen to a guy who performed audits for a living? A CPA? World's most boring profession. If Frank Bishop hadn't turned out to be a con man, Johnny could almost have empathized with him. A guy works hard for years and is at the precipice of a defining moment only to see it slipping away. How would Johnny have reacted to such a situation? Johnny thought back over the Frontier audit. He had been especially busy during the time the audit was performed. It was about a year ago. There was less audit work, but more legal entanglements to deal with. Many of the problems related to the earlier business failures of high tech companies audited by BCC. Some had run through court proceedings and dragged on without a resolution. He was involved in depositions, served as a witness at some court proceedings and assisted in negotiating settlements for BCC, as well as other injured parties. He was distracted enough to ask for assistance with the Frontier audit from one of the firm's offices outside of Chicago. He also remembered adding some people to his staff who he had not worked with before. A couple of them were responsible for overseeing the mailing and follow up related to the audit confirmations. Johnny had spent much less time than normal in discussions with top management and evaluation of their systems development. The words of Jonas Smith concerning his and BCC's culpability haunted him. Despite the procedures BCC had in place to insure the highest possible standards, Johnny had let the firm down.

....

Bill Palmer entered the restaurant the same way he had two days earlier. He looked serious, but seemed to have a quiet air of confidence. They shook hands and Palmer began by saying "This is going to take a while, Johnny. I simply don't have enough information at this point to give you what you need. But we'll get there."

Johnny responded, "After we met on Wednesday, I decided to fly to Reno and see if I could find the broker who handled all the bogus trades. I was successful, but I want to be sure about who orchestrated the trades before I decide what to do about it ."

Johnny repeated most of what Smith told him, including the part regarding Frank Bishop. Then he asked, "This may sound strange, but if I can get you the account numbers for Maria's joint trading account with her father, can you verify that certain trades were actually made?"

"Most likely," said Palmer.

"Thanks" said Johnny, "I can't explain right now, but knowing the truth about the trading activity will mean a lot to Maria." What he really meant was, "Once I know the truth I may or may not tell Maria."

"How do you want to proceed regarding Oak?" asked Palmer.

Can you see if it's for real and what's actually in the account?"

"That's just what I was planning on doing," replied Palmer. "Johnny," he continued "as I said on Wednesday, I owe Maria a lot, but this could get risky. It sounds like the people involved in moving this money around take their business seriously. Plus I don't really know how closely I'm being watched. This could get costly, too. If I pursue it further, we need to have an understanding regarding expenses and, I hope, some compensation."

"I understand, "said Johnny. "What do you propose?"

"Well, I'm willing to spend the time and advance the expenses involved to get the answers you need. That is, assuming I can find them and assuming I don't run out of money first. But if I can help recover any money that isn't ear marked for anyone else, I'd like a fifty-fifty split."

Johnny was puzzled by Bill Palmer's statement. "Mr. Palmer, you don't understand. Depending upon what we find, we'll have to return the money to the people it belongs to or possibly turn it over to the FBI.

"Oh, I'm sorry, I wasn't very clear," said Palmer. "What I meant was, any money I recover related to the matter of Frontier, Westpac or that entire business transaction will have to end up in the proper hands, don't misunderstand. But from what I can see, someone or some people may have set up an elaborate scheme to hide a lot of money. Chances are there is more being hidden that has nothing to do with your audit. Using off shore accounts generally takes a little practice. I'm guessing that one account will lead to another. I have no idea what I'll find, but would appreciate a little reward if I do find something that can be, say, unattached without anyone knowing about it."

"I see," said Johnny. "From my standpoint all I care about is making the people related to this matter whole. I don't want anyone to get hurt. And, I want my family cleared. Whatever happens outside of that really isn't my concern."

As they parted, Johnny asked Bill Palmer to keep him posted via cell phone. He did that specifically so he could monitor the feed back regarding the stock trading issue before anyone else found out.

Sixteen

On Monday morning, Johnny called Scott Borden and when Scott answered Johnny said, "I'm in. When can I start?"

BOOK II

Seventeen

Johnny told Maria of his decision shortly before he called Scott Borden on Monday morning. Her first reaction was to ask, "what are you going to tell Charlie?" The answer; "It'll probably make life easier for him, both because of what he knows and what he doesn't know." She intuitively understood Johnny's answer, but recognized that it would still be an emotional parting between the two.

On Monday afternoon, for the first time in a week and for the last time as an employee of BCC, Johnny entered the Gateway building and rode the elevator to the twelfth floor. As he strode the hallway to his office, the people he passed along the way and those who looked up from their work stations all asked how he was doing or smiled as if to say "we're with you." He had shared an administrative assistant with another partner and saw her as he was entering his office. He called her in and told her the news, but only mentioned that he had another job offer and not the name of the firm. She wished him well and said she understood his decision. He asked her to call Charlie's office and see when he would be available to meet with him. He then began to place his personal items in boxes he had brought with him.

He was told Charlie could see him right away and he left the unpacked boxes for his farewell meeting with his former mentor. His emotions started to get the better of him as he walked to Charlie's office. He knocked and then entered.

"Johnny, good to see you. I hope a little time off has cleared your head," offered Charlie.

"It has, but probably not in the way you would expect. Charles, I've received a job offer which, after careful consideration, I've decided to accept. I know you'll think I'm just reacting to the stress level around here, but I really need to make a change."

"I see," Charles replied. He paused for a few seconds and then continued, "Its important to me as I know it will be to Bill and Andy that you do this for the right reasons. You know the firm will stand by you through the Frontier thing. In fact, we've already hired a forensic accounting firm to review the facts surrounding the Frontier audit. Don't you think you should wait until we get some feedback on that before you make a decision?"

"Thanks Charles, I never doubted for a minute that you and the firm would cover my back, but it involves more than just the Frontier audit. The offer I have is from Investech. It gives me an opportunity to use my accounting knowledge of the tech industry and interact with many of the business people I already know. I don't view this as a step back, but actually a couple of steps forward. Let's face it, where am I really going here? Plus, my being out of the picture at BCC will make it easier to resolve the Frontier mess. Sort of like removing the cause of the problem." Johnny was careful not to mention the deal he was in the process of negotiating with Investech to ease the pain at BCC, because no details had been worked out yet. In fact Johnny didn't want Charlie to know about any of the maneuvering behind the scenes. He would make sure negotiations were handled by others, presumably Brad Worshaw of Investech with some assistance from Jonathan Blanchard.

"You know Johnny," said Charlie in an almost parental tone, "I really believe the problems we're working through are temporary. In fact, I think the worst is over. We'll get Frontier behind us and with the general business climate starting to pick up, you'll be riding high in no time. Bill tells me he has several new clients in the offing."

"Charles, I've given this a lot of thought and its true without Frontier I might not have even considered a change at this point. But the events of the past few weeks forced me to deal with reality. I haven't been happy for a long time. I'm actually looking forward to new challenges, and the earnings potential is intriguing. My only regret is not being able to work with you and some of the wonderful people associated with this firm."

"But you're a CPA and you've thrived on being able to apply your technical training in the most professional way. People respect you for what you are now," Charlie was clearly starting to press as he sensed he was losing the case. "I'll talk to Bill and Andy about additional compensation if that will help keep you here."

"No, but thank you very much anyway." Johnny responded, "Its not a money thing at its core. I know how much we both enjoy working together and the mutual respect we've developed over the years, but I think you can understand my decision."

Charlie's expression signaled to Johnny that he had thrown in the towel. A significant shrugging of his shoulders followed by a huge sigh. "I do Johnny, but it's difficult to accept."

"Charles, we won't be working together on a daily basis, but my office will be just down the street, I'll be representing some of BCC's clients, merely in a different aspect of business."

The discussion continued for some time and moved on to the matter of the forensic accounting firm that Charlie and Warner Simmons had hired. Johnny told Charlie he was sure the firm would find that BCC was only guilty of not thoroughly checking the source of some of the audit confirmations and there would be no implication of inappropriate application of Generally Accepted Accounting Principals. In that light, BCC could probably expect to absorb some financial repercussions, but would most likely be able to avoid any governmental sanctions. Johnny didn't explain the basis upon which he drew that conclusion and Charlie didn't mention he might have an ace up his sleeve in a former SEC investigator who might provide assistance to both BCC and Johnny personally.

Within seconds after Johnny left Charlie's office, Charlie picked up the phone and called Maria.

"Hi Maria its Charles. How are you dear?"

"I'm doing as well as can be expected," she replied.

"You're aware that Johnny has decided to join Investech? He asked.

"Yes, he told me this morning," was her response.

"You know I want the best for you and Johnny, but I can't help feeling he's over reacting to a difficult situation right now."

Maria replied, "You know Charles, the truth is he hasn't been that happy for some time. I'm sure you could tell, even if he didn't say anything. He could use a change, but I don't know how much I trust the people at Investech. Johnny likes Scott Borden, but hasn't said much about the other people at the firm. He also seems to think he can work out the problems related to our trading account with a little help from Investech."

"Did he say why?"

"No, he was a little vague about that and I didn't want to press him for details." was all she could say. "What do you know about Investech?"

"They're fairly new on the block. Their CEO is a well known industry guy who was in the technology business for years. He sold a company he started, made a huge profit and decided to underwrite mergers and acquisitions of other tech companies. There are rumors that the executive officers take large individual stock ownership positions in companies they advise, through entities that aren't related to Investech. I'm sure you know they're not supposed to do that because both parties to a merger need to have complete trust in their investment bankers. Especially when there are millions or billions at stake. If two firms are merging, the acquirer will be naturally suspicious that the target firm is hiding something. The whole process needs to be above reproach. No one has ever proven that the officers at Investech have benefited beyond the merger and acquisition fees they earn. Plus there's the matter of insider trading that would be a problem as well."

"So neither of us has a really good feeling about this, other than it could resolve all of our problems," she added half as a statement and half as a question.

"I genuinely think Johnny sees this as an opportunity." said Charlie, "But we would all have to be blind not to believe there are some risks involved."

"I see what you mean, Charles. I see what you mean."

Eighteen

THE WORLD OF MERGERS and acquisitions involves one interesting constant that is true above all else. There is only one party who is certain to benefit from a completed transaction and that is the investment banker. The investment banker is the chaperone of the dance, who sees that the music and the mood are just right so the dancers glide across the floor without tripping on each others feet. In the case of a potential merger, the dance partners are the target company and the suitor companies. The company to be bought and the possible acquirers. If the investment banker has done a good job, the dancers will be dancing the same dance. If not, one may be doing the Rumba while the other is doing the Fox Trot. It is the investment banker's job to ensure that the dance goes well enough for the dancers to want to continue dancing until a marriage takes place. For the privilege of arranging the dance, preparing the dancers in advance and hand holding during the courtship, the investment banker is paid a substantial fee, normally upon the successful completion of the marriage vows. In other words, it's generally all or nothing with big money at stake for everyone. Once the marriage is consummated, its up to the new, combined company to make it work, while the investment banker moves on to the next mating ritual.

....

Johnny arrived at Investech's offices punctually at 8:30 a.m. on the appointed day. As he walked through the glass doors into Investech's lobby, he immediately saw a banner over the receptionist's desk welcoming him, by name, to the firm.

He smiled at the receptionist and said, "Hi, I'm Johnny Brandt reporting for work."

Yes, Mr. Brandt, everyone is expecting you. Let me get Brad and Scott."

Within a couple of minutes the two walked into the reception area together and greeted Johnny warmly. They ushered him past the reception desk into the hallway leading to all of the offices and then into a decent sized office with modern furniture. His name was already on the door and the view of Lake Michigan from over forty stories was breathtaking.

Brad began, "Johnny, we've arranged for one of our most experienced people to serve as your executive administrative assistant. She'll have access to any and all research material you need. We have almost unlimited resources at your disposal, including a data base of every tech company in the industry and a support staff to generate whatever reports or presentation materials you need."

Brad picked up the phone and asked Brenda Holmes to join them in Johnny's office. Johnny guessed Brenda to be about forty. She was reasonably attractive with short to medium length light brown hair, very frank green eyes, a warm smile and a firm hand shake. She assured Johnny she would be pleased to work with him and was eager to get started. She had already placed research reports concerning some potential target companies on Johnny's desk. He was impressed.

With the introduction complete, Brad suggested they all sit down and discuss 'strategy'.

He began, "It would make the most sense for us to start with a couple of companies you've been auditing," he said to Johnny. "We know that Burgess Systems needs a capital infusion to develop their financial reporting software and that they're fiercely independent. We'd like to match them up with one of the big guys in Silicon Valley or Boston, but haven't figured out the best pairing at this point. We've talked to them about providing some equity, but that's as far as it's gone. Frankly, they're short of top level talent and could use a well positioned suitor. We know they have high regard for you, so we've held off pursuing any more meetings until you could arrange it."

Johnny responded, "I don't know how much interest you'll get from them concerning a merger, but they could definitely use capital to move to the next level. Their chairman has plans to bring his son on board in a few months and eventually turn the reigns over to him."

"Yes, we know that and it's part of what concerns us. It'll be difficult to convince our capital partners to back Burgess' expansion plans without an experienced management team to lead the way. Plus, they have another problem and that's marketing and distribution. Burgess has done a great job of product development, but that's really where their expertise lies. If they can't get the product to market, it's not going to do them any good."

Scott joined the conversation, "Johnny, just so you know, we've been shopping them around in terms of a debt and equity infusion and everyone we've talked to says the same thing. The potential capital sources are skeptical about our ability to get Burgess to the negotiating table. They know that, until now, Burgess regarded us as outsiders. We're confident they'll give their situation more serious consideration if they hear it from you."

"Your right, they're a bit of an introverted group compared to the typical tech players and I think that mentality is holding them back. I'll give Todd Pulaski a call this afternoon," said Johnny.

Brad went on, "The other firm we've identified as a takeover target is The Ronco Group. The problem is they're so big, the number of possible suitors would be very limited."

"Yes, and the winning suitor would have to have a lot of patience to repair the problems they've encountered over the past couple of years," Johnny came back.

All four looked at each other and nodded their agreement with the last statement. Ronco was well known in the industry for mismanagement of very lucrative government contracts. They had been in a public name calling match with the federal government over the past several months. In fact, Johnny had testified during an evidentiary proceeding that, fortunately for Ronco, was held behind closed doors. But Ronco was somewhat bullet proof in that they had the only software application available to support the latest version of satellites the government had been launching to complete the North American Defense System. The government could fight with Ronco about money, but ultimately Ronco held all the cards. Still their relations with a number of customers had become contentious and it was generally thought a new regime at Ronco would be welcome.

Johnny had to agree that the group at Investech had done a good job identifying two firms with significant potential for investment banking guidance. He also could see where has involvement might make the difference in landing one or both as clients.

With the strategy session over, Johnny was left alone to start the first day of the second job of his adult life. He felt out of place, although the warm reception provided by his new fellow employees certainly helped. He picked up the research reports and read through what several analysts had to say about Burgess, Ronco and a handful of other tech firms. He already knew most of what he was reading, but thought he ought to let at least half a day pass before he started calling for business.

During the morning, Brenda brought several people into Johnny's office for him to meet and at about 10:00 a.m., he got his first call. It was from Alex Franklin. He was sorry he could not be in the office to officially welcome Johnny in person, but he was on the West Coast meeting with some of the firms biggest clients. Johnny said he understood and would see Alex in a few days. Before finishing the call, Alex made a point of letting Johnny know that the firm was counting on him for big things and he was sure Johnny would deliver. Johnny appreciated the vote of confidence although he would have been even happier without the implied pressure that went with it.

Shortly after noon, Scott came by and invited Johnny to lunch. They went downstairs to a restaurant in the building and continued the conversation they had started in Johnny's office. As Investech's CFO, it was Scott's job to understand the financial position of the firm's clients and potential clients and Johnny always found Scott to be well prepared. He would be a good source of information.

As they were finishing lunch, Scott said to Johnny, "I know you'd like to move forward with wrapping up the Frontier matter, both for your family and BCC. One of the things Alex is doing in California involves business with WestPac and Blanchard's firm. He'll be able to update us when he gets back."

"Good," said Johnny, "the sooner the better."

With lunch finished, Johnny returned to his office, closed the door and started dialing for dollars. His first call was to Todd Pulaski at Burgess. He was told Todd was in a meeting and would likely not be able to return the call until tomorrow morning. Next he called Bill Mancini, the CFO at Ronco. Bill did not answer his phone, so Johnny left a voice message. Now what? Johnny made a mental list of the people he could call simply so he would feel busy, but not sound desperate for conversation. The first person he was able to actually get on the phone was a banker he had worked with on a small merger earlier that year. Johnny had helped interpret a portion of a client's financial statement for the banker, then stayed involved until the deal closed. The banker needed Johnny's involvement and had sent him a gift in appreciation of Johnny's efforts. The banker had heard Johnny left BCC and joined Investech. Johnny asked the banker what he knew about Burgess Systems and was surprised to hear that the bank had already been discussing a possible loan to Burgess. The banker couldn't talk freely about the transaction, other than to say the bank had some concerns about the depth of Burgess senior management. He also said that he believed that, under the right conditions, Burgess could be very 'bankable' but that he would want to partner with other investors to spread the risk. This Johnny found very interesting and he was happy he had garnered some information to share with his new associates. Johnny suggested they stay in touch and consider working together on a transaction with Burgess, if a deal could be structured. Could he be on the way in his new career?

His second day at work began with a meeting, including his entire team. Brenda had sent out an invitation by email to a total of fourteen people. The firm had a policy of rotating people among three different teams and anyone could be assigned to the A, B or C team depending upon their availability and the level of expertise needed by the team. The letter designations had no specific connotation involving competency or qualifications. Also, people could be added to or deleted from the team if there was a pressing need in a particular area. In order to give Johnny some confidence, Brad and Alex had decided to establish a team for him even though he hadn't started his first assignment. He would be able to get to know the people he'd be working with and establish some rapport before the heavy lifting began.

Although Brenda would help coordinate the team for Johnny, each key component had experts who would perform the day to day work. Jack Miller, chief of due diligence, would oversee a mini-team of up to six people who would essentially prepare a five year operating pro-forma of the target company. This would involve reviewing management financial data, contracts, SEC filings and the voluminous legal and related documents required as part of existence in the corporate sphere. This group formed the core of the due diligence team and Johnny knew that once an assignment began, they had a thankless job of long hours, extensive travel, meals at odd hours and maybe a few hours of sleep here and there. Before bids were placed by interested buyers, literally hundreds and possibly thousands of documents would be reviewed by this group and placed in a 'data room' which could be accessed on line by anyone who was given the pass code.

The remainder of the team included one of the firm's legal vice presidents and a paralegal who would be available to interact with the lawyers representing bidders and the target company. Along the way there would be confidentiality agreements to be negotiated, hopefully a merger agreement, often called an MA, together with disclosure schedules and press releases. The remaining members of the team would arrange financing for the merger and be available for hand holding along the way, whether they were holding a hand with a pen, money, or a wallet to put it in. The top executives of target firms in past several years generally received very lucrative severance packages, or offers to retain their positions after the merger closed. Faced with pressure to complete large, high profile transactions, they often needed emotional as well as professional coaching.

The meeting lasted a couple of hours and started with each of the team members introducing themselves and giving a little background information for Johnny to absorb. Investech had spared no expense in bringing in some of the finest talent from the best graduate schools in the country. Without asking, Johnny guessed Jack Miller and the other supervisory level people had reached the ripe age of thirty-something. But the rest of the troops were barely out of various MBA programs that would, no doubt, require student loan repayments for years to come. He also knew, given the current state of the investment banking field, they would have no trouble making those payments.

Johnny left the meeting with a good comfort level based on what had transpired. When he returned to his office, he had a message from Todd Pulaski, whom he immediately dialed and was put directly through.

"Johnny," I understand congratulations are in order."

"Thanks Todd," replied Johnny, "I'm really pumped about this opportunity with Investech. It's the right thing at the right time."

Todd went on, "we've been talking to Brad and Scott for some time, but I'd like to hear from you. We clearly have to make a move, but we've been waffling between doing a debt and equity offering, and considering a merger. The timing with you being on board is very good. When can we get together?

"How about Monday, first thing? I'll check the flights and get back to you in an hour."

....

From his office in the Chairman's suite, Brad Worshaw smiled as he viewed the screen on his desktop. His decision to bring Johnny on board was working as well as the voice interpreter Alex had installed in all the desktop computers and hand held devices at the company. The state of the art equipment converted verbal communication to written word and allowed the two of them to keep tabs on their employees. After all, he was techie at heart and what better way to test out an innovative product. Now, though, the only question was when to form the first off shore company to invest in Burgess. The way it looked, it was just about time to start the wheels in motion.

Nineteen

Scott Borden accompanied Johnny to Burgess' office the following Monday. As Todd Pulaski mentioned on the phone, there was a bit of a history between the two companies and Johnny wanted to hear the details. The plane ride to Denver would provide a good opportunity for them to talk. Normally they would bring a professionally prepared presentation with color slides comparing Burgess to its competitors, projecting their growth and profitability and then summarizing different industry measures that Wall Street analysts use to evaluate the potential success of a merger. The latter, Johnny thought, was part of a plan by the investment bankers to impress the boards of target firms with so many buzz words that their heads would spin. They all knew what EBITDA (earnings before interest, taxes, depreciation and amortization) meant but how about Implied Earnings Multiple or Nominal Enterprise Value. The pretty charts and graphs were sales tools to impress their potential clients, designed in part to convince them to put their companies on the market. That done, the investment banker would get a chance to use a different set of sales tools to sell the company to a suitor.

Scott had given Johnny a copy of the booklet Investech prepared for Burgess about six months earlier. The presentation was flawless and even though a few months had passed, still timely. There had been three meetings with either Brad, Alex or Scott and the top brass at Burgess. One of the meetings had included Burgess entire board of directors. In the months since the last meeting, there had been a couple of follow up conversations, but clearly the 'process' lost what little momentum it had going. Scott recommended against bringing another presentation booklet and suggested they handle the meeting as more of a heart to heart talk. After hearing all the details, Johnny now understood. The board was apparently interested in what the investment bankers had to say and understood the need to take some kind of action. But Investech had failed to gain enough trust to get a commitment from the board. That was now Johnny's job and illustrated why Brad and Alex had pushed so hard to have him join Investech. By the time the plane landed in Denver, Johnny was fully briefed and ready to go.

Johnny had gotten to know Todd Pulaski pretty well in the four years he was partner in charge of the Burgess audit. He had made it a point to schedule at least one winter business meeting in each of the last couple years at Burgess' office, so that he and Todd could go skiing afterward. Todd was in his mid fifties and in great physical condition. A true outdoorsman Johnny thought, liked to ski, hunt and mountain climb. He had graduated college with a degree in electrical engineering and later partnered with a couple of computer geeks to form a firm that pioneered some of the most sophisticated financial reporting software in the country. They targeted specific industries including real estate and insurance, did their homework, listened to their clients and rolled out what had become benchmark products for those industries. They focused heavily on product development, upgrading their products regularly and providing state of the art customer service. Johnny and Todd had talked about the potential for Burgess to expand upon the base it had already established. Todd had always been more concerned with serving his loyal customer base rather than looking for new business. Lately, though, some of the newer members of his board had been pushing for growth and Todd realized that Burgess had to expand or risk being overtaken by larger competitors. Competitors who could compete more effectively based on lower operating costs.

Johnny and Scott were escorted into Todd's office within minutes of their arrival. They were joined by Todd's son, Richard and Dave Rosen, Burgess' CFO.

"Johnny, good to see you and glad you brought Scott with you as well," was Todd's greeting. They shook hands warmly and settled into comfortable leather chairs around the round conference table.

After some guy talk about skiing and the recent trade the Denver Broncos football team had made, Johnny began, "Thanks for meeting with us today. On the ride out, Scott brought me up to date on your previous meetings and the general course of conversations you've had. My sense is that you and your team are ready to make some strategic moves, but you haven't gotten over the hump on which way to go. As you know, we'd like to help with those decisions. Frankly, we understand this will involve some pain in that it will require philosophical changes here, but as we've discussed before its more a matter of when, than if."

"You're basically correct, Johnny. The board's been more vocal than ever and I haven't followed up on my promise to them to make formal recommendations. I'm supposed to provide guidance regarding either expanding our technical capabilities or our sales network. Or both." Todd responded.

"I don't want to speak out of place Todd, but Scott and I believe there are two potential merger candidates for you who would be as close to a perfect fit as possible. We think at least one of them would be happy to have Burgess focus on the things it does best, while they handle distribution and funds for expansion. We haven't made any phone calls yet, but with your permission we could do that. We'd recommend, though, if you decide to go that route, you open up a broader competitive bid process to insure you come away with the best deal."

"What would we have to give up?" Todd asked.

"It all depends on what you can negotiate," Johnny responded, "and the comfort level you have with whoever you partner with. We really believe you're in a strong position. There are more firms out there who need what you bring to the table than the other way around."

Dave Rosen spoke for the first time, "To be honest with you Johnny, I'm very concerned about the extra work that process will impose on our people and the inherent morale issues. I know we have to provide the best possible results for our shareholders, but that could also mean some of our staff will be working themselves out of a job"

To this Scott replied, "We'd be less than honest if we said this wouldn't be a heavy load, especially on the accounting people. But we've already assembled a top notch team at Investech to help you through the wars. Fortunately, from what we can see, you're up to snuff on your legal documentation and Johnny says your accounting records are in great shape."

The conversation then started to focus on details of the process of finding a suitor or merger partner. Johnny realized that Todd, his son, and Dave Rosen were now talking as if engaging in the process had been decided and only the details, the vast, time consuming myriad of details, had to be worked out. Although Johnny didn't want to over emphasize the point, by the time the process was over, lawyers, accountants, investment bankers, lenders, senior level executives and analysts would know every square inch of Burgess' business. As clean as Burgess was, what little dirt there might be would become exposed somewhere along the way. And the suitors would use this to their advantage during the negotiations. Scott knew better than Johnny that if they made too much of this, it would discourage Todd and his people.

After meeting for some time, lunch was brought in and while they might now have expected to be talking about other topics, the discussion moved on to how to approach the board. Todd, as Chairman and CEO certainly had the board's trust, but felt that a formal presentation should be made by Johnny and a select group from Investech. Todd, Richard and Dave would have some preliminary discussions, especially with the key board members. They would prep them up so they would be ready to vote on the concept of exposing the company to either a formal bid process or a negotiated merger. A tentative date was set for a board meeting during the last week of May, in Denver.

The matter of Investech's fee was next on the agenda and there Johnny let Scott do the talking. He explained the commonly accepted industry method for computing investment banking fees and, based on Burgess assumed market value, Dave Rosen determined that the fee could be as high as twenty million dollars. Simple math. The more a company was worth, the higher the fee. Also, the industry standard had the suitor paying the fee, so, as the target, you didn't mind at all. It was almost perfect.

The meeting over, Johnny and Scott were driven back to the airport by limousine and caught a 4:12 p.m. flight back to O'Hare. With the time change, flying West to East, they would arrive back in Chicago at about 9:30 p.m. and be home, hopefully, within an hour. Long day. On the way back, Scott dozed and Johnny reflected on the events of the day. By all accounts it had been a huge success, with Johnny performing exactly as had been expected. He had to hand it to his new bosses. They correctly measured the response to his addition to the team. Johnny gave them the credibility to close a client who had been on the fence. There was no replacing personal relationships that had been developed over time. True, accountants had taken a hit to their reputation over the past few years. But those were nameless, faceless guys you read about in the papers, not your auditor who guided you through the inane SEC filings and provided solid advice when you needed it.

There was no joy in Johnny despite all of this. Although he realized he was overly critical of himself, he couldn't help feeling as if he had now become a salesman. Albeit, a high priced, sophisticated, technically oriented salesman. But, a salesman nonetheless. Brad, Alex and Scott had set the table and Johnny had moved them to where they could smell a twenty million dollar meal. Maybe it was too soon to go from being a partner in a public accounting firm to an investment banker and be comfortable with it. But the circumstances were wrong. It wasn't as if he had sought out a position with Investech. He had really acquiesced to a set of circumstances that were out of his control. How much did he trust his new employers? Nothing more had been said of the deal to be negotiated on his family's behalf. Then there was the matter of money. It was a little premature of him to place a lot of emphasis on it, but based on his employment agreement, a not so insignificant portion of the twenty million dollars would find its way into his pocket. He was as conflicted as he had ever been in his life.

Twenty

In Maria's mind, the risk profile hadn't gone away, but only shifted. What had started out as a threat to her and her father was now squarely on Johnny's shoulders. She might have been able to rationalize the fact that people make mistakes and the people who had made, or lost, a lot of money on the Frontier/Westpac merger reacted in a threatening way without first considering their actions. That alone would have been a stretch since she felt there was a message of implied physical harm to anyone who decided to pursue finding Jonas Smith. People who simply over react start out in anger and then, either let it dissipate, or move on to a more rational and well conceived plan for retribution. She had been followed and threatened, so that was apparently the anger phase. Then the mysterious Jonas Smith appears without any further effort to find him. He provides a rational and convincing argument for Johnny to join Investech. Phase two was now in progress.

She could not put her last conversation with Charlie out of her mind. The principals of Investech were thought to have violated securities laws by investing in companies that were about to become takeover targets. Of course, nothing had ever been substantiated. In her mind, this was a far cry from working for BCC regardless of whether or not the firm had been negligent in completing the Frontier audit. One constituted unintentional oversight and the other criminal activity. And, most likely, the difference between monetary fines and jail time.

There was more to it, though. She had to ask herself if it would be so bad if Johnny made a career change that got him out of a dead end job and into a new, lucrative position. Johnny was smart and perceptive and willing, now, to take some risk to break out of his personal confinement. But Maria knew Johnny might not be in the best position to know what he was dealing with. His natural tendency was to be more trusting than her.

Maria decided that she would monitor the situation, not from a distance but from as close to the inside as she could get. She let a few days pass after her phone conversation with Charlie and then began her research. Investech, as a registered investment banking firm, was required to be a member of certain professional organizations including the North American Securities Dealers association, or NASD. She went on line to NASD and navigated through the website until she found a registration statement for Investech. This included the background of all of its principals. Brad Warshaw was listed as Chairman of the Board and was a major stockholder. He was 59 years old and held a masters and a law degree from the University of California at Berkeley. He had previously been president of a technology firm in Silicon Valley and briefly practiced law with a firm named Blanchard and Stone in San Francisco, California. He had been Chairman since Investech's formation in 1995. Alex Franklin, age 47, was listed as president. The information indicated he had 'attended' Purdue University from 1972 through 1974. He then moved on to the US Marine Corp until 1979, when he joined a major east coast bank as a security officer, whatever that meant. He had a series of additional short term jobs before joining Investech. Maria found this strange in that his background did not fit someone at the top of an investment banking firm; one that specialized in the technology industry. Scott Borden was listed as chief financial officer. He was 42 years old, had graduated form the University of Michigan and worked for a big five accounting firm for most of his career prior to joining Investech. Some of the other officer's biographies were included in the registration statement, but these three were the only names she recognized.

Now to go on to the next step, she went into a Google search of individuals by name. There were five Bradley Warshaw's listed and she found her target as number three. He had graduated with honors from the University of California in 1969, completed his master's degree two years later and graduated from law school in 1976. He had held either vice presidencies or been president of three different firms in Silicon Valley and sold one of them in 1995. There were copies of articles published in local bay area newspapers discussing the sale and mentioning that the principals of the firm had pocketed almost $200 million. He later co-founded Investech and served as its Chairman. Nothing was mentioned regarding time with a law firm.

Maria concluded that Warshaw seemed like a solid citizen on the surface, but she needed to find out what other investments he had. This would be more difficult as she knew people didn't have to put these things in their own name. You could form a trust to invest for you, or put ownership in the name of your spouse. Or, you could invest through a foreign entity and by-pass United States laws entirely. She couldn't search the registration files in every country, so she would have to narrow the field down.

It occurred to her that she should start looking in whatever country the Oak Bank and Trust was domiciled. She wouldn't know that until they heard back from Bill Palmer. It had been about ten days since Johnny met with him and neither of them had heard from him since then. Johnny probably lost focus since he had become immersed in his new job and, apparently, there might be a resolution to their problems anyway. She decided she had nothing to lose by calling Bill and placed a call to his office in Kansas City. After several rings an answering machine announced that no one was in the office, so she left a message for him to call her at home.

She then placed a call to Charlie, mostly out of her frustration at not being able to proceed with any more fact finding. When he came on the line, she explained what she had accomplished and then he said, "Maria, I didn't tell you this the other day, but I was approached by a man who used to be with the investigative branch of the SEC. He offered his services to help us get to the bottom of Westpac allegations. I've held off doing anything until we hear back from the forensic accountants. I wanted to assess our risk before making the next move. That was before I knew Johnny was going to work for Investech. We may want to make that call now, although I can tell you, I'm sure there'll be a hefty fee involved for the information."

"I think we should pursue that," Maria responded. Then she asked, "Did you hear from the accountants yet?"

"We have a meeting with them in an hour. I'll let you know how it goes."

Maria asked, "Is there any exposure for Johnny?"

"I really don't know," was his response, "it depends on what they find, whether the firm is investigated and how good our bargaining position is."

With the conversation complete, Charlie left his office for a meeting with Warner Simmons before the session with the outside accounting firm. Warner had decided to hire the forensic accountants through BCC's outside legal counsel and have the findings submitted back to BCC through the same channels. This way BCC could assert that the accountant's report was privileged information and not subject to discovery. This would, hopefully, avoid the results being disclosed in the event of a legal proceeding. The meeting with Warner would be to discuss legal protocol before the results of the audit by the forensic guys were made known. Although it was firm practice to have its audits reviewed internally for quality control, this was the first time Charles could ever remember having an audit of an audit.

The forensic accountants arrived as scheduled and submitted booklets to each person at the meeting. They then proceeded with a power point presentation of the same material that was in the booklets. The first page outlined the procedures they followed in assessing BBC's compliance with industry standard auditing methods and the rest of the pages showed the results of their findings. Basically, BBC did not violate rules with regard to GAAP, (Generally Accepted Accounting Principals), however, the firm was not diligent in its implementation of audit confirmations.

The presentation included a full color chart and graphs which showed the number of confirmations mailed, the number of legitimate responses, the number of unsubstantiated responses and number of non responses. Unsubstantiated responses meant responses from companies that were found not to be bona fide operating companies, or had not executed orders for software as had been reported on Frontier's books. Or, they simply did not exist at all. Although the number of confirmations was about evenly split between real and fake, the dollar amount of the unsubstantiated confirmations far outweighed the legitimate dollars confirmed. This was clearly damaging to the firm. Someone had orchestrated an elaborate scheme to overstate the anticipated revenue stream of Frontier and thus its market value.

With a table full of lawyers and accountants there ensued a lengthy discussion of BCC's potential liability to the shareholder's of Westpac. BCC's outside counsel pointed out that some of Westpac's shareholder base consisted of institutional investors, most of whom had Silicon Valley connections. This meant they had a small number of sophisticated shareholders who would most likely not be interested in a high profile public law suit. He speculated that Jonathan Blanchard, with his firm's client base in that area, might be able to influence the amount of exposure this matter received and thus help keep it out of court. In other word's, Blanchard's claim that he represented shareholder's who were damaged in the merger might well be accurate. Working through Blanchard might be the key to a swift resolution. Whether it would be a reasonable resolution was another matter.

Charlie then asked "do you know if Blanchard's firm represents Investech?"

This was met with a puzzled look by most at the table.

"I don't know, but I can find out," was the response from outside counsel.

"Thanks, I'm just curious," was his comeback. He didn't want to go further with his reasoning in front of the whole group, but he was starting to connect the dots. Investech could be a major client of Blanchard's. Investech wanted

Johnny badly. Investech gets Johnny in exchange for Blanchard influencing the outcome of a potential dispute with BCC and promises Johnny protection for his family.

As the meeting concluded, the booklets that had been passed out were now collected and returned to the outside accountants. It would not be wise for this type of material to be floating around where it could inadvertently be found by anyone outside of the group at hand. The accountants also promised to keep the power point presentation under lock and key.

When all had gone, the three senior partners and Warner Simmons discussed their next course of action. Warner would fly to San Francisco and meet with Jonathan Blanchard. Obviously, Blanchard had a number in mind and if they could agree on it, they would avoid a nasty public spectacle and, hopefully, save the firm a fortune in legal fees. Then there was the matter of the audit confirmation fraud and what to do about it. It seemed fairly obvious that those who stood most to benefit from the sale of Frontier had concocted it. It was not something that BCC would want to take to the authorities. Hiring a private source would be best. It was then that Charlie produced the card of the man he had met on the elevator. The card with no individual's name, but simply a phone number to call. Someone who did not want to be known for who he was, but only for what he could do.

Twenty One

To say that life had not turned out as planned for William Palmer would be an understatement by anyone's standards. His father had been a well respected banker in Kansas City and, after graduating from prep school number five in a class of several hundred, he attended Kansas State University on an academic scholarship, or as his friends liked to say, on a 'full ride'. The scholarship was more a sense of pride to Bill than anything else, because his family could easily have afforded any college in the country. But Bill and his father, William Senior could never overcome a fractious relationship that seemed to start from the day he was born. That was the day he received the name William Palmer Junior and more than a label for life, it was, in young Bill's mind, the deed by which his father controlled his every move.

William Senior expected everyone in the family, his wife and Bill and his sister to live by a strict set of rules and there was no slack to be cut. No time off for good behavior. Although Bill took school seriously, he liked sports and wanted the usual down time with his friends. The latter came in small quantities when Bill was in prep school, as the house rule was four hours of homework everyday. Chores first, play later, if at all. This became a source of increased tension between Bill and his father, as Bill watched his classmates develop social skills and relationships that he sorely lacked. Bill's mother, a sweet and nurturing woman, did not have the stamina or desire to contest his father's dominance. So Bill determined to excel in school as means to achieve independence. Receiving the full ride to K State was his declaration of independence.

At K State, Bill majored in computer science, went at his studies with a vengeance, worked a part time job for spending money and had little time for anything else. His greatest fear in life was having to rely on his father for any means of support, because that meant giving up the independence he had worked so hard to achieve. That fear drove him to graduate college in three years and go on to the master's degree program in computer sciences. Part of the course work in that program involved performing as a teaching assistant or TA, which meant he conducted teaching labs for undergraduate students. One of his students was Laura Chambers, who, at nineteen, was three years younger than Bill, shared his intensity for information technology and was eager to learn anything she could glean from her course work. Being studious and introverted by nature, she seemed to have no life outside of school. Bill quickly became her mentor, best friend and eventually, after a short courtship that centered around discussing random access memory and gigabytes, her husband.

After college, Bill received a job offer from IBM, worked there for five years and started a small software consulting business. Laura worked in the IT department of a hospital in Kansas City, eventually becoming head of the department. Their first child, a girl was a very normal, happy tomboy, who was the apple of her father's eye. During her pregnancy with their second child though, Larua developed a rare form of blood disease that proved to be debilitating to the point where she was bed ridden for the last three months of her term. The doctors had warned Bill that although their child, a son, might be normal at birth, his genes could hold dormant platelets that would later produce the same symptoms as Laura's. Bill's immediate problem, though was Laura. Her condition did not improve significantly after the birth of their child. She required periodic transfusions, could no longer work, had a short attention span, lost all interest in sex and required psychotherapy.

Bill managed to find a way to adjust to Laura's condition as well as possible, as he now had the responsibility to raise two children. The financial and emotional stress was constant, but he persevered. That was until the second child began to exhibit the same symptoms as Laura. Bill saw that his son would not be able to attend school or live a normal life in any way. Eventually he might die from the disease. The medical bills escalated and the wheels started to come off. He became desperate for money and rather than ask his father for help, decided to expand his consulting practice into some unconventional areas.

Bill's clients included a handful of pharmaceutical companies and he offered to match one fledgling company with some experimental drug compounds he represented as being tested in foreign countries. His access to Abcon's formulas was the off shoot of his years at IBM, where he helped design security for some of the industry's most sophisticated applications. He was familiar with Abcon's security software, but needed a starting point. First he dialed the phone number for access to Abcon's computer and found that it had not been changed. Then he wrote a program that probed for access codes using the same sequencing model that he had helped set up. Every time a sequence of numbers was entered from his program that corresponded to a portion of an active code, that sequence was logged back into his system. The program started with a sequence of two numbers and each successful two number sequence was reentered with a third number until a match was found and logged in. After all successful three number combinations were logged, the program moved on to four number combinations and continued until it had found all successful seven number combinations, which is what Abcon's security wall required for entry. There were twenty eight active seven number combinations in all. Bill needed them because logging in under the same code on a repetitive basis would cause the system to notify the IT people at Abcon.

Bill forwarded the formulas to his client with cover sheets that made it appear as if they had been submitted by foreign drug companies for testing by foreign countries. Since Abcon had not submitted any of the formulas that Bill accessed to the Federal Drug Administration, there was no public record of them. Bill's sole payment for this information was to receive dosages of an experimental drug designed to balance certain blood platelets which would be developed from one of the formulas. As desperate as he was for money, his conscience would not allow him to accept more. The experimental drug might be a matter of life and death, so he proceeded, knowing the risk if he were caught. Guilt never left him. He told himself he had to hang on until the drug was eventually produced and approved for use by the public.

He researched the proper dosages of the drug to administer to his wife and son, starting with the smallest amount possible and then increasing the level to what was recommended. At first they responded slowly, but as time progressed the results were undeniable. Except for the financial pressure he was under, his life was turning for the better.

The investigation of his client lead to him within days, and he faced legal bills and certain jail time, until Maria interceded. After plea bargaining, he spent two years in a minimum security, with alternate weekends at home. The fact that he had not received financial remuneration from the drug company weighed heavily in his favor, but left him with no means of support for his family. Because of Maria, Abcon had graciously agreed to continue to supply the experimental drug at no cost, but his children would have to be cared for by his parents. Although he had escaped his father's control for years, he was right back where he started from.

He had just begun to regenerate his consulting business when the call came from Maria. Of course he would do anything he could to help her. Coincidentally, he was a man on a mission, although the parameters had not been defined. When he was released, he returned home, reopened his office, wrote letters to his clients asking them to trust him with their business and briefly explained his plight. He enclosed a clipping written by a friendly reporter for a local newspaper, telling Bill's side of the story; emphasis on, "Palmer neither asked for, nor received financial reward of any kind related to this case." The mini campaign to win back business was starting to work. Some of his old clients agreed to throw a little business his way.

More importantly, he had grown out of blaming his father for all of his problems. Although they would never have a close relationship, his parents, especially his mother had done an excellent job of caring for his kids. The drugs were working and being improved regularly. He was ready to move on to the next and, definitely happier, phase of his life.

The meeting with Johnny, though, perplexed him. This was not a simple consulting assignment and he wasn't sure he could really be of any help. On the other hand, he decided there was big money involved, and he needed to do a little research before drawing any conclusions. And, oh yes, he would be careful to cover his tracks. The matter of finding obscure, possibly, foreign banks was not his specialty. But, he did have at least one idea. The minimum security facility that had been his home for most of two years was full of white collar criminals, who surprisingly to Bill, were some brightest people he had met. One of the older, more friendly residents went by the name of Gus and was an expert in bank fraud. Gus apparently didn't have a last name he cared to use, and there was speculation that Gus wasn't his real first name anyway. Gus liked Bill and had been fascinated by Bill's knowledge of computers, a trade Bill assumed Gus would try and master as soon as he was a free man. For as long as that might be.

Bill likened Maria's situation to his own. Her family was at risk and she would do what was necessary to protect them. As much as he didn't want to set foot in jail again, Bill called the minimum security facility and found that Gus was still in residence. Since you didn't necessarily schedule appointments with inmates, Bill drove to see Gus, unannounced, and when Gus was led into the visiting room his eyes lit up when he saw Bill.

"William, to what do I owe the honor?"

"Good to see you Gus," said Bill, "You're looking well."

"It's the gourmet cuisine," he replied with a smile.

"Gus, I have an issue I hope you can help me with," said Bill as handed Gus the Oak Bank statement.

Gus looked at the statement as Bill explained everything he had been told by Maria and Johnny.

"I really doubt that Oak Bank and Trust is domiciled in the U.S.," said Gus. "I'm somewhat familiar with the Westpac case through what I've read. There was a lot of money lost and I can see where the losers want to recover what they can. There's been good speculation that the accountants will take a hit and, I suppose, if they can pin insider trading on anyone that will only help."

Bill replied, "I don't know about the accounting firm, but I really owe the Brandt's big time for helping me out. If it wasn't for them I'd still be here eating that gourmet food with you."

From Gus, "look for Oak Bank elsewhere. If I'd have raked in money on the sale of Frontier stock and I knew the deal was going to go South, I'd get the money out of the country as fast as I could. "

"Where?" asked Bill.

"The money havens out there tend to work for certain transactions and not for others. Its also a timing thing. I'd say this is a matter of moving money under the radar screen. I doubt tax consequences are an issue. That's where to start, computer man. Check out the Bahamas, Cayman, Barbados, and just keep going. The people who lost money want to lead someone, maybe even the feds to a bank account that may or may not exist. I don't know why. Maybe whatever money was transferred there isn't there any more. Maybe it was just a stop on the way to somewhere else. I don't know that either. Check the SEC filings to see if any large blocks of Frontier stock traded before the merger. Check Frontier out to see if it has any connections to foreign financial institutions. "

"And by the way," Gus went on, "how do you know your little accounting boy didn't set this whole thing up?"

Interesting question, thought Bill, as he realized his silence partially answered it. He couldn't be sure, although the logic of Maria calling Bill for help if that were the case made no sense. But, Gus was right for asking.

"OK, I'm going to follow through on the assignment. Then what?" asked Bill.

"Come back and see me. I'll buy you lunch."

....

When he returned to his office he had a message from Maria. He called her home number and when she answered said, "Hi Maria, its Bill Palmer."

"Mr. Palmer, thanks for calling me back so promptly."

He said, "Maria I've done what research I can in the last few days. Either Oak Bank exists in a foreign country or it doesn't exist at all. I have more work to do here before I can tell you anything."

"I wanted to let you know that Johnny accepted a job offer and he's not working at BCC anymore," she said.

"Interesting, where is he working now?"

"He's with Investech. They made him a great offer and they have a connection with a San Francisco law firm who they think can help us resolve the accusations against us and, maybe, even BCC."

"Wait a minute," said Palmer, "wasn't Investech the investment banker who put the Frontier deal together?"

"That's right," said Maria. "I really don't know if they're connected to the threats or not, but I'm really concerned about Johnny."

"What do you know about them?"

"They've been around for a while. Johnny worked with them on a few mergers. He likes their CFO. I never heard him mention any other names until a few days ago. I tried to get some background on their principals but all I could get was the usual stuff on the internet."

Maria gave him more details on Investech's pusuit of Johnny, including the conversation with Jonas Smith. Bill seemed to mull some thoughts around for a couple of seconds before responding, "Let's take a minute and review what we know. Frontier merges with Westpac and the owners of Westpac suffer a loss on their stock. It isn't necessarily a cash loss, but it's a large loss of value. A lawyer shows up at BCC and says the firm was negligent and produces a copy of stock trading certificates with your maiden name on them. They show trades in Frontier stock before and after the merger. You go to your lock box and find detailed statements of the same nature and an Oak Bank and Trust account statement showing large infusions of cash. You track down a company who provides you with the address of a trader who initiated the alleged trades. You go there and you're followed and told not pursue the matter further. Your husband searches for the stock trader, I think you said Jonas Smith. Smith finds your husband and assures him no harm is meant to any of you. He then convinces your husband to accept a job with Investech."

"Bizarre, but accurate," Maria responded.

He went on, "There is a connection between Jonas Smith, who set up the alleged trades and Investech. Investech principals are thought to invest in firms that are subject to mergers, although this has not been proven. They find ways to convince your husband to come to work for them, some subtle and some not so subtle. In any event, it works. Presumably he will help them land business for the firm which means the firm profits. If they do invest personally in the merger candidates, they profit individually.

"That's the same conclusion I drew."

"Maria," the tone in his voice more intense now, "are you ready to take this to the next level?"

"What do you mean, Bill?"

"I can start looking for some of the more likely places to find Oak Bank, but if it's in any of those places, we'll never get anywhere with this unless we have security or pass codes to access the bank accounts. It won't matter even if your father tries either. If he doesn't have the right code, he won't get anywhere"

"I understand," said Maria. "I need a little time on that one, Bill. I'll call you as soon as I have something."

Twenty two

HE GOT THE HERO'S treatment on Tuesday morning. Johnny didn't have an engagement letter to represent Burgess in hand, yet. Just a verbal agreement. But there was a quiet confidence in the smiles and the handshakes from his new associates.

He asked for and got an impromptu meeting at 10:30 a.m. with his team. A couple of people couldn't make it, but no matter, Brenda would follow up with a memo to all. It wouldn't be a formal meeting, but temporary assignments would be given and everyone would let Johnny know their availability going forward. Those people who had the most time now would start and be joined later by the rest of the team.

Johnny would work with the lawyers to draft an engagement letter and Investech's general counsel would send Johnny a couple of sample letters from other deals to look at.

Jack Miller's team would contact Dave Rosen and set up a time for a meeting to discuss the financial proformas. It would take weeks to prepare, review and finalize the detailed schedules that could be released to prospective merger candidates and eventually appear in an SEC filing. Johnny would also review each schedule before it was released, but thank God he didn't have to do the grunt work. Everything, literally every number, had to be supportable. Not necessarily perfectly factual, but supportable. This was an important distinction he would have to get used to. Accounting financial statements summarized events that had passed. There were historical facts and written contracts underlying everything that was booked. The rest was based on established formulas. Proformas were based on what you could get people to believe. There was some room for artistic interpretation depending on how good you were. Jack Miller was known to be the best.

The actual board presentation would be coordinated by someone from the public relations group who would report to Jack. They could start on the structure now. The written portion which would include background on Burgess, its principals, its products and its history could be drafted in about a week. It was agreed that Jack would have a preliminary 'Executive Summary' or very brief overview of the five year financial proforma in two weeks. That would give them less than a week to refine, edit and distribute the paper booklets to the board before the Burgess meeting in Denver. The PR guys would be sure the charts and graphs were of the highest quality, with the most striking colors and clarity anyone had ever seen. The requisite number of investment banking terms that no one else understood would be included.

By Tuesday, Johnny had a night to get his head on straight and decided he needed a break from too much thinking. He had looked Todd Pulaski in the eye, shook his hand, and for better or worse, he was Todd's man now. There was no telling where Burgess, its officers and staff as well as its shareholder's would end up. Once you started the process it could get a little out of control. Suitors might want to simply buyout all the shareholder's for cash. Some might want to exchange their stock for Burgess' stock. There could be a deal done with some combination of both. Some might want to keep Todd and his people around. Some might not. Either way, the senior officers at Burgess were assured of coming out OK. They would get severance packages or hefty employment contracts, depending on the structure accepted from the winning bidder. There might even be an offer from Todd and the management team backed by a private equity firm. Assuming one or more definitive bids was tendered, the board would decide on the winning offer, if any. Before it was final, Burgess shareholder's would approve the board's action by voting on it.

Once a company hired an investment banker and began soliciting offers to merge, that company was known to be 'in play', in industry jargon. There was risk to Burgess' senior management that an offer could be received that was so favorable to the shareholder's, the board would be obligated to accept it. But, there could be no assurance that such an offer would result in the type of outcome sought by senior management. Todd had told Johnny he and his team wanted to remain with the successor firm after a merger. The bidder might have other ideas. Todd could end up at odds with his own board if he wasn't offered the top slot. In some cases the egos of top management drove them to fight for a Chairman or CEO positions even if a severance offer was more than fair. When billions of dollars were involved, people could get irrational.

This was an awesome responsibility and Johnny's first deal as an investment banker. He owed it to Todd and Burgess to avoid distractions and focus his efforts on a successful result for all concerned.

Scott Borden came into to see Johnny shortly after lunch. "When do you want to start contacting the banks?" He asked.

"I'd like to find an excuse to call a few bankers and see if they ask us about Burgess. I'm reluctant to start the conversation until we get the engagement letter signed. We're going to have to negotiate with Todd on how far he'll let us go with fees. I assume if only one bank is involved they'll want us to step aside. If we have to put a consortium together I'd think we're entitled to an additional fee?"

"Generally correct, Johnny, depending upon what the eight hundred pound guerillas will let us keep," Scott replied.

Johnny knew that Scott was referring to a few of the large banks who would want to form the banking group. It would be a tug of war over fees with some of the banks, but ultimately it would get resolved, because they all needed each other.

"I'll make a few calls," said Scott. "I always have reasons to call bankers. You should sit in on some of the calls to get an idea of what they already know. Word spreads fast."

This suited Johnny just fine.

The next topic was the fairness opinion, which is a document issued by a financial services firm. In essence, it says that the financial terms of a transaction are fair based on similar transactions in the marketplace. The fairness opinion is an appraisal related to a financial transaction. This has to accompany the forms filed with the SEC and sent to each shareholder to solicit their votes to either approve or reject a merger bid. Johnny always laughed at the fairness opinions he read, because they contained so many disclaimers regarding the liability of the preparer. It really made you wonder if there was anyone willing to take responsibility for the expert conclusion they put on paper. And got paid for. There were always some people who were skeptical about investment bankers preparing fairness opinions for their own deals, because obviously they had fees at stake. Johnny and Scott decided they would include language in the engagement letter regarding the alternative of retaining an outside firm, if the need arose.

Scott and Johnny talked briefly about data transmission and availability. They called Jack and agreed this could be discussed with Burgess during Jack's first visit to their office. The key would be to determine the compatibility of Burgess' IT system with a data room provider. By the time bidders were asked to begin working on their offers, virtually every document on Burgess' system would have to be accessible via the data room web site. This meant moving massive amounts of data electronically. If all went well, Burgess would download data onto disks and those disks could be read into the data room server, or eventually forwarded to a bidder. If not, some or all of the data would have to be converted before it could be downloaded. Depending upon the volume, conversion would add to the cost and time in moving the process along.

By the end of the day Tuesday, Johnny felt confident he had a great team that would ensure the best possible result for Burgess. He was struck by how intense the team was, without being uptight. The only one who had not been through this before was Johnny. He hadn't really thought about it, but in some businesses no one started to work on an assignment until a contract or some form of legal document describing the scope of services and legal fees had been signed. Not so in investment banking. Time was clearly of the essence and no one even questioned if the engagement letter would be signed. It was a foregone conclusion.

The days that ensued were energizing for Johnny. There was a lot of activity; meetings, phone calls and brief conversations involving minor decisions. It was easier for him to stay focused than when he was only half busy at BCC. He liked the action. Alex Franklin had returned from his business on the West coast for one day, was in meetings that entire day, and was back on the road again before Johnny could talk to him. He was a little frustrated that the matter of a potential criminal complaint was not top priority for anyone else at Investech. He decided against calling Alex on his cell phone or approaching Brad. He would conduct business as usual, but when Alex returned from his most recent trip, Johnny would make sure everything was moving in the right direction. Johnny also had not forgotten about his need to talk to Henry Dann. But since he couldn't think of a seemingly informal way of approaching the subject of insider trading with his wife's father, he simply put the matter aside. Eventually, he would have to deal with it.

Johnny had received a return phone call from Bill Mancini at Ronco and, although Bill didn't see an immediate move by Ronco into a potential merger or restructuring, he mentioned he'd like to see Johnny anyway. Johnny told Bill he had another meeting scheduled in the Washington D.C. area the following week and could swing by if it was convenient for Bill. They arranged to meet at Bill's office. Johnny would work with Brenda to prepare a brief, informal presentation booklet for Bill so he could leave something behind for Bill to think about. The other meeting, of course, didn't exist.

As the week progressed, Johnny really wasn't exactly in or out of the comfort zone. His promise to himself not to over think his personal problems was holding up. But he felt he had let Maria down from an emotional standpoint. She had been through a lot the past few weeks and, no matter how serious the problems, she had come through remarkably well. More than that, she had taken the initiative to step right into a potentially dangerous situation without concern for her own personal safety. She would think of everyone else first and herself last. Of course. That was Maria, the one constant in his life. He really hadn't done enough to help her recapture her identity after the birth of Josh. Too busy buried in his own mire. It was time to start planning that romantic getaway they had talked about. Not a trip, but a vacation. Sex on the beach and anyplace else they could think of. Sorting through life would be easy after that. He would have to help her shop, and encourage her to buy anything that would fit easily in her suitcase. The less, the better. You certainly didn't want to wear too much on a tropical island did you? Fortunately, he knew she would be game.

Twenty Three

The change in Johnny's demeanor was noticeable if not pronounced, Maria thought. Her husband had always told her that men were simpler creatures than women and she knew he was right. For most men, it didn't take as much to balance their lives as it did for women. She didn't believe he thought that all of their problems were over, but he did have a new sense of purpose that buoyed him for the present. For her, there were red flags all over the place.

Bill Palmer had helped her focus on her next move, but putting any kind of a meaningful plan together would be a major challenge. The information she sought was controlled by people who only wanted to be found on their own terms. She could think of two possibilities. Talk to Charlie about hiring the former SEC investigator, or find a way to gain access to the personal records of Brad Worshaw and Alex Franklin. She would pursue both.

What did she know about Worshaw and Franklin? They were principals in an investment banking firm with apparently no determinable flaws in their background. Well educated, if not necessarily well respected. Well compensated in their profession and maybe outside of it too. They lived in a high tech world so she guessed whatever scheme they were running she could gain some insight into it through access to their computers. It might not be on the surface, but it would be there, somewhere.

The people at Investech had no idea what she looked like, which was to her advantage. When Johnny told her he would be going to Washington D.C. for a day, she had the perfect opportunity for phase one of her plan. She would need business cards and an East coast phone number. The cards, of course, were easy. For the phone number, she went to the library, found a New York City yellow pages directory and looked under the heading for Executive Suites. There, she found several phone numbers for firms offering secretarial services. She called four of them and on the fourth call, got what she was looking for. A company that would provide a phone number and answering service for $250 a month. No contract necessary. When she asked if the phone number could be set on call forwarding the answer was yes, she could provide instructions either way.

She would call Brad Worshaw's office and leave word that she was Elizabeth Blake, an attorney with the firm of Howard and Fine. The name of the law firm and the individual lawyer came from the Martindale-Hubbell guide she found at the library. They were a small, no name firm specializing in securities law. If Worshaw did a cursory check into her background, it would hold up. If he decided to dig deeper, it could mean trouble.

As timing would have it, Elizabeth had an overseas client who was interested in placing as much as ten figures with one or more promising technology firms in the U.S. The name of the client could not be disclosed, but they would pay a substantial fee for the right relationship. She

THE LAST AUDIT • 159

would be in Chicago the following week and hoped there was a chance to meet face to face with Mr. Worshaw.

Maria wondered if Worshaw's secretary had caller ID, and if so, would she find it strange that a New York Lawyer would call from a Chicago area exchange? She thought about having the secretarial firm make the call, but rejected the idea, in case there were questions that only she could answer. Plus, the appointment with Worshaw had to occur at a specific time and she would have to explain why. It occurred to Maria that most people were familiar with area codes in their immediate vicinity. If an area code popped up on a screen that was not familiar to the recipient, they would most likely not give a second thought as to where the call came from. Maria also decided that a firm like Investech received almost all its calls from major financial centers like New York, Boston and San Francisco. She could drive to Rockford, Illinois, about an hour from her house, but with a different area code. From there she would find a pay phone and make the call.

In Rockford, she stopped at a shopping mall just off Interstate 90. She dialed the number and asked for Bradley Worshaw. When his secretary answered the phone, in her best New York accent Maria said, "Yes ma'am, my name is Elizabeth Blake, an attorney with Howard (the "r" disappeared as she spoke) and Fine in New Yok City. I would like to speak with Bradley Woshaw on behalf of my client."

"I see," was the response. "Mr. Worshaw is not in right now. May I ask the nature of your business?"

"Yes, I represent a major European investment fund looking to place money with one or more growing technology firms in the U. S. Mr. Woshaw was recommended to me as someone who could be very helpful in that area." She then added, a little less formally, "My client is not opposed to paying top dollar for the right investment advice."

"Very good, Ms. Blake, I'm sure Mr. Worshaw will be happy to meet with you. When would you like to meet?"

"I'll be in town next Wednesday. I have to make it late in the day, as I have a number of appointments and can stop by on my way to the airport."

"Where can I call you to confirm the meeting?"

Maria had set the New York number for call forwarding to her cell phone, so she gave that number and added, "I'm at a client's office now, but it's best to call my office and leave word with my assistant. I think 5:00 p.m. next Wednesday will work well."

Maria had a little time before she had to get back on the road, so she took the opportunity to do some shopping. She wanted an outfit that made her look professional without being too provocative. She found a business suit that she thought looked good on her, but made a statement, "I'm all business in a New York power chick way."

Later that day his secretary called to confirm the appointment, with Maria adopting a different phone voice as Elizabeth Blake's assistant.

She waited a couple of days and called Charlie to see how the meeting with the forensic accountants had gone. He told her it went pretty much as expected and that Warner Simmons was going to fly out to San Francisco to meet with Jonathan Blanchard, the attorney who represented the Westpac shareholders. Until then they had decided to hold off on calling the former SEC man.

The name Blanchard stuck in her head, but she couldn't place it. She thanked Charlie, but told him nothing of her plan to access Worshaw's computer. He would never let it happen. It was later that day that she remembered the reference to Blanchard and Stone, the law firm in San Francisco that appeared in Worshaw's resume.

....

She entered the Investech offices on Wednesday, punctually at 5:00 p.m. and produced her business card for the receptionist. Because she was on her way to the airport, she had a small roller suitcase with her. She took a seat as she waited and within a minute of her arrival, the cleaning crew began walking in, as scheduled. She had called the receptionist a few days earlier posing as the office supervisor of the cleaning crew. She wanted to verify that they had been arriving on time at five o'clock and that they had been wearing their uniforms. She was told they were always prompt about starting at five o'clock, but that they always wore blue jeans or other work clothes, but no uniforms. Maria told the receptionist she'd check into the uniform situation. Maria would not have to worry about getting a work uniform, but old jeans would do.

Brad Worshaw's secretary came for Maria within five minutes and soon she was shaking hands with her husband's boss.

"I'm sorry for the rushed nature of the visit Mr. Woshaw, but I did want to take this opportunity to introduce myself and start a dialogue. I know how long it can take for an investor and operating company to get together on a deal. But the discussions have to start somewhere."

"I understand completely, Elizabeth," he responded. "I appreciate you're stopping by. Are you able to disclose your client's name?"

"I'm afraid not. I'm sworn to secrecy until we have a specific opportunity. My clients will fly here from Amsterdam to meet with you when the time comes. If they're interested in what you have to propose."

"That's fine. In fact we're working on some exciting things right now. I may be able to provide a couple of possibilities for you in the near future."

"Well, Mr. Woshaw, since I'm not able to tell you anything about my client, I can't expect you to say anything about yours."

"It really would be too soon, I agree. But tell me about yourself. How long have you been practicing law?"

"Its been about eight years now," she said. "I graduated from New Yok City Law School."

"And you've been with Howard and Fine all that time?" he asked, looking at the business card she had given him.

"That's right. I was in intellectual property for a few years and moved over to mergers and acquisitions. I represent mostly clients who are in the technology industry or are investing in it."

Worshaw came back 'Funny, I know most of the law firms doing securities work in New York and I've never heard of Howard and Fine."

She felt her back get hot but kept her composure. "You know that's just why we were asked to represent the client I'm here to see you about. They're very low profile and they don't want a lot attention drawn to them. If word gets out they're investing in the U.S. they'll be inundated with calls."

He seemed to accept her response and they made small talk for a few more minutes. Then she said, "You have an interesting desk top set up," referring to the flat screen attached to a rectangular black base on his desk.

"We've added a few bells and whistles here. We deal exclusively with people in the technology business so we want them to think we're a step ahead when they come to see us."

"And are you, Mr. Woshaw?"

She had challenged him and found he was happy to share a little information. She knew the right questions to ask. This would help her skip a couple of steps when she logged into the Investech system.

She couldn't let too much time pass, because she needed the cleaning crew to be around when she left. She thanked him for the visit and said she would have to be on her way. He walked her to the reception area, said good bye and turned to go back to his office.

She entered the hallway and wheeled her suitcase around to the women's rest room. No one was there, so first she removed all her make up. She then entered a stall and changed into a pair of blue jeans she had bought at a thrift store. They were huge on her size two frame, had no style whatsoever so she had to cinch them at the waste. She pulled an old oversized sweatshirt on, tied her hair in a bun and placed a large baseball cap on her head, so that none of her hair and almost none of her face could be seen. What was even better was that whoever had taken the clothes to the thrift shop had left a little of themselves behind to smell. She then pulled a couple of oversized garbage bags out of the suitcase, zipped it up and walked out of the stall with the garbage bags in hand. She left the suitcase behind.

When she walked back into the reception area at Investech, the receptionist had already gone, so she was free to move about. She had noticed Alex Franklin's name on the office next to Brad's and decided that was where to head. She heard Worshaw on the phone, but his door was closed. The cleaning crew had opened all the other individual office doors, so if she went into Alex' office and closed the door, it would look strange. With no one else around, she closed all the doors on the corridor as if the offices had been cleaned.

Thanks to Brad Worshaw, she was able to navigate her way around the desk top without worrying about what operating system Investech used. She had also questioned Johnny in an offhand way about how he logged in at the office. When she got to the point where she was prompted to enter Alex Franklin's user name, she followed the pattern Johnny had explained, and entered what she thought Alex would have used. It worked and she didn't have to worry about his password because he had left a command for the system to remember it. She had sensed that Alex, because of his background, would not want to waste time entering a password every time he logged in and she was right. Being a security officer in the Marine Corp had nothing to do with guarding confidential data stored on one's computer. She was curious as to what he really did do for Investech, though.

There were icons she recognized and some she didn't. She skipped the obvious ones and went to something called 'communications log'. The screen came back with a list of calls made during various dates in descending order. She clicked on the current date and the screen flashed a log of calls and listed an internal extension number and the outside phone number it was connected to. She clicked on one of the entries and the screen flashed either an extension number or the outside phone number and after each was what appeared to be the typed version of a telephone conversation. She clicked on a few additional entries and found more of the same. Brad was right, they had added a few bells and whistles. They were monitoring the phone calls of some or all of their employees.

She tried a few more unfamiliar icons, but discovered nothing of any importance.

Then an idea hit. First she checked the print out of all the employee extensions on Alex' desk. She went back to the communications log to see if either Brad's or Alex' extensions were included anywhere on the call log. Not surprisingly, there was nothing from either of their phones. She would not likely be able to figure out how to program their phones to record their calls, but Bill Palmer might. She found something called communication log set up among the icons and clicked on it. It prompted the user to enter the Investech extension number to be monitored. She tried to enter Alex' number but the system responded that the extension was not a valid communication devise. Same result with Brad's. Even if she had been able to set up their extensions for recording, where would she have the information stored? This would take a little more work.

She looked around Alex' office for anything she could find. Alex did not appear to be a man who spent much time in the office. Way too neat. Virtually every drawer to every piece of furniture in his office was locked. She now understood what security officer meant in Marine terms.

She heard voices in the hallway and decided she had maxed out her research time for the day. So far, all had gone well. No one had seen her and she could probably slip back in another day, maybe when Brad was out of town. She heard office doors being closed in the distance and waited as the voices and the door closings stopped. She opened the door to Alex' office, closed it behind her and made her way to the main entry door in the reception area. It was locked. She didn't need a key to unlock the door from the inside, but had no way to lock it again from the outside. She could simply leave it unlocked, but when the first group of employees arrived in the morning they would be alerted that security had been breached. If Brad was still in the office, he'd know even sooner. She had an answer for that one, but it would mean a return to the rest room. She would have to change back into her lawyer suit, take her hair down, put on some lipstick and add a little color to her face. She did this in record time and was out the rest room door and into the elevator to the lobby so fast, she could barely catch her breath. On the way out, as she passed the security guard in the lobby she said, "I just left a meeting at Investech and I noticed the main door was unlocked. I don't know if the cleaning crew forgot or what."

The security guard asked, "did you lock it ma'am?"

"No I was just visiting, I don't work there. I don't have a key. The person I was meeting with is on the phone and looks like he might be there for a while."

"What's your name ma'am?"

She reached in her purse and handed him a business card announcing her as Elizabeth Blake.

He checked the sign in log and saw that she had entered the building at five o'clock. He handed back the card and said, "I'll send someone to lock up. Thanks for reporting it ma'am."

Twenty Four

Specific plans for the meeting in Denver started to take shape about a week before the scheduled day. It would be a big meeting, probably too big to get much detailed work done, but the focus would be on getting board approval for Burgess to sign the engagement letter. That would be the main event. Johnny and the lawyers would stay until all the language for the engagement letter was finished and Todd and he could sign for the respective firms.

From Investech, the attendees would be Johnny, Scott, their general counsel and Jack Miller. Jack told Johnny that he traveled about 60 per cent of the time and Johnny could see it was true. He was a work horse and Johnny was grateful to have him on the team. Investech's general counsel mentioned that Burgess' in house lawyers asked for a recommendation for outside counsel to guide them through the maze of merger and securities laws they would encounter. With Burgess' general counsel also in attendance, the deck would be stacked with at least three sets of lawyers. "That should insure the process will grind to a halt," thought Johnny.

When the full complement of people was counted it totaled sixteen. Four from Investech, Todd and his board totaled seven, then add Dave Rosen, Todd's son and their GC. The outside lawyers for Burgess would add two more.

The traveling team from Investech would arrive from Chicago and be driven to Burgess' headquarters as they had three weeks earlier. They arrived at mid morning and were ushered into a large conference room with a square table. It appeared as though they were the last to arrive as the room was already populated, with several informal conversations in progress. Johnny surveyed the room and in the distance he saw the profile of an attractive woman with long blonde hair. She was turned with her side toward Johnny, listening to an older man speak. As Johnny walked into the room, she turned toward him while the man continued to speak. It was the woman who accompanied Jonathan Blanchard to the meeting at BCC's headquarters in Chicago. The meeting which Johnny hadn't attended. But he had positioned himself so he had a good look at all of the accusers before they walked into Bill Lewis' cramped office. The meeting which heralded the beginning of the end for Johnny at BCC. Well, the official end anyway.

Great, Burgess had hired Blanchard's firm to represent them. As he looked at her across the room, she smiled at him and held the smile for an extra second. She was about three inches shorter than Johnny, had perfectly straight hair, blue eyes that looked too good to be real and a body that gave new meaning to the term women's business attire. She was certainly dressed appropriately, not gaudy, but she filled out every inch of the light blue skirt and jacket she was wearing. She looked even better than the last time Johnny had seen her and he was definitely impressed then. He would be working with the enemy who, as it turned out, was a fox.

Small talk continued for a couple of minutes, when Todd asked everyone to take their seats so the meeting could begin. They followed business protocol for the meeting; they would go around the table with each person introducing themselves and giving some professional or personal background information. Burgess' board was well qualified with the right mix of tech people, a lawyer, accountant and financial consultant. Todd had a good rapport with the board, but they were known have strong opinions of their own. The blonde's name was Ellen Caulfield. She had graduated from the University of Idaho Law School, spent two years with the SEC in Washington DC and joined Jonathan Blanchard two years ago. Johnny guessed she was, maybe, thirty. The other lawyer who accompanied her was even younger than Ellen.

Johnny began the presentation to the board. Each person had a booklet they could refer to, but the same material was shown on a screen at the front of the room. He followed the outline of the presentation, but added comments to make his points. It was a great time to be in Burgess' position. Recent mergers greatly favored the target companies. Pricing for good acquisitions was at record highs. The targets could push hard for favorable structuring. Translated that meant the senior executives should end up in a good bargaining position.

On the downside, Burgess had some needs as well and this would affect the decision regarding the ideal suitor. The perfect fit might not involve the highest bidder, but a firm with the ability to address marketing and distribution of Burgess' products. Something to keep in mind. Johnny then asked Jack to discuss the proformas with everyone. Jack took over and was careful to explain that his team had a few weeks of work left to complete the final numbers and his presentation was based on what had been generated to date. He explained that pricing of a target company's stock was based on multiples of either projected GAAP earnings or EBITDA or even other forms of measurement, depending upon the suitor's point of view. His team's job was to come up with the highest projected results and support them. His charts showed that Burgess stock could be worth as much as twenty five per cent more than it's current trading price. When he was done, there was a discernable silence while everyone digested what had just been said. Johnny suggested that they hear from Scott regarding financing before going into a question and answer session.

Todd and his people had done a good job of preparing the board, and their questions reflected this. The member with a financial background told the rest of the board that he was familiar with a few of the mergers that had recently taken place and the preliminary numbers were not out of line. That was because suitor companies could base their valuations on estimated future earnings growth. After the question and answer session, the board excused themselves to meet in private and vote on authorizing Todd, as CEO, to sign the engagement letter.

While the rest of the group waited, lunch was served and they talked among themselves. Johnny stood in the buffet line and Ellen walked up behind him. "Johnny, I'm sorry we didn't have a chance to meet while I was in Chicago. I hope you're doing well." She almost sounded as if she meant it.

"Yes, actually I'm doing very well. Being with Investech seems to agree with me."

"Good. I'm looking forward to working with you. I know everything is going to turn out for the best."

He wasn't sure what that meant. Did she mean for Burgess and Investech, or him personally? He wanted to ask, but didn't.

The board was out for about an hour. After lunch, there was time to make a few phone calls and return a few emails for those who had laptops or blackberry's. When they returned, the meeting resumed. Todd announced that the board had voted to proceed with executing an engagement letter. Essentially, the formal part of the meeting was over and everyone was free to go except for Johnny and the lawyers, who would negotiate the final wording of the document. A draft had been circulated a couple of weeks earlier, had already received some comments and been redrafted. They were in a good position to finish it that day. Scott and Jack would fly back to Chicago and, depending upon the timing, Johnny would fly back that night or the next morning.

The open items in the engagement letter related to fees, financing and cancellation provisions if Burgess wanted to stop the process before it was completed. When everyone else had gone, the five who remained moved closer together. They repositioned the plates and glasses that remained from lunch so they could spread their papers out and get to work. Johnny wasn't sure who would lead from Burgess' side so, as he spoke, he moved his eyes among Burgess' general counsel, Ellen and the kid who had accompanied her from San Francisco. "As I believe you've seen, we provided you with a spread sheet showing all the merger activity in the industry over the past two years. Our fee request is based on the fees earned by the investment banker for those transactions in the dollar range we expect to occur here."

After a brief pause Ellen said, "Johnny, the fee proposal in your letter is really at the top end of the range, if you consider all the facts." She then produced a schedule prepared on Blanchard and Stone letterhead which she handed to all. She went on, "The six most relevant mergers were the ones we highlighted in blue and were taken from your spread sheet. As you can see from the notes we provided, three of them involved foreign capital and there were tricky tax issues which had to be resolved. We know because we consulted with the investment bankers on those deals. The fees earned on those three were the highest in the group. The remaining three were all done domestically and the fees paid were at the low end of the spectrum. My client doesn't want the fees to be a point of contention and understands that the buyer will pay them, but wants the fees to be based on all the relevant facts."

Her voice was matter of fact as she spoke and not meant to be anything but business like. Johnny was becoming more impressed with her by the moment. She had her points down and knew how to present them. Although she hadn't said anything he didn't already know, this was all part of the game and she played it well.

She continued, "In talking with Todd, what he would like to do is set up a fee schedule that will reward you for performance. In other words the percentage of the price paid for your fee will increase as the overall bid increases. Here is what we have in mind." She then distributed another schedule which showed five different price ranges per share of Burgess' stock and the fee as a percent of the price. It demonstrated what she had said. It started out with a fee at the low end of the range and moved upward as the stock price increased.

This seemed to Johnny like a fair proposal. Investech would, of course, push for the highest price possible for their client. But having additional incentive certainly didn't hurt. Rather than agree right away though, he said, "Alright, I understand what you're saying. But lets review the rest of the open items before we finalize the fee structure."

The next item was the matter of fees which could be paid for arranging financing for a transaction. Ellen said that her client was concerned that the same people who had access to confidential information about Burgess could also be out trying to put the financing together. There might be a possible conflict of interest. Burgess preferred that Investech not pursue financing, but rather let one of the Wall Street firms work on that.

Johnny didn't want to press the point with her, but he also didn't want to give up a possible source of additional revenue for Investech. He knew that the bidders would each be looking on their own for financing. He proposed that if Investech was approached for financing by a bidder, they would assign someone in the firm who was not on Johnny's team and therefore not involved in the bidding process. Only that person would work on financing and would sign a confidentiality agreement as to specific financial institutions to be approached. If the lenders or the bidders were willing to pay a fee to Investech, then Burgess wouldn't object. Everyone found that acceptable, and they moved on.

When it came to the matter of cancellation of the engagement letter, Ellen's associate finally joined the negotiations. "Burgess would simply like the right to stop the process if they feel it isn't going in the right direction. Since the board doesn't have to accept any bid, it makes sense not to waste anyone's time if they've changed they're mind about a merger, before the bidding begins."

This was typically how it was handled, so Johnny really had no objection. But, he found a way to tie the fee schedule into Burgess' right to cancel. He said, "I agree, but since our fee is only earned when a transaction closes, depending on the timing, we should receive a portion of our fee for termination of the engagement. As you know we'll be putting a huge number of man hours into the process and we'll need some cost recovery."

They negotiated back and forth on that point until they reached agreement on an appropriate termination fee to be payable at different stages of the process. Johnny then accepted Ellen's fee schedule and the engagement letter had been agreed to by all parties. Ellen's associate had been writing notes on his copy of the draft and then left the room to enter the verbiage into the word document so they would have a final clean copy to sign.

As they waited, it was back to small talk. Johnny asked Ellen how she enjoyed living in San Francisco and she responded with a glowing report on her last two years in the city by the bay. She had spent a lot of time as a ski bunny in Sun Valley Idaho as a teenager and won a couple of junior downhill events along the way. Went right to the SEC from law school. She would have sounded like an overachiever to Johnny, except she seemed to have a pretty strong skill set in life. Johnny managed to interject a few words about himself into the conversation without forcing it. The other attorneys in the room added quips when relevant and then the talk turned to prior merger and acquisition war stories they had all heard. Ellen's associate returned with the document, which they all reviewed and agreed it was ready for signature. Burgess' general counsel called Todd's office and his secretary said he would be down to sign it in a few minutes.

By the time everything was signed and sealed it was after six. Todd asked them if they would be interested in going out to dinner and all agreed they were ready to eat; and a minor celebration would be fitting. They walked a couple of blocks to a brew pub in downtown Denver. In May, before the intense heat of summer overtook the West an early evening walk in the thin atmosphere of Denver was a just reward for a hard days work. There was a light breeze and with the sun blocked by the tall buildings, the temperature was ideal. In the distance were the snow capped Rocky Mountains. Although Johnny wasn't much of a drinker, a beer seemed like a necessity and everyone in the party joined in. The brew pub was especially proud of their proprietary blend and served it in extra large portions. If you finished the first, the second was on the house. By the time you were done drinking, it didn't matter whether you agreed with their assessment or not.

Dinner was more of the same small talk, but with the addition of beer, the stories got funnier. After dinner, they walked back to Burgess' office so they could collect their brief cases. Todd's secretary had made hotel reservations for Johnny and he would grab a cab in front of the office. As he said good bye to all, he shook Ellen's hand. This time she held his hand in hers for an extra couple of seconds. "Johnny," she said, "I'd like to talk to you in the next few days about some of the documents we'll need for the SEC filing."

Twenty Five

"The question is," Bill Palmer began, "is the voice conversion devise programmed into each phone or in a central system somewhere?"

"I'm going to guess it's in the base that hold's the flat screens on their desks," was Maria's response. "I noticed their phones are wired to the same base. But that means we have to figure out how to add Brad's and Alex' extensions to the list of recognized devises."

"We need somebody on the inside, Maria," he said. "You're going to have to tell Johnny."

"I really have to tell him anyway. I can't let him say anything on the phone that can be used against us. But asking him to find out how to program a voice converter so we can spy on his bosses ups the ante a bit. I don't have any idea what to tell him to look for."

"It has to have a microphone to receive the verbal input from the speaker and the earpiece. I'm guessing it will have a microphone and then be hard wired back into the IT system from each desk top. It has to be a self contained box or something." was Palmer's conclusion.

"So if I'm right, we have to see if the little box is installed in the bases in the two offices we need bugged. If not we have to figure out how to find them, install them and program them," Maria said. "Oh, and one more thing, we have to figure out how to retrieve the data."

"Maria, if Johnny can find the devise and get me a name or model number, or anything, I can almost certainly track it down and figure out how to use it."

She promised to get Johnny on it as soon as he got back in town.

She knew Johnny would be skeptical when she told him what she had found. She wished she had had time to access the log containing his calls when she was at Investech, so she could prove it to him by repeating some of his conversations, verbatim. But she hadn't wanted to press her luck. She knew the first visit might be reconnaissance only, so now it was a matter of taking what she had learned and putting it to use.

When he got home from Denver and the kids were in bed, she said, "I was in your office at Investech a couple of nights ago."

All he could say was, "what?"

"I went in just after the cleaning crew started and blended in with them. If I show you what I wore, you'll believe it."

"Why" from Johnny this time.

"Because they're hiding something and we both know it." As she said this she bore in on him with her intense dark eyes as if to say, "get back to reality mister. While you're out doing mega mergers, I'm covering our asses."

"That's what we have Bill Palmer for," Johnny's tried to take some of the self imposed pressure off of her.

"I'm working with Bill," said Maria. "There's only so much he can do. He thinks the Frontier money went through a foreign bank. He'll narrow down the possibilities for us but we'll never get access to specific accounts unless we have security pass codes."

What she said made sense. She continued, "they have your phone tapped with a devise that turns your conversations into a written log that's accessible on their desk tops. Who knows maybe on mobile devices as well. Convenient for the frequent traveler who wants to monitor what goes on in the office." The reference to Alex was unmistakable.

Now he was dumbfounded, but knew better than to doubt her on this one.

Maria repeated her conversation with Bill Palmer. When she was done, Johnny searched his mind for any incriminating phone conversation he might have had over the past few weeks. He was sure there were none. He had thought about calling his father in law and breathed a huge sigh of relief that he had not made the call. He had been all business since starting at Investech. But his little bubble was bursting. The insulation he had started to feel by focusing so hard on business was stripped away. He felt a wave of anger come over him and wanted to be mad at Maria for peeling back his mental coat of armor. But why? She was willing to put herself on the line; where were his guts? If she were that interested in rocking his boat, she would have asked his permission before going up to Investech. They would have had a fight and probably resolved nothing. She had taken it upon herself to back up her suspicions and present her case to Johnny instead of just speculating. Based on what she found, she had to tell him. He let the wave pass and they talked about what to do next.

The first move was obvious. Johnny would inspect the black rectangular box on his desk to see if he could find a microphone. It wouldn't be the same thing as a speaker contained in the phone. It would have to be in the box. He could do this first thing in the morning. If he found anything, he would have to either call Maria from a phone outside of the office, or wait until he got home. It would be cumbersome, but it was the only way. He couldn't disconnect it because whoever was monitoring his calls would immediately become suspicious if the call logs ceased.

He made it a point to arrive an hour early the next morning. The box sat on four small rubber feet which held it slightly off the surface of the desk. It was heavy and with the flat screen connected to it, awkward to move around. He tilted it so the bottom of the box faced him. Underneath, he could see the box was vented. It was impossible to tell if anything was connected without looking inside. There were no screws or other visible means by which the box was held together. It appeared to be self contained.

Johnny realized the hunt and report method could take forever, without a way to communicate with the outside world. He waited until nine o'clock and told Brenda he had arrived at work early, without breakfast, and needed to go downstairs for quick bite. Once outside the building that housed Investech's office, he walked quickly to the nearest cell phone store about a block away. He was fortunate to beat the crowd and receive immediate attention. Within twenty minutes he left with a new cell phone registered to himself at his home address. Cheapest phone and calling plan available. Just enough to by-pass some of the most sophisticated equipment in the world, he thought.

He stopped on the street, called Maria and told her he couldn't figure out how to get the box open.

"Probably needs to be programmed," she said.

"Of course," He replied.

She told him to look for any icons on his screen that referred to systems maintenance or that had anything to do with changing or adjusting devices. Then simply probe around until he, hopefully, found something that would lead him to a command to open the box.

By the time he got back to his office the full day's activity had begun. He had calls to return, meetings to attend and letters to write. He waited until the lunch hour when things settled down a bit and went on with his mission. He went to the desktop page on the flat screen and found an icon that said "system utilities." He clicked on that and then continued to click on various options based purely on guesswork. It occurred to him that if there was a devise installed in the black box and the box could be opened through a program on each person's computer, each person could discover it for themselves. But who would know what to look for or have any reason to look? Everyone called tech support when they had a computer problem.

Finally, he was prompted to a devise called "system base." This he clicked on and was given several options including "base access". He clicked on and heard a noise similar to the sound when the portable disk drawer to a laptop opens. He tilted the base toward him again and the bottom vented portion swung open. It was hinged on the inside. There, staring him in the face, was a silver square about two and a half inches around. The part of the square that was next to the vented portion of the box had a microphone. It was connected by little silver wires to larger colored wires running out of the black rectangular box and into the Investech central processing unit. On the side of the silver square were the letters ESS and the words model # 17784097.

He quickly closed the bottom vented portion of the box and tilted the box and screen upright which he placed back on his desk. He excused himself for lunch so he could call Maria. He walked to a restaurant three blocks away and as he pulled out his new cell phone he looked around to be sure no one he knew was watching him. He gave her the information then returned to the business of making deals.

....

Maria called Bill Palmer and repeated what Johnny had told her.

"ESS is an acronym for Electronic Systems Solutions," he said. "They're a small firm out of Ohio. I have to get some specs on the devise before we can figure out what to do with it. Give me a day or two."

....

It was the next afternoon before he called her back.

"The devise is called a voice to data transmitter, or VTDT for short," according to Bill. "It's self programmed for stealth operation. Johnny will have to get into the bases of the phones you want to tap. He should find VTDT's have been installed but not activated for outgoing transmissions. They will have to be there because the voice transmission can't be converted to written text without them. They can be set up to transmit only, receive only or both. He'll have to activate the VTDT's for outgoing transmissions. I don't know if they will work outside of Investech's IT system, so I assume he'll have to direct the transmissions to his desktop."

"There's no way we can direct it to our PC at the house?" Maria asked.

"I can't be sure Maria. We might be able to get it to work, but we could waste valuable time trying."

"OK, when Johnny gets home tonight, we'll call you for instructions."

....

They called Bill Palmer as soon as Johnny walked in the door.

"You'll have to open the base connected to the phone you want to tap and disconnect the VTDT. It should be fastened with a clip. When you remove it, you'll see a small screen on the side with a toggle switch. Press the switch until it prompts you with 'outgoing devise'. Then enter the extension number of that phone and press the switch again. It should say 'outgoing entered' and display the extension number. It will ask you to confirm the entry. Press the switch again and it will say "incoming devise'. Since your phone is already being tapped, you should find your extension has already been entered, probably along with everyone else in the office. You may be prompted to confirm all the extensions again. After that you will be asked to activate the VTDT."

He continued, "You'll have to disconnect the VTDT on your phone and go through the same process. You should find that the outgoing devise or devices have been set, but not the incoming. You can enter as many incoming extensions as the VTDT will let you. I think it will go up to a hundred. Be sure to activate it again when you're done.

You'll have to go to your computer and bring up the correct file in order to review the transmissions. I think Maria said to look under 'communications log'. If it says 'devises inactive', it's not working. It should prompt you with call logs for various dates and then let you access the logs for each extension you have forwarded to your phone."

Palmer added, "I know I don't have to tell you this, but if your employer went to the trouble of bugging your phones, they'll probably do a periodic check to make sure everything is working properly. My suggestion is, you forward as few phones to yours as possible. If we find something we can use, I would deactivate the VTDTs you programmed and switch yours back to transmit only."

Johnny replied, "Great work Bill, but I have a couple of questions. When I disconnect the VTDTs do I have to worry about how to rewire them?"

"If they're not color coded, find a way to reconnect them as they were originally. I don't know if it matters, but why take a chance."

Johnny's next question, "Is there anyway to intercept emails using the VTDTs?"

"No, but I'm guessing what we're looking for will not be something these people want to put in writing anyway. If the principals at Investech have a little side business going, the odds are strong that the money is going into numbered accounts and they will have the numbers memorized. Or they're under lock and key somewhere. But if so, they will have to call in their deposits and use a security code. Once we have something to go on, I'll get more details."

....

With the technical part of the plan in place it went back to logistics. Johnny and Maria weighed the merits of having Johnny go it alone, or finding a way for one of them to stand guard while the other programmed the VTDT's. They opted for the team approach and decided Johnny would have to work on the upcoming weekend in order to catch up with his backlog. On Saturday, with the kids at a neighbor's house, they drove downtown together. Johnny went up to the office while Maria waited in a coffee shop around the corner. Since she could be recognized as Elizabeth Blake, she donned her cleaning crew outfit. When Johnny was sure the coast was clear, he would call her and she would appear to clean the hallway in front of Investech's reception area. As soon as she was in position, he would enter Brad's and then Alex' offices to take care of business. If anyone decided to come in on Saturday, she would call on his cell phone which was set to vibrate and not ring.

On Friday before he left work, he waited for the cleaning crew to open all the office doors and he turned the inner lock on the two doors so, when the crew closed them, they remained unlocked. He checked again as they were leaving to be sure they remained that way. When he entered on Saturday, the doors were unlocked, so he entered with no problem and called Maria on his cell phone.

He went out to the reception area, called security so they would let her in the building and waited until she got off the elevator. She had cleaning polish and rags for the handrails in the hallway and began working as he went back into the Investech offices. If nothing else, the halls would shine.

He started with Alex' office since he wouldn't have to worry about a password. He logged in and went through the steps he had followed to unlock the bottom panel of the base of the box in his office. It worked just as it had earlier in the week. He tilted the base so the bottom faced him. Knowing he would need two hands free, had brought a cushion from the couch in the hallway and leaned the flat screen on the cushion. He had brought a pink and a black magic marker with him and rubbed one on each of the silver connecting wires to correspond to the like color of the IT system wires. They were joined with mini electrical connectors which he unscrewed. He found the clip which fastened the VTDT to the inside of the box and pressed the connecting piece until it was free.

With the silver square in his right hand he pressed the toggle switch and was prompted with "outgoing device". He entered Alex' extension number. If it worked, Alex' calls would be received by his desktop, which he had already programmed as an incoming device in his VTDT. Then, it occurred to him that since he didn't have Brad's password, he should enter his extension as an incoming devise on Alex' VTDT and maybe the VTDT would forward Brad's call log as well as Alex." He would do the same with Scott Borden's not knowing what to expect. When he got to the prompts for incoming devises the VTDT flashed, 'incoming devise #16'. This made sense to Johnny as Alex had probably already tapped 15 other phones. He took a minute to think and realized that if he entered Brad or Scott's extension for the first time Alex would begin to receive print outs of their calls and discover his VTDT had been tampered with. He had to go back and see if either of the two extensions were already entered. But how to do that? He rolled the toggle back and forth and it went up and down, but would not position the cursor over the number 6 in 16. If he could change the 6 to 5, he hoped the extension number that had been entered would appear on the screen. He pressed a small red button next to the screen and rolled the toggle. It positioned the cursor as he had hoped. Then he pressed the red button again and the 6 changed to 7. Oops. He pressed the button twice and the 7 changed back to 6. Two more presses and it changed to 5 and displayed an extension he didn't recognize. He went through the process and discovered Scott's extension had been entered as number 5, Brad was number 1.

Maria had entered Johnny's cell phone number in hers so all she would have to do was press the green key if someone entered the Investech office. She was starting to polish railing number two when the elevator door opened and a casually dressed man stepped out and put his key in the lock to open the main door to the reception area. She reached into her pocket, grabbed the phone, and pressed the green key. The phone immediately registered that the call had failed. She tried again with no luck. She was in the interior of a large concrete and steel building and was blocked from access to a cell phone tower. They hadn't figured on that. She waited until the man moved past the reception area into the hallway and saw he was walking in the direction of Alex' office. She followed him and said in a very loud voice in the most broken English she could muster, "Meester, Meester, you need cleen, you need cleen?"

Johnny heard the ruckus and moved to the door to Alex office. He opened it just a crack to see one of the guys on Jack's team turned to face Maria. He was staring at her with a blank expression. Maria could see Johnny out of the corner of her eye. He nodded to her, closed the door and locked it. In the hallway, the man shook his head at Maria indicating either that he didn't need cleen, or had no idea what he she was saying. She shrugged her shoulders and walked out to her post.

Back at work, Johnny reconnected the wires, clipped the VTDT in place, closed the base and placed the flat screen in its original place. Since Maria had alerted him that there were people in the other offices, he opened the door to Alex office very slowly and looked around. If he had any thoughts about trying to get into Brad's system, he abandoned them knowing he was not alone. He was careful to lock both offices before he went to the reception area. He left the building alone and was joined five minutes later in the parking garage by Maria.

Time would tell if Johnny could add 'installer of electronic eavesdropping devices' to his resume.

Twenty Six

THE PROBLEM WITH FLYING across the country for a face to face meeting without any preparation is that you could be wasting a lot of time and money. The meeting could last for hours or minutes. There was no way of telling. Such was the dilemma facing Warner Simmons. He didn't want to spend a lot of time on the phone with Blanchard or his associates 'pre-negotiating' anything. He didn't see that as dealing from a position of strength which, frankly, he wasn't. But, he could walk out of the meeting at any time since he was on the road. He did at least have that going for him, if the proposed terms of the settlement were ridiculous.

Simmons had joined BCC ten years earlier before the previous two mergers and before the accounting profession had been dragged into some very high profile business scandals. Or, maybe it was more appropriate to say, had done nothing to stop them. He preferred to think that the bad judgment of a few had affected the future of many. The profession, as well as the firm, had taken some hits. One of BCC's four peers was now gone, having been dissolved in the face of the most sensational example of disregard for the investing public America had ever seen. Interestingly enough, in the aftermath of Enron and the other major failures, the remaining large accounting firms had more business than they could handle. The result of the failure to protect the public was that the accounting firms were given additional responsibilities to see that their clients towed the line. No one said the work was productive, or the rules were clear, but the fees poured in anyhow.

Warner had the awesome responsibility to see that BCC did not go the way of the dinosaur Having heard the results of the forensic accounting engagement, he didn't think BCC would incur the wrath of the government. He assumed they would be able to reach some sort of a financial settlement and continue on. But even if the settlement were confidential, the firm would suffer a major black eye. The senior partners were all nearing retirement age and he had heard that a group of younger partners wanted to take control of the negotiations with Blanchard. He recognized that when he returned with Blanchard's proposal he might have to sell it to more than the usual group of three. Beyond that, he understood there could be pressure for a change at the top no matter what the result. The management, business practices and name of the firm were all subject to change. The firm had a much better chance of staying in tact if he could negotiate a reasonable settlement and close it quickly.

The offices of Blanchard and Stone were located in an old converted house on the outskirts of downtown San Francisco. The house had been built in 1896, renovated three times since, and then a fourth time when the law firm purchased it in 1988. The interior was finished in conservative wood trim with comfortable trappings, but avoided the appearance of stodginess. Warner was asked to have a seat in the reception area and, while he waited, he perused the annual reports of a few technology firms that he found on the table tops in front of him. He assumed Blanchard's firm represented those firms, and that was confirmed as he flipped to the back pages of the reports where the professional relationships are disclosed.

"Good of you to fly out and see us Warner." Blanchard said as he ushered his visitor toward a seat at a circular conference table where they were joined by a male associate of Blanchard's. One of the group who had been at the meeting in BCC's office.

"Glad we could get together on short notice," was his response.

They talked briefly about law, accounting and San Francisco and then got down to business. "I'll get right to the point," Blanchard began. "You know we represent the majority shareholders of Westpac, who are prepared to institute a law suit if we're not able to reach an acceptable financial resolution to this matter. Westpac bought Frontier with the expectation of income to be generated from orders for its software. Orders that were confirmed by your firm. Orders that never existed."

"I need to correct you on a couple of points before you continue, Jonathan. First, many of the orders were valid and did exist. Second, there was never any assurance that the orders would be filled before they were cancelled. BCC never gave an opinion on the future revenue stream of Frontier. Whatever method Westpac used to determine the price it paid for Frontier was based on its own internal valuations"

Blanchard came back, "I really don't think we would have much trouble convincing a court that you were negligent, although I'm not going to tell you that's our preferred way to handle this. We've computed what we think the damages amount to and my clients are prepared to accept a reasonable settlement."

With that Blanchard's associate produced a schedule and handed it to Warner. The schedule started out by showing the potential income for Frontier over a three year period, beginning on the date of the merger. It was divided by three and from that number was subtracted a line item labeled 'Income from Non Existence Sources.' The net of those two numbers was called 'Determinable Income'. That number was then multiplied by 15 and the result called 'Confirmed Value'. From the Confirmed Value was subtracted the 'Price Paid', resulting in an 'Overpayment' of Eight Hundred and Fifty Million Dollars.

Warner Simmons studied the schedule then looked up at Blanchard. "So what are you proposing?"

"My clients will accept Five Hundred and Fifty Million dollars if we can get it done in two weeks."

The numbers didn't shock BCC's general counsel. He expected Blanchard to start with a high number that would be more than BCC could afford to pay, but not so high that BCC would refuse to negotiate. Further, with that kind of money being kicked around, BCC's insurance company would get involved and then the prospect of closing something quickly and painlessly would be out the window. The insurance company would bring in a team of lawyers and they would go to war. Blanchard knew that and would clearly accept something less, although he was assured of a huge pay day whether they went to court or not. But the question for Warner was whether he would stay and attempt to negotiate a deal or simply thank Jonathan for his time and tell him he'd get back to him. He decided to add a dash of humor to appear not overly concerned about the outcome. "Our petty cash fund is a little short this week, you know."

"If you're saying you want to pay it out over time, we can work something out," was Blanchard's response.

That wasn't what Warner had in mind, but he had received a concession without asking. "Not really," he said. "It's not a number we'd realistically consider. We don't think there's that much exposure for us here."

"Warner, I don't want to press this any further than I have to, but there's still the matter involving Johnny Brandt. You need to factor that in when considering your exposure."

"Again, that's really unsubstantiated at this point," was his response. "You'd have to prove the paperwork you have is legit and the trades really took place."

"We can do that with ease," said Blanchard.

"I'm sure we don't want to debate the merits of our respective cases here, Jonathan. Even though I think your number is beyond consideration, I'll present it to our senior committee and call you in the next couple of days."

With that Warner Simmons left for the airport feeling as though the trip had not been in vain. True, the initial proposal was out of the question, but the message was "we don't want to bury you." The real wild card was BCC's professional liability insurance carrier. Involving them raised the stakes. They would bring more money to the pot, but make the plaintiff's law suit much more difficult if it came to that. He knew Jonathan Blanchard was in a tactical bind. He wanted to move quickly and maximize his client's recovery without getting bogged down. The question was, what did that translate to in terms of numbers?

Twenty Seven

THE NEWS OF JONAS Smith's death would have escaped almost anyone outside of the Reno area. It was covered in a small fifth page article in the Reno Gazette - Journal. Apparently, Mr. Smith had decided to party late and then drive in the dangerous high country around Lake Tahoe at night. Bill Palmer had set up his own mini night desk to filter data relevant to whatever matters he might be working on. He regularly received the online version of daily publications including the Wall Street Journal. After he undertook the initial steps to help Johnny and Maria he ordered the daily newspapers from Reno, San Francisco and Chicago to keep tabs on any suspicious activity involving the players. He had written a program which allowed him to enter names or key phrases and then that program searched the publications for a match. He made sure he received as much background information from Maria as possible before entering it into the program. If and when a match occurred, he received an alert message on his computer screen. Until now, there were a few unimportant matches involving the initials BCC or the name Billingsly Carlton and Craig. Once, Bradley Worshaw was cited as donating a substantial sum of money to a charity. But that was it.

Seeing the article sent a chill down Palmer's spine. He didn't know anything about Jonas Smith except what Maria had told him. He lived in Reno, so presumably he knew where and where not to drive at night. There was no mention of whether the police suspected foul play, or if this was your typical drink and drive event. "Way too coincidental for me," Palmer thought. He would have to get more information on the police investigation, but for now, as much as he didn't want to, he simply had to call Maria. He knew the call would unnerve her, but it had to be made.

Johnny had already left for work when the call came in. Maria was shaken and Palmer apologized at having to break the news. She thanked him nonetheless and he promised to let her know as soon as he had more details. She had to get word to Johnny and it would not go through the Investech phone system. Johnny was in a meeting when he felt his cell phone vibrate. He resisted the urge to answer because there was only one person who knew he had the cell phone and she wouldn't call unless it was important. As soon as he could, he broke form the meeting and went to the men's room. He waited until he was sure he was alone and then called Maria. "Smith's dead," she said.

The words shot through him like a cannon. Maria repeated her call with Bill Palmer to Johnny. He was speechless for a few seconds and then realized he had absolutely nothing to say. He couldn't undue anything he had done over the weekend. He also wasn't sure if he was in more danger by having done it, or less. Tapping the phones might provide critical information that could solve problems or save lives. Or, it could get him killed. He promised Maria he would be careful and returned to his office.

The days were getting busier as the Burgess process picked up steam. Even though Ronco wasn't a go, Johnny had his team doing research and periodically sending it to them anyway. People in the firm were taking advantage of Johnny's expertise and so he gradually became involved in other deals ranging from mergers, to structuring complicated financing, to the sale of a Midwestern toll road to a foreign pension fund. The latter proved to be a coup for Investech, but made Johnny uncomfortable. What incentive did the Aussies have in making sure he didn't drive over pot holes anyway?

Jack Miller's team was in and out of intense meetings with the accountants at Burgess, as well as various department heads. His people flew back and forth to Denver or were on the phone continuously. Some of the contact was with BCC, as Burgess' auditors and it gave Johnny a chance to work with his former colleagues. Each department at Burgess had to provide detailed documents for Investech to perform due diligence required of a first rate investment banking firm. Jack had anywhere from four to eight people reading memos, contracts, copies of emails, prior SEC filings, software patents and more, all supplied by Burgess. They would check and cross check the written documents to be sure they supported the proformas to be included in the offering memorandum, or OM, which would be distributed to potential bidders. Any critical information contained in these documents would be included in the OM as well.

The OM started taking shape during the week after Johnny returned form Denver. It began with a history of Burgess and included a time line of the introduction of its major products. Most were still in production, although some were into their third, fourth or fifth generation. The PR guys had come up with an innovative way to present

Burgess' most popular soft ware. When you turned the page displaying the product, a screen popped up affixed to a fold out. The screen was made out of shinny aluminum and contained a replica of a spreadsheet which had been developed by Burgess. At the bottom of the screen, printed on the page, was a set of faux computer keys which spelled out the word B-U-R-G-E-S-S, and then below that said, 'the key to your success'. The OM also included a section with detailed proformas, a section for charts and graphs and finally, detailed biographies on all of Burgess' senior officers.

When he could, Johnny, checked the communication log program on his desktop computer. The VTDT worked perfectly and did forward calls from not only Brad's and Scott's phones, but the other thirteen phones that were tapped by Alex Franklin. He didn't want to spend any more time than was absolutely necessary reviewing the logs and once he determined that a call contained nothing of any importance, he moved on. He was struck by an interesting question though. Had Alex tapped Brad's phone with his knowledge? Was Brad even aware that several office phones had been tapped? Scott's calls produced nothing of an incriminating nature, so Johnny wasn't sure how to tell the good guys from the bad. It was an excruciating waiting game, but there was no choice.

A meeting was set to finalize the OM. It would take about a week to run though production and in that week Johnny, Brad, Alex and Scott would contact prospective suitors and negotiate confidentiality agreements. Each party would have to execute a confidentiality agreement before an OM would be sent. A draft of a standard form confidentiality agreement had been prepared and was ready to go out. All hands at Investech were present at the meeting, including Brad and Alex. Jack had received all of Burgess' comments to the OM and now the finishing touches would be agreed upon and the OM would go to press.

After the meeting, Brad and Alex asked Johnny to stay behind. When the three were alone, Brad began, "Johnny, I know we haven't followed up on our commitment to report back to you on our progress on the Westpac matter. You know we've all been busy as hell around here, but Alex was in to see Jonathan Blanchard last week and we can up date you now."

It was Alex' turn. "That's right Johnny. According to Jonathan, BCC's general counsel was out to see him and they talked about a settlement. No decision was reached, so that matter is on hold until he gets a response. We told Jonathan we would use our influence with the Westpac shareholders once we know they get close on something. It will be a little easier for us to do that if we can get a deal together on Burgess and close it as soon as possible."

Johnny was confused. What did one have to do with the other? Then he got it. Either they were using the Burgess deal to put additional pressure on Johnny to produce fees, or they were buying up Burgess stock in anticipation of a price increase once a merger was announced. Or both. They hadn't been extremely subtle in getting the message across. He was just slow on the uptake.

Johnny was upset and wanted to lash out, but he saw an opportunity. "Alright," he thought, 'I'll bait the trap, even if it's my trap.' He said, "You know, I'm absolutely convinced we'll get a deal for Burgess at $56 a share. I've been getting calls left and right. Even though the OM isn't out yet the big tech firms are really hungry for a merger. In fact I hear there's a Dutch group that's already putting pension money together to make a preemptive strike."

"$56," said Brad, "that's another ten percent on top of the twenty five we're hoping for. Are you sure about that Johnny?"

"Of course, I can't guaranty anything, but with all the liquidity out there chasing deals, I think its going to happen. Plus, the Dutch are under pressure to get their pension money invested before the accounting rules change. I think they'll up the stakes."

"Thanks Johnny," said Alex. "Brad and I want you to know we think you're doing a great job. Keep us posted on anything you hear related to Burgess. Oh, and we'll have your written bonus agreement on your desk next week."

Johnny left the meeting ready to fight. When they were recruiting him, of course, nothing was said about strings being attached to the offer to intercede with Jonathan Blanchard. Now he was expected to close the Burgess merger so they could profit handsomely from his first deal. But really, could he have expected anything less? If the answer was yes, he was kidding himself and he knew it. But they had put their plans out there for him and he would take advantage of whatever opening they gave him. It was the first time he sensed a slight shift in the balance of power, although a wrong move at any point would negate that shift, big time.

When he returned to his office, Brenda handed him several phone messages, including one from Ellen Caulfield. She was two hours behind him on Pacific time, so he waited until late in the day and returned the call, It certainly would be a good idea to maintain solid relations with Blanchard's firm. When she came on the line she said, "Hi Johnny, how've you been?" with genuine sincerity.

"Good Ellen, and you?"

"Can't complain, sweat shop and all aside."

"I heard Jonathan can be a real slave driver," he said.

"Oh well, I guess its job security," she responded. "Anyway, we're working on a draft of a merger agreement for Burgess and I wanted to see if we could get together and review it. Their general counsel asked me to fly over next week and work out of his office. Can you meet us there?"

The merger agreement or MA was the cornerstone document in the entire merger and acquisition process. It was the legal document by which parties obligated themselves to either pay or receive the largest sums of money normally exchanged in any single business transaction. In recent years, many billions of dollars exchanged hands based on what was written in the MA's. A great deal of time and precision would be spent on the MA before anyone signed it. However, a completed draft would be forwarded to all bidders so they could see what they would be expected to sign, if their bid was accepted.

It would have been standard procedure for the lawyers to knock heads over the first draft and then ask Johnny to review it. He didn't want to read too much in to Ellen's invitation to join them. She had seemed especially friendly the last time they were together. Was it related to the Westpac matter or did she find him good looking? He had no idea what women saw when they looked at him. A few weeks earlier he was a sad sack with a low self esteem. Now he was back to his old self. At least that was what he wanted the world to see. A confident guy, still young, physically attractive, in his prime. He was on the offensive now and maybe she sensed it. With everything he had on his plate, he didn't want to commit to a trip just then. He told Ellen he'd check his schedule and get back to her tomorrow.

When he got home he repeated the contents of his brief meeting with Brad and Alex to Maria. She nodded knowingly when he described their almost direct appeal to him to make sure they had the right timing with regard to investing in Burgess' stock. He emphasized his mention of the Dutch investor and she picked up on that right away. "So you're saying Elizabeth Blake should expect a call from a certain investment banker in the near future," she said, more of a statement than a question.

"I would think so," he replied.

"Mar, I really should go back to Denver next week. I have to keep the ball rolling on the Burgess deal. I want to maintain the appearance of business as usual. I'll probably be gone one night" He tried to convince himself he meant it as he said it.

"OK," she said, "I can take the kids and stay at my parents' house."

They talked about how she should handle the call if it came from Brad. Her original plan was to become Elizabeth Blake for a total of about 30 minutes. Enough to get in, survey the office layout, figure out what she could about Investech's IT system and then become a cleaning lady with a serious foreign accent. Now, Johnny had found more use for Elizabeth. "Give me a day or so and I'll have a plan," she said.

....

The meeting in Denver was scheduled for the second Thursday in June. Johnny arrived at the usual time and took a cab to Burgess' offices. He was greeted warmly by the receptionist, who now knew him by name. Burgess' general counsel sent his secretary for Johnny and he was escorted to the same conference room where they met a couple of weeks before. The weather had warmed up considerably since his last trip, with the thermometer expected to go over a hundred degrees by mid afternoon. It was warm in the conference room as the late morning sun bore in. A sun shade had been pulled, but it was only marginally effective. Papers were spread over most of the conference room table. The general counsel had removed his jacket and was in shirt sleeves. Ellen had removed her jacket as well and wore a tight fitting white blouse made out of material that clung closely to her skin. Johnny could see that the blouse was cut to reveal a more than adequate amount of cleavage, even though she was seated.

With serious work in progress, he didn't want to disturb them. They both started to stand up to greet him, but he said, "Please don't let me interrupt."

"Johnny, my secretary is updating the first fifty pages of the MA, I'll have it here in about fifteen minutes. It would be a good place for you to start your review," said the general counsel.

Ellen looked pre-occupied with work, but excellent nonetheless. He had looked forward to their next negotiating session, as he found her to be bright but reasonable. In this case they would be working together on the MA for Burgess so it would be teamwork instead of negotiations. He couldn't wait to get started.

He made a couple of calls on his cell phone while he waited for the document. When it came, he was able to focus in on the issues immediately. He had reviewed numerous MA's related to other deals, so his job would be to help conform this MA to fit the Burgess transaction. He made notes in the margins of the document and passed them to the two lawyers. They asked a couple of questions, but generally understood what he wanted.

With the first fifty pages complete, he excused himself and found Jack and his team meeting with Dave Rosen. A few issues had come up regarding presentation of numbers in the proforma and they wanted his opinion. Apparently, Jack's team had taken what Dave thought was an aggressive approach and they wanted to review it to be sure it would standup to scrutiny. In the end, Johnny suggested they add some footnotes to the numbers to clarify the position they had taken. The reader could draw his own conclusion.

Johnny returned to the conference room. The lawyers had finished the MA and were now discussing the disclosure schedules. These were the exhibits which listed any and all exceptions to the audited financial statements as well as clarified much of what was in the MA. The schedules were probably even more important than the MA itself. And maybe thicker. Finally, at six o'clock, Burgess' general counsel said, "I have a previous engagement tonight, so I have to leave now. You both can stay and work as late as you like. I'll notify security that you may be here awhile."

As soon as he left, Ellen looked at Johnny and said, "Let's get outta here."

They walked out into the still very warm late afternoon and remembered there were several choices of places to eat along the route to the brew pub they had visited a couple of weeks earlier. They found an upscale Italian restaurant, went inside and within minutes were seated. Dinner started off with a glass of wine and Johnny felt the edge coming off after a few sips. By the time he finished the first glass, he was a new man. Ellen was right there with him. They moved on to the second glass without even thinking about dinner. As they drank, the conversation became easier, the questions faster and the laughs a little bit louder. Ellen filled Johnny in on what it was like to grow up in a ski town. Johnny mentioned that, growing up in the Midwest, all you ever did with snow was try and move it out of the way. At one point Ellen said, "Johnny, I'm really sorry about the matter with Westpac and the whole meeting with Blanchard at your office. I really haven't been involved with it at all. My background is in securities, not corporate or criminal law. It's just that Jonathan likes to take me on the road with him whenever he can."

Johnny didn't doubt anything she said and responded, "I believe you Ellen. And we're gonna get it all of worked out."

"If there's anything I can do to help, just please let me know" was her reply.

Johnny thought about asking her to talk to Blanchard and see if she could persuade him to expedite the negotiations with BCC, but decided against it. It was a card he might play at some point in the future.

With dinner over, Ellen convinced Johnny they needed an after dinner drink and ordered two for each of them. They came in small glasses with little bean looking things at the bottom of the glass. One big swallow and each drink was gone. They ordered another round. Finally she said, "Lets go."

"Where?" he said.

"We can do a little walking or go back to my hotel if you prefer," she presented it in an innocent sounding way.

Johnny stood up to go and his legs felt momentarily heavy. His brain told them to move forward, but instead he rocked slightly to the side and he placed his palms on the table for balance. He wasn't in danger of passing out, but the drinks had definitely found their mark. Ellen saw this and walked around the table to Johnny's left side. She wrapped her right arm around his back, with her hand against Johnny's side under his right arm. She pulled him gently close to her so she could help him as they walked. He felt her breasts press against his side and he turned toward her, their faces only inches apart. Control officially went to Ellen.

"Correction," she said, "you're place."

The doorman helped them into a cab and as they settled in the back seat, Johnny turned toward her and moved slowly enough to telegraph his intention to kiss her. He gave her plenty of time to turn her head away. Instead, she accepted the kiss without hesitation. He wanted to be subtle and not rush the physical part, but once he sensed the green light, all that was forgotten. In his mind, she started it, made sure they had enough liquor to break down their inhibitions and left it up to him to take it as far as he wanted. There was no turning back.

They made their way up to his room and the clothes started to come off before the lights came on at all. They fumbled with their own clothes, each other's clothes and back to their own, fighting the effects of the alcohol. When they were completely naked, he put his arms around her and pulled her close to him. He kissed her again and this time she gave him her tongue. Her breath was warm and sweet with the same taste as the after dinner drinks. He felt himself get hard as her nipples, pressed against his chest, confirmed her own willingness to keep going.

She led him toward the bed and they were on their sides, facing each other. He could feel the suppressed drive in her body waiting for him to take command. But with the long day and the drinks behind him, he felt his energy start to ebb slightly. He couldn't think straight and wasn't sure if his mind had decided to shut down and let his body finish up on its own. He held her close to him and melted completely into her.

....

The dull ache in his head was accompanied by the first dim morning light curling around the edges of the curtains in his room. Something told him not to open his eyes too quickly so he lay on his back, eyes shut, and moved his left arm to see if she had stayed the night. The gentle hissing of the shower could have given him the answer, but he was not awake enough to notice. His left hand found a small amount of very light weight fabric on top of the sheets and he clutched it and opened his eyes slowly. He held a bra and a swatch of lace that couldn't possibly have covered much of anything. He sat up and turned toward the bathroom just as she walked out. She was toweling her hair, with nothing on. In the dim light he could see what he had held the night before. At the sight of her taut body, he was instantly ready to go again, headache or not. He stood up and kissed her and she held him tightly but, when he started to move her back to the bed, she stopped him.

"I have to get to my room and change for work. I still have a couple of hours to get in before I fly back."

Johnny thought about making a case for a little action before breakfast, but decided not to push it. "OK, counselor, but I'll need another day in court if you can get me on the docket."

"We'll see what we can do," was her response. And then, with her blue eyes taking him in, "Johnny, thanks for last night."

Twenty Eight

IF THE LITTLE MEETING Johnny had with Brad and Alex before his trip to Denver denoted a chink in their armor, the first serious break came on his return. He made time between meetings and sometimes while he was on the phone to check the call logs. Brad had made a call to a phone number in Las Vegas, which Johnny could tell because of the area code. The person in Vegas answered the call by saying "hello" and Brad then said, "Hi Sammy, its Brad. We need to think about getting liquid for the Burgess deal."

Sammy responded by saying, "I'm gonna need about two weeks. How much are we talking about?"

""You can do some research and let me know what you think."

"That's what I pay you for and before I make any commitments, I want some of that money from the accounting firm before I stick my neck out again."

"There's a Dutch group who came to see me about investing in a tech firm or firms in the U.S. They're under a lot of pressure to invest their funds as soon as possible. The word is they'll pay a premium on top of a high multiple.

I think we can match them up with Burgess. Once word gets out, the stock will go through the roof. It'll be too late," responded Brad.

"Don't let word get out until we're ready," from Sammy.

Brad responded, "I can keep it under cover and leak word later, but I have a short window"

"You need to lengthen the window until we see some return on the Westpac investment. Better yet, get the deal done with the accountants"

"I'm working on it, I'm working on it," was all Brad could say.

The call was over.

Bingo, thought Johnny. Brad and his 'investors' are going to recycle the settlement proceeds from BCC to buy Burgess stock. If Brad gave Sammy wiring instructions for the investment, they could find the receiving bank. It might be Oak Bank. But even if it wasn't, money would now be flowing in, and then out and somewhere along the line they'd find the final resting place. He was convinced whoever was framing his wife and father in law had wired a large sum of money in their name to Oak Bank and then moved it out to wherever they wanted it to go. It was the perfect plan. Get the money out of the U.S. in someone else's name. Why not have it be a relative of a person who had inside knowledge that a merger was soon to be announced. Especially if that person happened to be a partner in a deep pockets accounting firm. And, oh yes, along the way orchestrate a smoke and mirrors series of audit confirmations, mostly from firms that didn't exist or were shell companies. You pump up the value of the target company, sell the stock before the shit hits the fan and set up the accounting firm for an easy kill. It was a brilliant plan. Win win. If you were in the middle of it, you made money on the sale of Frontier stock and on the recovery from the accounting firm. Plus, you had an insider trading case in your back pocket as insurance.

Johnny might have figured out part of the game, but not the whole. It was becoming clearer that Jonas Smith had pitched him during their little get together in Reno. What's more, whoever set up the plan, Bishop, Worshaw, maybe both, was working off of other people's money too. And, what about the losers? Sammy sounded like he could be one of them. Taking on outside investors added a dimension of risk. Lose your own money and its one thing. Lose someone else's it another. Especially if they had a low level of risk tolerance.

There was something else Johnny needed to sort out. He had gotten caught in a trap and was angry at himself and racked with guilt at the same time. The pressure of the past few months had built to a level inside him that desperately begged for a release. The liquor had made it easy for him to let his guard down and give in to the testosterone driven night with Ellen. He had seen it coming and instead of trying to avoid it, he simply let it happen. He wasn't in the habit of beating himself up over things he couldn't control. But this wasn't one of them. It was the deception that bothered him. It was understood that after fourteen years of marriage, his ego would be stoked if a woman like Ellen wanted him. The prospect of physical gratification with beautiful flesh he had never experienced pushed him to the limit. But Maria was his soul mate and had never let him lack for anything, intellectually, or physically. Why had he not been able to stop? He asked himself this question over and over again without finding the answer. He knew he never would.

Maria and Johnny decided they had to make some of their phone calls to each other over the office phone instead of all their calls on their cell phones. Whoever was monitoring his call log might find it suspicious if he never talked to his wife during the day. He picked up the phone and dialed her at her parent's house.

"Hi Mar, when are you coming home?"

"I'll be home in time for dinner, but I think the kids want to stay for a couple of days."

"OK, then lets have dinner at Franco's," he said.

Franco's was a restaurant a few blocks from their house, so they decided to meet there at 7:00 p.m. A date with his wife without the kids would give them a chance to talk through some things and make some major decisions.

Once they were seated and had glanced through the menu, Johnny told Maria about Brad Worhaw's call to Las Vegas. Then he explained his theory regarding the entire tie in between Westpac, BCC, the plan to involve Johnny and their family. "Burgess could be a way to bail out the losers," he said.

Maria listened intently and finally nodded her agreement. Then she said, "the pressure will be on Worshaw to move the Burgess deal along." And, "Johnny let me ask you this; is it possible for two companies to arrange for a merger without the target company going through a bid process?"

"Yes," he said, realizing that she had asked the right question. "The board's obligation is to make the best deal for its shareholders. Normally that's accomplished through a competitive process. But it doesn't have to be. If they were wowed by a pre-emptive offer and were afraid of losing it, they could accept it. Another firm could always make a topping offer, so the target really can't lose." Johnny went on, "If you think about it, all the due diligence we're doing now would be available to anyone the board wanted to give it to. The OM is done. It could really move a deal along rather quickly."

"Then I need to be ready for Worshaw's call. If he's under as much pressure as it seems, and he has the OM ready, he'll want to know who my client is. It wouldn't be surprising if he pushes for a negotiated deal with the Dutch, to accelerate Burgess"

"We have to buy enough time to get routing numbers to the bank accounts they're using," Johnny said. "I got the impression Brad or Alex might have to wire some money back to Sammy before the BCC thing gets resolved. "

"OK," she responded, "He'll get antsy, but I'll hold him off as best I can."

"Another thing, Mar, I need to talk to your father and find out what he knows. We really should think about going to the FBI. There's only so much risk we should be taking."

"I agree. In fact I was thinking that we should have a private security firm watch the house," she said.

"Let's do that. It's only a matter of time before we take this as far as we can go. Then we have to turn it over to the authorities. If your father wasn't involved, I would say we should do it now, but I don't want to expose him if he's really at risk. We have to know that first."

"We'll drive up this week end and pick the kids up. That'll be the perfect opportunity to talk."

....

The call came the next morning. She still had her calls from New York forwarded so it was no surprise when the screen on her cell phone flashed a 312 area code. She quickly adopted the thick accented voice of her trusty secretary and said "Ms. Blake's ouffice, may I help you?"

"Yes, this Brad Worshaw for Ms. Blake."

"I'm sorry Mr. Woshaw, but Ms. Blake is at a client's office."

"I see. Well, could you let her know I'll be in New York next week and I'd like to meet with her?"

"Well, I know she has a particularly hectic scheduuule next week, but I'll let her know you caulled."

"Thank you. It's very important that I speak with her."

"Why yes, of course, I know that," Maria thought. "But I didn't expect you to be in New York." That certainly creates a problem. What if he wanted to come to her office? She could probably continue to stall him on the identity of her client. But logistics could be an issue. He might be coming to New York to check her out and see if she was legit. After all, he said he hadn't heard of Howard and Fine. She was trying to buy time, but waiting too long to call him back was not a good idea. There was also the matter of her phone number showing up on his caller ID, if he had one.

After thinking about it, she decided email would be the best route for a while. It was always a good way to stay in touch without letting things move too quickly. Bill Palmer had helped her set up the email address Eblake@HowardFineLaw.com. Emails would go through his system and automatically be forwarded to her. She could generate emails in the same manner. That afternoon she sent an email saying, "Mr. Worshaw, thank you for the call today. I will be out of the country starting tomorrow morning for ten days. However, I am still able to conduct business while I am out. Is there anything in particular you would like to discuss?"

The response came an hour later: "Yes, I have specific information regarding a firm we represent who will be accepting merger proposals in a few weeks. I can give you a preview of that information. Where can I send it?"

The next morning she replied: "Can it be sent by email?"

Before noon she had received the OM by email. Doing business in the computer age was wonderful, even if it was monkey business. She had dodged a bullet, but for how long?

....

The drive from Chicago to Madison, Wisconsin takes two and a half hours and moves you across some of the richest farm land known to man. In between Rockford, Illinois, Beloit, Janesville and then Madison are miles of open space that gently changes from prairie to land that was covered by ice during the last ice age. As the ice melted, it left behind kettle moraines or undulations in the earth's surface, Even if you're a true son of Illinois, you can't help wishing the ice had made it a little further South. It endowed the land with character that was unmistakable, if short of spectacular. If you appreciated the Upper Midwest for what it really was, you understood the character of the land and the people ran together. Wisconsin was settled primarily by immigrants from Germany and Scandinavia. No nonsense, hard working, steady people who knew that the system worked if you contributed more to it that what you took out. Get a good education, work hard, live within your means – that was life. Johnny didn't know anyone from Wisconsin who didn't consider it an honor to be called a "cheesehead."

Johnny and Maria arrived at her parent's house early on Saturday afternoon. Henry Dann had followed the rules. He started in the family's building supply business just out of college. When he took over the business with his brother, they made the necessary innovations and product decisions to keep the business successful in the face of stiff competition. First it was the myriad of smaller guys selling material out of the back of their trucks, then the bigger well capitalized chains. Henry and his brother bought out any of the competitors they could and established relationships with almost every builder in Central to Northern Wisconsin. They provided construction design service, expedited delivery, warehousing, whatever it took to keep their customers happy. Over the years the Dann's had prospered and although not super wealthy by current standards were certainly comfortable. Henry was semi-retired now and finally able to travel with Maria's mother several months out of the year. Johnny had great respect for Henry which was what made it so difficult to have the conversation that had to take place.

Johnny normally looked forward to the drive to Madison in the summer months. Usually it was a time to unwind and finally see some pleasant scenery. But, not today. He really didn't know how Henry would react to the questions he'd be asking. After lunch Maria found a way to get her mother and the kids involved in a project which gave Johnny a chance to catch her father alone.

"Henry," Johnny began, "I need to ask you a question and I'll explain where all of this is going in a few minutes. But I have to tell you, what we're discussing here is of the utmost importance."

The gravity in Johnny's voice rang through to Henry and he looked squarely at Johnny as he spoke.

"We've been over to Sea First Bank a couple of times in the last few weeks. We found settlement statements pertaining to your joint account with Maria that show excessive trading in a stock called Frontier Data Systems. The stock was bought before the Westpac merger with Frontier. Then it was sold just after the merger was announced. The profits were huge, in the millions." Johnny stopped to let this sink in.

Henry had a look of puzzlement which seemed genuine to Johnny. He shook his head as he spoke. "No, Johnny there must be a mistake. I don't remember that at all."

"Think hard on this Henry, We need to be very sure."

He did that for a few moments before responding again, "You know I don't usually invest in anything unless I have some background knowledge first."

"I worked on the Westpac/Frontier merger at BCC and Maria or I may have said something to you."

A slow look of recognition came to Henry's face. "Johnny, I don't know if this has anything to do with it or not. You know Maria's mother has small occasional bouts with memory loss. It's nothing serious but I have to keep an eye on her. A year or so ago, a man called the house while I was out. He told her I had asked him to buy some stock for us but forgot to give him our account information. She couldn't remember if I told her to provide the information or not, so trying to helpful, she went ahead and gave it to him. I only know this because I found a note she wrote but forgot to give to me. I thought she meant she gave out the account number for my personal trades. I had that number changed immediately. I haven't touched the joint account in years, since we set it up for the kids."

Henry's explanation made sense. Other than the Frontier trades, Johnny remembered there was no other activity except for interest and dividend payments.

Having started the discussion with Henry, Johnny had no choice but to finish it. He told him of the events of the past couple of months and was finally able to give him the real background on his move to Investech. Predictably, Henry was shocked and then worried. Johnny told him they had hired a security firm to watch the house and, when Maria went out with the kids, to follow her at a distance.

"Henry, we're going to go the FBI, but before we did that, I had to know what your involvement was. We really didn't want to expose you to anything. This was really tough on us. We never thought for a minute you were involved in insider trading, but I had to make you aware of what's been going on. If nothing else you probably have a right to know."

Henry said, "I guess I really don't know what my exposure is. I assume the FBI could trace the money flow and clear me. But if it went to an offshore bank, they might hit a dead end."

Based on what Henry told Johnny, he had to agree. Maria's mother had given out the joint account number which meant that the trades actually went through the joint account. Since neither Henry nor Maria made any trades, they didn't bother to check the monthly settlement statements. The FBI would want to know why no one reported the suspicious activity before now. It wasn't a good fact pattern for any of them.

Johnny promised to keep Henry in the loop as things progressed and they both agreed that Maria's mother should not be told anything. He would be sure Maria knew that.

....

The security patrol Bill Palmer recommended was set to start at 5 o'clock on Sunday night, although Johnny told them they would not be home until a couple of hours after that. He wanted them to watch the house to see if there was any suspicious activity before they arrived. He was told they would do that and he might not see any evidence of the patrol when they got to the house. They would call him to confirm they were on duty. Since no one knew if the Brandt's home phone was tapped, they would hang up after one ring. Twenty minutes after they walked in, the phone rang once.

Twenty Nine

On Monday morning, William Palmer starting checking the motor vehicle accident reports filed on line by the Reno police. By Wednesday, the report did not appear, so he called the police department and inquired as to their procedure. He was told that, normally, a report is filed within forty eight hours of the accident, unless there were extenuating circumstances. So when the report did not appear by Friday, he knew something was up. He also knew if there was more to the story than was printed in the paper, he had little chance of getting it on the phone.

If the police were conducting any kind of an investigation into the death of Jonas Smith they would never reveal anything to him, unless of course, he had some reason to be told. He remembered what Maria had said to him about portraying Smith's wife. She had also given him Smith's address and phone number and mentioned that Johnny was sure he was a bachelor based on what he saw when he was in Smith's house.. He went to work creating a form he called "Request for Benefits Payment Upon Death of Insured." He entered the insured's name, address, phone number and then details regarding fictitious life insurance coverage. This included the name of the insurance company, the amount of the policy, the policy number and name of the beneficiary, which was Gina Polarski Smith. If the police said they had no record of Smith being married, he would shrug his shoulders and tell them he was just doing his job. That is, verifying that the accident was real so he could authorize payment of the benefits. He made sure the amount of the policy was only ten thousand dollars so it would not cause undo attention.

There was no doubt in his mind he owed it to Maria to find out all he could about Jonas Smith's death. He flew to Reno and went directly to the police department, holding the form in his hand. He said to the receptionist, "Good morning ma'am, I'm Bill Palmer, an insurance adjuster investigating the death of Jonas Smith who was killed in a car accident about a week ago. I just have a few simple questions regarding the accident."

She grabbed a file on her desk, looked for the name Smith, and when she found it she said, "I'll call up to detective Finnegan's office and see if someone can talk to you."

He took a seat and waited for about ten minutes until a young man in his mid twenties approached him. "Mr. Palmer?"

"Yes," said Palmer.

"I'm Andrew Finnegan, How can I help you?"

Palmer began, "I'm an independent insurance investigator. The insurance carriers send me one of these forms every time one of their insureds dies in a car accident. Normally, I just access the police report and send it along with the form and that's it. Problem is I've been looking for the Smith report and haven't been able to find it."

"We're just about done with it. It should be posted by tomorrow."

"Any reason for the delay?" asked Palmer

Detective Finnegan looked at him and spoke as if he expected him to read between the lines. "We were waiting for the blood work to come back from the lab. We wanted to check the alcohol level before we completed the report."

"Oh," said Palmer, "and what did they find?"

"Well, all I can tell you is Jonas Smith liked to eat at Ruby's Steakhouse in Incline Village," said Finnegan.

Palmer was left to interpret the non answer for himself. Obviously Finnegan couldn't say much more and he wasn't going to push it. He thanked Finnegan for his time and asked if he could call him to follow up, if necessary.

He went back to his rented car and got directions to Ruby's. It was about a forty minute drive from Reno and he made it there right in the middle of the afternoon. If he were going ask about Smith; who might have seen him and how much he had to drink that night, his chances of getting some answers would be better if he hung around Ruby's until dinner was served. He had just enough time to drive around Lake Tahoe, stop for a couple of minutes at the South end of the lake and make it back to Incline Village for dinner. He made a mental note to himself to bring his family back for a ski trip that fall if they were physically up for it. It would be a great way to signify the end of one phase in their lives and the beginning of the next. One in which their lives would take a decided turn for the better.

Ruby's carried forward the building tradition of Incline Village and looked like a large open ski chalet. Palmer was seated by a window overlooking a stand of pine trees before a steep drop in the terrain. He decided to order first before starting to ask the questions. When his appetizer came he asked the waitress, "I'd like to ask a question, miss. I was friends with a guy named Jonas Smith. I know he was involved in a car accident about a week ago and I was wondering if anyone remembers seeing him in here before the accident."

"Let me think," she said, and after a pause, "I think he usually sat at Betty's table. Let me get her."

In a minute, a middle aged blonde haired woman came to his table and said, "I understand you're a friend of Jonas Smith?"

"That's right. My name is Bill Palmer and I went to school with Jonas. We usually talked once or twice a year and whenever I made it up here we'd get together."

"A real pity about him. He was good customer. Came here pretty much every week. I was so sorry about the accident."

"I never knew Jonas to drink that much, but there's some implication he was in a drunk driving wreck," said Palmer.

"He was here the night it happened. Had two beers and some dinner with another guy. I know because I waited on them."

Palmer thought fast. "Maybe he was having dinner with his brother. He's a little shorter than Jonas with thinning hair?"

"No, this guy was big, short dark hair mixed with gray. He looked to be about forty or a little older and I'd say an ex athlete or military man."

"Doesn't sound like his brother." And then, "You don't happen to remember what time they left do you?" he asked.

"Well Jonas always came in fairly early, before the crowd. He was usually done and out of here by eight or so."

"Thanks so much for talking with me about this," he said. "I'm trying to put a little closure on it. It was kind of a shock."

What he really wanted to do was ask her if she over heard any of the conversation between the two, but realized his questions would sound more like an investigation than interest from a semi-grieving friend.

"For me too," she replied. "Such a nice man."

He had taken the conversation with her as far as it could go. Smith was with another guy, didn't drink enough to be classified as a drunk driver and left about eight. As soon as he could get a copy of the accident report, he would find out the time of the accident. Or, to be more precise, the time of death.

Palmer stayed the night in Reno and checked the Reno police files first thing in the morning. He found what he was looking for. The police report put the time of the accident at 11:45 p.m. on Saturday, May 29th. So Smith crashed his car over three hours after leaving the restaurant. Also, the police were suspicious enough of the circumstances to order a blood alcohol test. If he only had two beers before eight o'clock that night and it was determined he was over the legal limit at the time of the accident, it means he would have had to do some serious drinking, then, go driving around afterward. But Betty, the waitress said he liked to avoid crowds, so Smith didn't sound like the partying type. And, with an ex athlete or military man?

On the accident report, Palmer looked for the address where the accident occurred and then checked Smith's address. He found both locations on the map and they were twenty miles apart. He decided to drive to the site of the accident and found it to be a very hilly, somewhat isolated area. So on top of everything else, Smith was driving in a hilly area, at night, while most likely under the influence and many miles from home. Smith knew the area well, so why take a dark isolated road?

Bill Palmer's version of insurance investigation work was over. In his mind, the circumstances surrounding Jonas Smith's death were way too suspicious to be considered an accident. He was sure that's what Detective Finnegan had tried to say, without saying it. He had no idea if the police planned to investigate the matter any further, but if they did, he really couldn't wait around for the results anyway. All he could do now was report his findings to Maria. She would be surprised that he went to Reno, but he was glad he had gone. If the Westpac, Frontier, Investech matter advanced to the next step, he would honor his commitment to Maria and Johnny from a very low profile base. In fact he would be darned near invisible.

He called Maria on her cell phone and filled her in on the details.

She said, "The military man is Alex Franklin."

Thirty

Warner Simmons really didn't have to call the three partners together for a meeting so much as they dropped in on him the morning after he returned from San Francisco. It was a short get together. The number given to him from Jonathan Blanchard was significantly beyond anything they would consider paying, but merely set up the question of what to counter with. Charles now told Andy and Bill about the visit he received from the former SEC man and it was unanimously agreed it was time to give him a call. Charles and Warner would call him together. For now, none of the other partners would be involved.

From Warner's office they dialed the number on the card. A voice on the other end simply said, "please leave a message. Your call will be returned in exactly one hour."

Charles left his name, but Warner's number, as he preferred to handle everything related to Westpac through him. Since they didn't expect the man to give his name to Warner's secretary, they told her to put all calls through to his office, regardless of who called. Charles left, but returned five minutes before the expected call and was there when the phone rang. Charles answered the call and the caller said, "Mr. Stein, I appreciate your call. How can I help you today?"

"I'm in the office of our general counsel and I'd like to put him on the speaker phone with us, if that's acceptable."

"That will be fine."

"OK, His name is Warner Simmons."

They switched over to the speaker and Warner said hello, to which the caller responded in kind.

Charles went on, "We've had our first meeting with Jonathan Blanchard and he's given us a settlement proposal."

"I see," was the response.

"Before we proceed we'd like to talk with you about your offer to help."

"Very good. Now you have an idea how much is at stake. Did you have a chance to do research on the information I left you with?"

"No," said Charles, "I wouldn't know where to start."

"OK. First, let me tell you how I work. Basically I sell information for a living. What you do with it is your business. I'm not greedy, but the only way you could be in a position to know that is to understand your risk. I will quote you a price and ask for a deposit up front. If you don't think the information is worth the price, you don't pay the balance."

He went on, "knowing the facts surrounding the Westpac, Frontier merger, I would guess you've been quoted a settlement number of between five hundred and seven hundred and fifty million dollars." My fee will be one percent of the lower number. The deposit will be twenty percent."

Charles did the math. The fee was five million dollars. They would have to pay one million to find out if this guy knew anything worthwhile. He responded, "that's a lot of money, without knowing if it will help us at all."

"There's a lot of money at risk. My guess is you'll be tempted to negotiate back and forth, engage in some give and take. That may not be your best approach. I will be able to supply critical input as you need it. If you don't believe you're making any progress with the information I give you, simply don't pay the balance of the fee. However, if you don't make incremental payments, I won't have any more information for you."

"Let us discuss it among ourselves and we'll call you back tomorrow."

"I'll wait for your call. If you decide to proceed I will give you an account number where you can wire the deposit. Once I have confirmation that the money has been wired, we can get started right away."

Sending a million dollars to an unidentified man wasn't something Charles would decide to do on his own. It would a matter for the senior partners together. He would have to reconvene the partners meeting, which he did that afternoon. He repeated the conversation he and Warner had with SECman as he had been dubbed. Andy was the first to speak. "What do we know about this guy? Nothing. This could be another scam for all we know."

Said Bill, "Apparently he knows we're in negotiations with Blanchard. He must have some inside knowledge. We need to be sure we use every tool available to us when dealing with the firm's money."

"I have to agree with Bill. I hate spending the money, but it's very small amount when compared to what's at stake here," were Charles words.

"It's going to be pretty embarrassing if we pay the first million and we never hear from SECman again," from Andy.

"We all agree Andy," said Bill, "but this is like insurance. Think about all the insurance premiums we pay without ever knowing if we'll get anything in return."

After a brief silence Andy went on. "What if we start negotiating on our own and call SECman later if we need him?"

Charles responded, "He seemed to imply we might lose some of the advantage he could give us if he isn't involved from the beginning. It may have been salesmanship, but I don't know."

The conversation went back and forth for quite a while. There was some talk about involving a few of the younger partners in the decision, but that idea was rejected, the three reasoning that if things didn't turn out well it wouldn't matter if they had made the wrong call on this one. They'd have bigger problems to worry about. In the end Bill and Charles out voted Andy, and BCC would be wiring out the one million. They knew it was a pure gamble, but under the circumstances, one worth taking.

Charles called the next day and the SECman said, "wise choice Mr. Stein. I'm sure you'll be happy with the arrangement." He gave Charles a bank account number, routing number and domestic bank name for Charles to use for the wire. Shortly after the wire was generated, Charles received a federal reference number to use in tracking the funds and he passed that along to SECman. At that point he mentally crossed his fingers and waited for a return call. It came minutes later.

"We're in business, Mr. Stein. My advise is for you too respond to their offer at a number that's high enough to show them you want to resolve this issue without going to court, and not so low that they'll be tempted to file a law suit. They really don't want to do that, but if you're number is too low they may feel like they haven't got much to lose. Later on, I can help you lower the number even below your first counter offer, but for now we have to play the game. Since you didn't tell me my estimate of their proposal was wrong, I assume I was within range. In that case, I would tell them you'll settle at two hundred and fifty million."

Charles listened carefully and then asked, "How do we know they won't go ahead and file the suit as a negotiating tactic to put pressure on us?"

"Once that suit gets filed they lose some control. Blanchard represents a select group of investors, but not all of them. He's really only concerned with what he can get his clients. If he files suit, any of the other shareholders can tack on to it and it'll become a full fledged class action suit. Many lawyers will benefit from Blanchard's work. It will wind through the court system forever. Eventually his guys will have to split the pie with everyone. That's why you want to offer enough to make them think they'll get more out of it if they don't have to file."

Charles got the message. BCC's investment in SEC-man might just pay off after all.

....

Armed with the information Charles gave him, Warner Simmons called Jonathan Blanchard that afternoon. After they exchanged lukewarm greetings, Simmons began, "Jonathan, I've discussed your proposal with the senior members of the firm. They, again, want me to let you know they don't feel like we have much exposure here. However, they recognize the climate is such that accounting firms are prime targets whenever someone decides to cry uncle about a bad investment they made. In order to avoid a long drawn out battle, they've authorized me to settle this matter for two hundred and fifty million dollars."

Blanchard did his best to sound indignant on the other end of the line. "Well Warner, I can talk to my clients, but as you know, we've already adjusted our number. I don't see why they'd agree to anything less than what we proposed."

"That adjustment was based your assumed diminution of value, which doesn't take into account future business which can be generated by Frontier. There's no way of telling today what Frontier might really be worth. It takes time"

"I really think, Warner," Blanchard retorted, "no court is going to look into a crystal ball when computing value."

"No, they're going to look at the results of other mergers and see that very few of them lived up to their pre-merger billing."

"The phony audit confirmations will speak for themselves."

Simmons wanted to say that BCC was planning to look into that matter a little further, on their own, but didn't think it would be appropriate for the current conversation. Hopefully SECman would be able to help with that. Instead he started to close off the conversation. "We'll await your response to our offer," he said, matter of factly.

"OK, I'll see if my client chooses to respond," said Blanchard. And the call was over.

Thirty One

A WEEK HAD PASSED since Johnny returned from Denver and his team was deeply involved in the Burgess pre-bid process. Twelve prospective bidders had signed confidentiality agreements and received offering memorandums. Despite, or maybe because of, all the data that had been posted in the data room, questions from the bidders were coming hot and heavy. The due diligence portion of the team was putting in the crazy hours now, including nights and weekends. When the consumption of pizza and Chinese food became rampant, you knew it was getting close to crunch time.

Some of the questions could be answered fairly easily and some took time and research. They all required that someone from Investech work with someone at Burgess. Each time a question was asked, it was added to a question and answer file maintained in the data room. Answers were posted as they became available. It was Investech's job as the investment banker to make sure the flow of information was in constant motion. The number of questions averaged between fifty and a hundred a day. But all were answered in a timely manner.

Some of the potential bidders requested face to face meetings with Burgess' senior management team. Scott would attend the meetings, and he and Johnny would prepare Todd and his people in advance. Scott had been through this experience numerous times before and would take the lead. The PR guys were already working on a well orchestrated power point presentation that would assist the Burgess executive team in their presentation. But much of the meeting would be about sizing up the strengths and weaknesses of Burgess' top people and who would be asked to stay on after a merger.

Johnny was surprised he was able to maintain any level of concentration at work while his personal life was in upheaval. Through Maria, he had received Bill Palmer's report about the circumstances surrounding Jonas Smith's death and his dinner companion that evening. Johnny tried to remember if Alex was out of town the Friday before the prior weekend, but drew a blank. During the last week, he received two phone messages from Ellen, but had not returned either call. First, he couldn't risk having what she might say recorded on the company call log. Further, what was there to say to her? Thank you and I feel like a complete ass? He knew she wanted to work with him on the merger agreement, but he didn't want to end up alone with her again. He would have to call her, but would do it from his cell phone.

Maria, or more precisely, Elizabeth maintained a dialogue with Brad Worshaw via email. Brad was increasingly intent on arranging a meeting with her Dutch pension fund investors. He pressed and each time she got an email she showed it to Johnny who helped her prepare a response. They were fighting a stalling action but they had to make the communication seem like it was leading somewhere. Elizabeth asked questions regarding material contained in the OM. For many of the answers Brad had to come to Johnny. Some of Brad's responses brought more questions from Elizabeth; the kind a serious investor would ask. When Brad expressed frustration over the pace of the dialogue with Elizabeth, Johnny calmed him down and reminded him that Europeans are not accustomed to moving as fast as Americans. But once they were on board with a deal, they generally paid top dollar. Still, Johnny told Maria he thought they had a few more days, at best, before Brad became suspicious. Sooner or later he would start checking into Elizabeth Blake and the law firm of Howard and Fine. He told her she could start including tentative dates for a meeting in Amsterdam in her mails, and that might placate Brad until they got what they needed.

That brought him to another dose of reality. They were pinning their hopes on a thread. If Sammy or another of Brad's apparently anxious Westpac investors put enough pressure on him, he would have to start funding their returns out of his own pocket. Johnny guessed Brad had 'guaranteed' some sort of pay out of the expected settlement with BCC. With that held up, he might have to literally buy some time by making an installment payment or two. That would in turn lead them to either the source, or destination, of the funds. It was that trail Johnny hoped would lead them to the evidence that would clear them from any suspicion of insider trading. But what if that never happened? Or if it did, what if the bank account information was transmitted in such a way that Johnny couldn't intercept it? He assumed Brad would not want a paper or electronic trail with that kind of information, so it would be handled over the phone. But there was no assurance of that. In any event, Johnny and Maria decided they were only days away from going to the authorities. They would give up what little control they had, or thought they had, over the whole mess. But if they waited too long they might be giving up a lot more.

Johnny had one other motivation going. He felt as though he had let BCC down. It would be a stretch for anyone to put the entire blame for the botched audit squarely on his shoulders. But he had heard the rumblings about a partner mutiny and was aware, through Maria, that settlement talks were in the works and substantial money was at stake. He didn't want his legacy of fourteen years at BCC to be that of the partner who caused the firm's demise. He owed Charlie his best effort to make sure that didn't happen.

If Johnny and Maria went to either the FBI or the SEC, he couldn't be sure he wouldn't be arrested, or at least held under suspicion. If that happened, he would be done at Investech on the spot, although his employment there was in its last few days anyway. But he also had an obligation to Todd Pulaski at Burgess to see them through the merger. He felt that Scott could finish the job from here on out. That is, if Investech didn't implode first. As much as it troubled him, he realized that the Burgess merger might be a casualty of war that couldn't be avoided. He was certain if that happened, another investment banker would swoop in and pick up the spoils. Investech would have done the heavy lifting and its successor would only need to consummate the marriage. In fact, the remainder of Johnny's team would probably be retained by the new firm in what could be a positive result for everyone.

It was now a matter of who blinked first.

Thirty Two

Bradley Worshaw was a man who ultimately needed be in control. If he was that way by nature, his tutelage at the hands of Jonathan Blanchard completed the formal part of the process. He was a product of the great technology ramp up that began in Northern California in the middle to latter part of the last century. Growing up in San Jose, he was an honor student in high school and then attended the UC at Berkeley. From there, he partnered with some of his classmates in a handful of start up tech companies that either ultimately fizzled, or were eventually bought out by the biggies. Within fifteen years of graduating college, he had accumulated a healthy net worth for a relatively young man. It set the stage for things to come.

In the mid Nineteen Nineties, one of his companies was pursued by the largest computer chip manufacturer in the United States. He sought out an attorney to represent the company in the transaction and was introduced to Jonathan Blanchard. Blanchard was not only able to help Brad negotiate a very profitable sale, but showed him how to make some extra money on the side. After the sale, with Brad looking for a way to fill his time, Jonathan Blanchard made him an offer to join his law firm as a technical consultant. From there, the two came up with a brilliant business plan. Brad would form an investment banking firm specializing in serving technology companies. The firm would provide financing, equity capital and merger and acquisition expertise. Blanchard alone, with his industry connections could supply a long list of clients. To the extent Brad generated clients on his own, he would refer them to Jonathan for legal representation. Blanchard, through one of his companies outside of the law practice, would be a part owner in the firm.

The new firm, Investech, prospered from the beginning. Brad, the entrepreneur, realized the more he knew about goings on in the high tech industry, the better for business. He wasn't content knowing about what was already public knowledge. He wanted to know what went on behind closed doors. For that he needed a specialist in opening those doors. Enter Alex Franklin. Alex could be as visible or invisible, as charming or devious as circumstances required. He was equally as adept at handling delicate business matters as he was with covert fact finding. Brad never concerned himself with Alex' methods. Alex simply produced results that Brad needed.

From his spacious office at Investech's headquarters, Brad looked out at the blue expanse of Lake Michigan as he spoke with Alex. "I'm not sure what to make of her," he said as they talked about Elizabeth Blake. "She could be for real or she could be a phony. I have to believe if she represented the Dutch we'd have heard from them by now. Burgess is too good of an opportunity for them to pass up."

"I really should check this out," Alex responded. "If she's a phony we need to find out what she wants. Did you do any background on her?"

"The law firm is listed in New York and she's on their roster of practicing attorneys. That's it."

"So all she really has so far is the Burgess OM. That's available to anyone who signs a confidentiality agreement. Nothing special there."

"Right," said Brad. Then after thinking for a few seconds, "Maybe the law firm is free lancing. It's a small firm. What if they're taking everything they can get their hands on and using it to talk someone into bidding? They can generate some business for themselves along the way."

"How is she communicating with you?" Alex asked.

"Right now by email. She's out of the country."

From Alex, "Does she seem knowledgeable?"

"Yes. I would say from the questions in her emails, she's zeroing in on some key issues. She's asking the same questions I would ask."

"OK, give me a couple of days and I'll get back to you."

Brad responded, "Alex, you know how much pressure I'm under to get our friends off my back. You need to do this as quickly as possible."

"Roger," he shot back, all business. "I'll be in New York tonight.

....

The first indicator that all was not right was when Alex called the main number for the Law firm of Howard and Fine. He did not use the direct line to Elizabeth Blake that Brad had given him. The receptionist rang and the real Elizabeth Blake's secretary answered. Alex announced that he was with Investech and was calling to inquire when Ms. Blake would be returning to the United States. Her secretary sounded confused and responded that Elizabeth was at a client's office in New Jersey and would back first thing in the morning. "Oh," said Alex, "that's great. I'll be in your area tomorrow. Do you know if she can meet with me then?"

"Let me check with her. Can I say what this is about?"

Alex responded, "Its about the Burgess merger. If she isn't familiar with it, then I'd appreciate a few minutes of her time to explain. I may have need for representation. You can tell her I was referred by Abe Woodward."

"OK. Let me put you on hold. I think I can get through to her now."

Alex was proud of himself for doing a little bit of homework. In researching Howard and Fine, he discovered that they represented a client in a small merger earlier that year with Elizabeth as the attorney of record. The opposing attorney was Abe Woodward of Greene, Arthur and Platt. From what he read, the deal closed successfully so he assumed the two attorneys were on good terms. He also assumed if he could get in and out of an early meeting with attorney Blake, she wouldn't have time to call Abe Woodward for confirmation that he knew Alex.

Elizabeth's secretary came back on the line. "If you can come in at 10:00 a.m. tomorrow, she can see you."

"Thanks very much, I'll be there."

....

Alex arrived at Howard and Fine's offices promptly at ten the next morning. After a brief wait he was greeted by a generally unattractive brunette woman who he judged to be about thirty five to forty years old. She ushered him back to an office with the name Elizabeth Blake on the door. Brad had described Elizabeth Blake as a pert, attractive, dark haired woman, probably in her early thirties. He thought the woman who greeted him was Elizabeth's secretary, but when she walked around and seated herself behind the large, paper laden desk, Alex had his first question answered without even asking it.

"How do you know Abe?" she started the conversation.

This was not a subject he wanted to spend much time on. "Oh, we were involved in a small deal a few years ago. I would have asked him to help me, but he's got a conflict on this one."

"I see," she responded. "So you're thinking about making an offer for Burgess?"

"Yes, are you familiar with them?"

"I only know what I read and hear."

He spent a few minutes giving her some general background on Burgess. As he started to conclude what he was saying, his cell phone rang. He apologized for the interruption, but told Elizabeth he would need a couple of seconds for the call. With the phone to his ear, and without her knowing, he snapped off three quick photos of her while he was talking.

When he finished the call, he concluded what he had been telling her by saying, "One of our clients located in New York wants to put in a bid for Burgess. They asked us to make a recommendation regarding an attorney. I called Abe and he suggested I call you."

"I'm flattered," she said. "Who's your client?"

"It's really a small consortium," he responded. "If you're available, I'll email you all the information."

"Yes, I would be. Once I hear from you on that, I'll do a quick check to make sure our firm is comfortable on the other side of the table from Burgess. But I'm sure it won't be a problem."

"Good, either my secretary or I will get back to you later today."

The meeting over, Alex stepped out of the law offices and quickly emailed the photos of Elizabeth to Brad. Within minutes Brad called Alex and confirmed what he already knew. In Brad's words, "That is not the woman I met with."

....

Alex had spent the night before he left for New York reviewing Brad's call log for the time period in which he was first contacted by Elizabeth, or someone who represented herself to be Elizabeth. The first call was made from a phone number in Rockford, Illinois to Brad's office. That caller left a return phone number with a New York area code. It was the same phone number that appeared on the business card left by Elizabeth's imposter. Brad also called the New York number a few days later, but was told Ms. Blake was out of the country.

Alex thought about calling the New York number but realized he might tip someone off that he was getting closer. For now though, that was not what he wanted. He operated on the theory that the person or people he was looking for were based in Illinois, but had set up a number in New York to receive calls. The messages were then conveyed back to the Illinois party. It was not a coincidence that after the first couple of calls the communication shifted to email. Whoever Elizabeth's imposter was did not want to make any more outgoing calls than the bare minimum. Did not want a phone number to show up on someone's caller ID screen. This meant there was no one in New York who was actively part of the plan. It would take a little time and some luck to position the Illinois connection where he wanted them. But the trip to New York confirmed it. Maria Brandt was on his team, she just didn't know it. Alex would report back to Brad, but, of course, the pictures told the story. At least the part Alex wanted him to know. The rest would go elsewhere.

He truly marveled at Maria's ability to figure out how to manipulate the VTDT system in the Investech office. It had to be her. A slender, attractive dark haired woman, early thirties, very knowledgeable in computers and able to figure out some basics about their system. She was a perfect fit with the description and background contained in the report he ordered before Johnny joined the firm. She had all the advantages too; input from Johnny, and unknowingly, from Brad as well. That was worth a good laugh. The computer guru was so anxious to impress her, he helped her mess with his mind. This was good for Alex. She would do the equivalent of the high tech heavy lifting. He would do the tracking. Each doing what they did best. Until she took him just where he wanted to be.

He was the only player in the game who had time on his side. Going to New York at Brad's direction was the perfect use of a day to confirm something he already knew. Now he could justify staying there for another day or two 'looking for the real Elizabeth Blake'. He could make his calls to San Francisco and Las Vegas and see how high the offers went as time passed.

....

The call to Brad from Sammy left no doubt as to where he stood. The time for action was now. Brad had kept him updated on the status of the BCC negotiations and the Burgess merger, but as time passed with no tangible results, Sammy expected Brad to make good on their deal. Although it troubled Brad to dip into his own funds, it was only temporary, until their other 'investments' paid off. This he was prepared to do. He always honored his commitments. It was how and why he made his living. People weren't afraid to invest money with him because they knew he could be trusted to deliver, one way or the other. Besides, he needed Sammy for some of the really big money down the line. He told Sammy he would have twenty million for him as soon as he could wire funds from one of his accounts. He always followed the same procedure: proceeds from any of his deals went into an off shore clearing account. From that account he wired money to other off shore accounts for different investments. This created a wall between the accounts which would be almost impossible to penetrate. Money going back the other way would require the same procedure, in reverse. Sammy told Brad he didn't want any of the money coming back into the United States, so Brad offered to set up an account for him at the bank he used for his clearing account. When the account had been set up and the money received, Brad would call Sammy with the details. It would take a day or two. Later, Sammy could change his pass code as he saw fit.

Thirty Three

THE RETURN CALL FROM Jonathan Blanchard came faster than Warner Simmons expected. SECman had been correct. The other side wanted to move this along before word leaked out that a settlement was in progress. In reality that was what BCC wanted as well; as long as it didn't mean giving up the store. But Warner saw risk with the plan outlined by SECman to backslide on their counter proposal. That would delay the outcome and potentially force Blanchard into filing suit. He wanted to ask SECman what he had up his sleeve. For now though, they had paid their nickel, or in this case one million dollars and he could only hope they got their money's worth.

"We've considered your counter offer to our proposal, Warner, and my clients don't want to be unreasonable," Blanchard started. "If we can resolve this today, I'm prepared to fly out to Chicago tonight and wrap up the paperwork tomorrow. We'll accept four hundred and fifty million."

"Jonathan, I can assure you if we had any thought of agreeing to your number, we'd have to take this matter to our professional liability carrier. That would delay things even further. We're still a long way off."

Blanchard responded, "I think we need to get in a room and negotiate something we can both live with."

Simmons needed time to bring Blanchard's new proposal to the executive committee and then to call SECman. "Let me see when I can arrange that," was his response.

As soon as he could, he reached Charles and relayed his conversation with Blanchard. They called SECman's phone number and left a message. The call was returned within minutes this time.

"I think they'll settle for fifty million or less," said SECman. "I know you'd like to get this over with, but you can't move too quickly. Wait until tomorrow and call Jonathan Blanchard back. Tell him, as part of the settlement, you want a release for Johnny Brandt and any members of his family. Tell him you want to review the rest of the evidence they have regarding their insider trading case. You won't know what the release language should cover unless you see all the evidence. They probably won't be in a position to give you what want, so they'll start to cave. At a minimum, it will slow them down and frustrate them."

Simmons responded, "At what point do we frustrate them so much they decide to just go ahead and sue us?"

"You've got a way to go," was the answer. "Look at it like this; you're not prepared to pay them anything close to what their asking. If they do file suit, you can always settle after you see how strong their case is. Filing a suit will be more for posturing than anything else. For now, you haven't seen enough to pay out close to half a billion dollars."

There was definite logic to his comments, except for the matter of public disclosure a law suit would bring. This was the gamble they would be taking. Warner Simmons didn't believe Jonathan Blanchard would file a suit without threatening it several more times. He could remember once or twice in the past when an adversary's lawyers prepared filings and waived them in his face while demanding a settlement. The preparation of the lawsuit was nothing more than a show. The lawyers were, in effect, saying, "look, we've done all the work. All we have to do now is go down to the courthouse and see the clerk." He was sure Jonathan was capable of such a tactic.

SECman had one more comment for them before the call was over. "Gentlemen, I think you can see the benefit of my knowledge will save you many millions. Please be prepared to wire another million to my account before we talk again."

Thirty four

Bill Palmer had made arrangements to be out of the country for several weeks. He told his wife he'd be on a salvage operation for a major client, managing all of the IT requirements. The timing was propitious. She was well enough to care for herself with minimum assistance and his kids were still with his parents. As soon as he got home, they'd be back together under his roof. His equipment was virtually packed and ready to go. Now all he needed to know was where.

Maria called Bill daily now and if things went well he'd have bank account numbers at any time. From there, he would take Gus up on his lunch invitation and find out what to tell his travel agent. But knowing the name and location of the Oak Bank or whatever bank Brad Worshaw kept his clearing account at was only the first step. He'd have to be able to trace outgoing and incoming transfers to and from that account to find what they were really looking for. The bank account numbers where the cash ultimately ended up. Then he could tie that information in a bow, hand it to Maria, and she and Johnny could take it to the police. Having her joint account number as part of the package, would show that Brad Worshaw controlled all the money that she or her father supposedly made on his trading activities.

There was no real way of knowing how big a salvage operation this would be, although Bill liked the use of the term as it related to the business at hand. First, he was clearly helping clients recover something that had been lost. Something that, for the Brandt's, would be worth more than money. Their innocence, their respectability, their freedom, in short – their lives. As in any salvage operation, you didn't know how deep you would have to go, how difficult it would be to find your target, and once found, how problematic it would be to extract the treasure. If he was lucky he could use his systems capabilities to find his mark. But more likely it would be a combination of technology and human ingenuity. As in salvage work, no amount of planning would ensure initial success. He had to expect some measure of trial and error along the way. He thought about discussing this with Maria. Depending upon where the trail led, the operation could require two people instead of just one. But he didn't really have any details for her and having the conversation now might put undo pressure on her. Especially when she was concerned with the safety of her family. Bill realized at some point she might have to make a painful decision about whether or not to leave her family behind and join him.

....

The job of managing the Burgess process, Johnny found, was much easier than managing his anxiety. With his team operating at full efficiency, Johnny could participate in meetings and duck out periodically to check the call logs in his office. This did not arouse any suspicion since he was pursuing other deals, including Ronco. There had been two calls between Brad and Sammy in the last three days and he expected the main event to occur at any minute.

The only question for him was whether he would take the bank account numbers with him and walk out of Investech forever, or stay on in case he had to monitor additional conversations recorded on the call logs. Or, watch Brad to see how he would handle the Elizabeth Blake matter.

All that Johnny and Maria were able to plan for was twenty four hour security. They made sure they had hired a well qualified firm with attentive people who understood there was more than passive risk to them. Bill had done a good job of that. If Johnny left Investech for good, he could be with his family under the protection of the security service. But he gave up that safety net if he stayed on. It would be a last minute decision when the time came.

....

Maria had gone from the comfortable life of house mom to her children, who she loved dearly, to the pregnant wife of a recently deceased securities broker, if that's what he really was. Then she went on to her brief career as a New York City lawyer followed immediately by the foreign cleaning lady who spoke only broken English. Now she was back to square one. But something had clearly been taken from her. Her life would never really be the same. If circumstances could change as fast and dramatically as they had for Johnny and her, there really was no comfort zone. It was a mind set thing. She found herself looking for the next effect before the cause. She didn't want it to descend upon her. She wanted to be a step ahead of it. Or, at least prepared to deal with it. She was confident they would get past anything and everything to do with Westpac, Frontier and Investech. But then what? She was worried about Johnny. He had just started to recover from the dark days at BCC and soon he would be out of Investech after a total of six weeks on the job. What would be left in its wake? She expected that when the truth came out about the whole matter, he would be cleared of any wrong doing and might even be a hero of sorts for exposing the crooks. She knew he wouldn't want to go back to public accounting and was concerned that he would simply drift, after their problems were over. To her it was part of the irony that had become their lives. The accusations against them and the knowledge that they were dangerously exposed had given them a sense of purpose together. Where would they be when that sense of purpose waned?

....

The words, or more appropriately, the numbers they were all waiting for came on the third Wednesday in June. Brad called Sammy to let him know he had set up a bank account in the name of his foreign company and deposited the twenty million they agreed on. As soon as Johnny had the numbers, he left the office and called Maria. She relayed the information to Bill Palmer. Bill called the minimum security prison and left word for Gus. He would come the next day at lunch time.

"So, William, when we get done with you, you'll not only be a computer geek, but an expert in international monetary transactions as well," said Gus as he peered above the reading spectacles set down on his nose.

"With your help Gus. I might be ready for a career change after this is over." Bill had decided to eschew the prison food and stopped to buy a pizza for them which he handed to Gus.

As the aroma filled the air, Gus related to Bill that he'd be missing an unforgettable experience in the prison dinning facility, but would nevertheless settle for the pizza. As they began to eat Bill reached in his pocket and unfolded a piece of paper with a bank account and routing number on it.

Gus pulled the reading glasses up and took the paper from Bill, "I can tell you the country where this account is located by looking at the routing number, although you'll have to find the bank. Each bank has its own set of account numbers just as in the U.S. You may have to open an account in a few different banks until you find the right sequence."

"OK Gus, that's what I'm here for," said Bill.

"William, before I tell you what you want to know, I have to say a few things. First, the person or people who set this account up have gone to a lot of trouble to avoid being found. You realize the risks inherent in what you're about to do?"

Palmer responded, "My client in this case has done more for me than I can tell you. If it wasn't for them, I'd still be here full time instead of as your lunch guest. Worse, I really don't know if my wife and son would have been given the opportunity to participate in the experimental drug program that may have saved their lives. I'm in this for the long haul no matter how it comes out."

"OK then," Gus went on, "let me ask you this: have you considered that if you fail to find what you're looking for and, somehow aren't eliminated by who you're looking for, you may be found guilty of bank fraud?"

This really hadn't occurred to Bill. He thought about it for a few seconds and understood what Gus was telling him. If the bank which housed the accounts he was looking for caught him trying to crack their security wall, they would report him. He didn't know anything about the authorities in any foreign country, so it was impossible to assess what that might mean. At worst, he could be in a position of having to go on trial in an unfriendly court system. His record in the U.S would not help at all. He realized his story regarding representation of a client in a matter of recovery and restitution would be laughed at.

Bill shook his head. "You certainly paint a pleasant picture, Gus, but there's no turning back."

"All right then, let me give you a few pointers on how to cover your tracks. But remember, this is coming from your ex fellow inmate. Past failure is no guaranty of future success."

Gus went into details of some of the tricks he had used when he was 'on the street.' Bill could relate to many of them since they involved programs designed to defeat security systems similar to what he had helped design. It was as good an education as he had ever received in school. When it was over, he had a new found respect for Gus. He also understood why Gus was always interested in talking shop with Bill. Gus was a man who had learned to adapt a counter punch on the run. He wished he could take Gus with him to wherever he was going.

With the education complete and lunch over, Gus gave Bill what he had come for. He was about to leave Kansas for the journey of his life.

....

From his car he called Maria. When she answered her cell phone he said. "It's on the Isle of Man."

"What is that?"

"A small Island off the coast of Ireland."

Book III

Thirty Five

The Isle of Man is an island country located about halfway between Britain and Ireland, in the Irish Sea. It measures about 30 miles in length and 15 miles in width and has an unusual history which makes it ideally suited for off shore banking activities. In the eighteenth century, the island's off shore independence made it a major center for smuggling, causing a significant loss of revenue for the English treasury. Although the island was eventually purchased by the English government, by the mid 1800's it had gradually started to regain some control over its internal finances. Today, with the transformation complete, the Isle of Man, now has its own independent democratic government in place.

While the island's economy includes farming and ranching, one statistic stuck out immediately as Maria researched everything she could about a place she had only heard of minutes earlier. In excess of fifty banking institutions have a presence on the Isle of Man. That's a ratio of about one bank for each 1,500 residents. In fact a search of the websites of some of the banks revealed many of them touted their 'private banking services, or customized relationship management.' It would be hard to believe many of the 75,000 people living in the Isle of Man were wealthy enough to need such services. Certainly not enough to support up to fifty banks.

The little country appeared to Maria to have gained a very favorable financial climate due to its unique geography and history. Its located near a major European business hub in London, but not necessarily constrained by the same banking rules. From what she could see, the relaxed banking laws allowed that an 'Offshore Banking License' could be granted to any banking business located outside the Island. All that was needed was a management agreement with a bank domiciled in the Island. To her this meant that, maybe, Brad Worshaw was pumping money in and out of his own bank. A bank named Oak Bank and Trust. Or, maybe he had more than one bank.

Maria and Bill Palmer discussed their plans in some detail before his plane took off. He would fly from Kansas City to New York and then on to Dublin. From there, he would either get a flight or ferry to Douglas, the largest city in the Isle of Man. He would find a hotel and report back to her with his location. He made sure his cell phone had international capabilities. He took with him his laptop computer and several disks with as much security infiltrating software as he could. It would not be the same as operating from his office, which allowed for more sophisticated applications. This is where Maria would have to provide support as necessary. If it came down to it, she would go to Abcon and tell them her story. She hoped they would let her use their system, but couldn't be sure. They might tell her to go to the authorities and, if so, they would probably be right.

The trip from Kansas City to Douglas would take most of the day for Bill. While she was waiting for him to check in, Maria gave some thought to what she had read about the banking laws and how it could affect them. If Worshaw had set up his own bank, was it possible the managing bank would reserve a specific sequence of account numbers or a separate routing number for his bank only? Bill's first task would be to go to as many banks as necessary and open up accounts. He would ask for temporary checks for each account, which would include that bank's numbers. When he found the bank with the routing number and same account number sequence as Brad had given Sammy, they would know they had found their bank. That wouldn't work, though, if the numbers were reserved for Brad's bank only. In short Bill could spend a lot of time searching and come up empty.

When Bill finally called, it was three thirty in the morning in Chicago. Maria managed to shake off the effects of being woken in the middle of the night to explain to him what she had discovered. "Bill," she said, "we can't go to every bank. We had no way of knowing it, but there are banks within banks. It could take weeks and we could come up empty handed."

"Any ideas?" he asked.

"Yes. There must be a public record of all the banks that are licensed to do business on the Island. That's where to start."

"You mean look for an offshore license in the name of Oak Bank?"

"That's it," said Maria.

"I'm on it. Call you back in a couple of hours."

....

It was seven thirty when he called back.

"There's no Oak Bank," he said.

"Is there anything in the public record that gives the names of the stockholder's or owners of the banks?"

"I checked that too. The answer is also no," he replied.

'Ok, so that means we have to try something else. Let me think. I'll call you back in an hour."

Bill said, "while I'm waiting, I may as well go open a few accounts and see if I get lucky."

....

She called back as soon as she got Lindsay off to school. "So if there's no information regarding ownership of banks on the island, What CAN you find out about the banks?"

"For one thing, you were right, there's a lot of 'em. They give you a print out of all licensed banks. That's it. From there you have to go to the Incorporation Charter for each bank. For the off shore banks, they have to register as a foreign corporation. That form includes the number of shares issued, total capitalization, the name of the managing bank on the island and the home country of the foreign corp."

"OK," she said. "Let's go with that. Wouldn't you think some of the local banks are more interested in picking up managed account relationships with foreign banks than others? Maybe we should focus on those banks for starters."

"Good thought," was his response. "I'll need to go back through the records and see which local banks have the largest number of management agreements with foreign banks." He paused for a minute and added, "You know we're assuming Worshaw has an off shore license. Maybe he found a way to incorporate on the island."

"Could be," she said, "but we better take the most logical route first."

Bill agreed, and set off to do more research. He went back to the log of active offshore banks licensed to do business on the island and copied the first few pages. From there he went to the book which included the registration statements for the foreign corporations. By matching the two records he found that five banks with full scale banking licenses seemed to dominate the 'managed account' business. He was happy at having narrowed the field down, but by the time he had the five names, all of the banks had closed for the day. He would go to the five banks the next day and open money market accounts.

    Maria struggled to a find a way through the apparent road block. The pieces to the puzzle they had were the routing number and account number where Brad had deposited Sammy's money. The missing piece was the name of the bank. The puzzle was further complicated because the bank they were looking for was a foreign bank, most likely managed by a parent bank. Logic told her the parent bank, as part of the management agreement, would provide camouflage for the managed bank. She remembered that Bill told her he thought whoever was behind Oak Bank only wanted to be found on their own terms. And, when they were ready. The facts that she and Bill were dealing with fit this scenario perfectly. Worshaw could easily have started his own bank, which accounted for the Oak Bank statements having no address. Why should they? It was his bank and he knew where to find it. Plus he had all the advantages of a full service parent bank which allowed him to wire money in and out of his bank at will.

    She rolled all of this around in her mind and came up with a possibility if all else failed. She or Bill could start calling the banks and attempt to wire money out of Sammy's account, using only the account number and pass code. They didn't have the name on the account, so that would be a problem. It was a long shot, but if they even so much as got a confirmation that the account existed, they would have their bank.

....

It wasn't until the next day that Maria heard back from Bill.

"Hi Maria," he said, the discouragement evident from thousands of miles away. "No luck. I went to the five banks we targeted and the numbers just don't match up at all."

She told him her idea regarding the wire transfers and he agreed that was all they had to go on at that point. They would make up a list of banks domiciled on the Island and start calling. It would be an arduous task and neither of them was particularly optimistic about the possibilities.

Thirty Six

Johnny was day to day, hour to hour, minute to minute. He knew as soon as he walked out of Investech and didn't come back, he would jeopardize the work Maria was doing with Bill Palmer. It would only be a short time until Brad and Alex started to put the clamps on their operation.

He called Ellen back from his office phone, but made sure he called first thing in the morning Chicago time so she would not be in her office. He left a message saying he had asked Investech's general counsel to work with her to finish up the merger agreement. He would then be available to review the final draft. He thanked her for all her hard work and said he would see her in the next few weeks, as the bids came in and serious negotiations between Burgess and the winning bidder took place. He could say that because he knew he would absolutely be gone by then.

Meetings were now taking place between Burgess senior management team and a few of the interested bidders. None of the meetings were in Chicago and Johnny would like to have attended, but his main job was still to monitor the call logs. Scott was really driving the process on that front anyway, so no one minded that he didn't attend. As he told Scott, he felt he was more valuable to the team if he monitored the data flow and questions and answers from the Investech office. He didn't believe that for a minute, but he was not going to spend any nights away from home.

Within a couple of weeks, bids would be in, negotiations would be whittled down to a couple of the most qualified investors and the merger agreement would be signed by Burgess and the eventual winner. The merger agreement was drafted in such a way that there really weren't any contingencies to the deal. The bidders had to include evidence in their bids that they had arranged adequate financing to fund the cash portion of their offers. They had to represent they had received approval from their board of directors to consummate a deal and that no other requirements had to be met for them to complete the transaction. Essentially, once the merger agreement was signed, the deal was done except for approval by Burgess' shareholders. Johnny didn't foresee a problem with that.

Johnny stole as much time as he could to look at the call logs. There were no new calls between Sammy and Brad. But Brad and Jonathan Blanchard had a couple of heated calls regarding various 'off balance sheet investors' as Blanchard put it. From what Johnny could gather, Blanchard accused Worshaw of "expanding his shareholder base" without consulting Blanchard. Johnny found those calls very odd. He knew that Investech had a more than close relationship with Blanchard's firm. Blanchard and Stone seemed to represent almost all of Investech's clients. In some cases, if the client firms had other attorneys, they represented the opposing company in a transaction with the client firm. They also represented Investech. How is it that Blanchard would care if Worshaw took on investors in Worshaw's business?

Another thing Johnny noticed after a couple of weeks of monitoring call logs; he had never seen one call from Alex' extension. The calls that were forwarded to Johnny's phone came from the other extensions in the office which Alex had programmed. Even though Alex was rarely in the office, you'd think he'd at least make some calls from his office phone. But, maybe, since Alex was the architect of the VTDT installations, he had a natural aversion to using his office phone.

Maria and Johnny made a point of talking on their cell phones at least a couple of times a day. The calls would be meaningless until they found Oak Bank. But, if nothing else, talking helped them keep their spirits up.

The emails back and forth between Maria, as Elizabeth, and Brad had completely stopped. The last from Elizabeth, included a couple of suggested dates in Amsterdam for them to meet with her client. Brad would only have broken off communication if he suspected her of being a fraud. Johnny couldn't be sure if Brad was suspicious of anything in particular or, decided Elizabeth was simply trying to generate a little business for herself. In fact, he detected that Brad was much more closed door than usual. Not that Brad was the outgoing type, but he occasionally mingled with the troops so he could keep his hand on the pulse of the organization. For a couple of days running he had barely come out of his office. When he did, he looked deeply rooted in his own world. Johnny wondered if Brad would take some evasive action if he felt his security had been penetrated.

Alex, of course, was no where to be found.

Thirty Seven

THE BREAKTHROUGH CAME ON Bill Palmer's fourth day on the Isle of Man. He wanted to wait until a reasonable hour in Chicago before calling Maria, but he was too excited and thought, by now, she was probably used to being awakened at all hours. That is, if she got any sleep at all.

"I found it," he said without even saying hello.

"Great, where was it," she replied.

"I decided to hang out at the office where the public records are kept and just go through everything I could find. It turns out Oak Bank changed its name to Cayman Enterprises Bank. It's managed on the island by Wilshire Trust Company."

"Good work Bill," was her reply.

"Maria, the name change was put in place late last week, just a day before I got here. You know what that could mean."

She did. It meant that Brad was spooked and decided now was not the time he wanted his banking empire to be uncovered. "I got it Bill. Where do we go from here?"

"Now the fun starts. If I get lucky, they'll give me a statement with all the activity for Sammy's account. It should show the account number and name of the source of incoming deposits. From there, I'll go to that account and look for the same information until I uncover the whole money tree."

"And if not?" she asked.

"Then we do it the hard way. I'll either hack in or find a way to do it manually."

"Call me back after you try getting the statement." She said.

"You'll be the second to know." With that, he was out the door on his way to Wilshire Trust.

He walked the four blocks from his hotel to the stately white colonial style building located on Athol Street, one of the main thoroughfares on the island. In fact the downtown area of Douglas contained one bank building after another, housing the fifty plus banks and, no doubt, the banks within the banks. He couldn't help but feel that if he wasn't under intense pressure to provide results for Johnny and Maria, he would have enjoyed his time on this island. The weather was perfect, the rolling hills as green as he had ever seen and the people among the most courteous he had met, anywhere.

Upon entering Wilshire Trust, he was greeted by a receptionist who asked if she could help him. "Yes," he answered, "I'd like to request a print out of the activity in my account, please."

"Certainly sir," was the response, "please have a seat and I'll have someone to help you." The dialect wasn't quite English or Irish, but it was interesting and, at least, somewhat challenging.

Within a couple of minutes a short man with a full head of curly gray hair, a pleasant smile and wearing a suit from the nineteen fifties walked up to where Bill was sitting. "Sir, my name is Shane Fergus. I'd be happy to help you with your banking needs today. If you'll just follow me." He turned and directed Bill past the reception area across a large room with tellers to a small cubicle. The desk had a computer screen on it together with a few loosely strewn papers. Shane asked Bill to have a seat across from him while he seated himself behind the desk. The smile never left his face as he spoke. "I understand you'd like a print out of your account activity?"

"That's right," said Bill.

"And may I ask your name sir?"

"Yes, of course. William Palmer," he said as he shook hands with the banker. Bill had no choice but to give his real name. He hadn't made any provisions to disguise his identity. There simply was no time. He hoped that the account number and pass code he could provide would get the job done.

"And is the account in your name, sir"

"Well no," said Bill. "I'm an auditor for the owner. I'm working on his taxes. He has a number of accounts on the island and he sent me here to gather all the necessary information."

"I see," said Shane, smile still firmly in place. "And you have all the relevant account numbers?"

"Yes sir," Bill said as he handed him a piece of paper with the account number and pass code on it."

Shane fiddled with his keyboard for a few minutes. The screen looked like it came from the same era as Mr. Fergus suit and Bill guessed if the rest of the system was that old he could crack it, given a little time. Shane seemed to be trying to enter and re-enter the same numbers Bill had given him, with no luck." The smile faded as he labored on. After a few minutes he said, "excuse me," and left Bill alone in the cubicle.

With the banker gone, Bill casually stood up and walked to the entrance to the cubicle. No one was nearby, so he turned slowly and walked around to the side of the man's desk to an angle where he could just see what was on the computer screen. It was nothing but a home page for the bank. Apparently, the account number or pass code Bill had given Shane wasn't working. Bill hoped it was simply a computer glitch. He had no choice but to sit down and wait.

Shane returned and said to Bill, "apparently the pass code was changed a couple of days ago. The number you gave me was valid prior to then, but won't allow me to gain access now."

"Uhm," said Bill, a puzzled look on his face. Thinking quickly he said, "I bet I know what happened. The owner told me they were going to change the pass code on each account after I finish my review. I've been sending them a list of the accounts I review every day and I bet they accidentally changed this one before I got to it."

The smile now returned to Shane's face. "Sounds like a simple solution, Mr. Palmer. Let's just call them and get the new pass code."

"You know the problem is its the middle of the night where they are and I won't be able to reach anyone until tomorrow."

"I see. Can this wait until then?"

"Yes, of course" said Bill. "I'll have the new pass code by then."

....

"So close," thought Bill on his way back to the hotel. "But so far."

He called Maria as soon as he returned and gave her the news.

"So we have the right bank, but we can't get to the account," she said.

"Right," was the response.

"So let's go back through this," she said. "How did he know the pass code had been changed?"

"I don't know. He got up, left his cubicle for a couple of minutes, and came back with the news."

"So there's another computer or print out somewhere with a record of old and new pass codes."

"Yes," said Bill.

"It sounds like this is turning into a two man job now, Bill," She said. One to create a diversion and another to find the pass code entries."

"I might be able to get into their system and access the program for changing the pass codes. It could take hours or days. Or it might be never. I can't be sure. What are you thinking Maria?" he said.

"I think Johnny or I need to get over there and help you before we run out of time. As soon as he gets home from work, we'll call you."

"OK, in the meantime, I need to look around the whole bank and figure out where their systems are located. I can do that first thing in the morning."

....

When Johnny got home, he and Maria called Bill. It was 2:00 a.m. on the Isle of Man and fatigue was starting to set in, especially for Bill. The three of them talked for a couple of hours as they considered alternative courses of action. In the end, Johnny and Maria decided they should both go to meet Bill. Maria's parents would pick up the kids and take them up to Madison, with the security patrol in tow. They would arrange for a flight the next day which meant Bill had a day to figure out a way to case the bank. Johnny had spent his last day as an Investech employee without even saying goodbye. He was leaving so he could gather enough evidence to put his boss away for a long time. How many employees would like to be in his position?

By the time they finished their call it was after 4:00 a.m. for Bill. He told Johnny and Maria he would be going back to the bank promptly at nine, local time. He wanted Johnny to be available to pose as the owner of Sammy's account, via telephone. Bill would call him from the bank. Bill prepped Johnny for the phone call before he hung up. The call would come at approximately 2:00 a.m. Chicago time.

Bright and early the next morning, Bill returned to the bank and was reunited with the affable Mr. Fergus. "I tell you Mr. Fergus, I talked to my people and they swear they didn't change the pass code. Are you sure there isn't some mistake. Maybe it's the wrong account that was changed. The owner is available by phone if you wouldn't mind calling him now."

"Certainly, Mr. Palmer. If you give me the number I'll make the call."

Bill gave him Johnny's number and after he dialed it, he handed the phone to Bill. When Johnny answered, Bill went through the routine they had rehearsed. He said he was calling from Wilshire Trust and would like to introduce Johnny to a Mr. Shane Fergus, who was helping him try and access the account in question. He then handed the phone back to Shane Fergus. Johnny, of course, assured Mr. Fergus he had never changed the code and no else could have done it either, because he hadn't given the code to anyone. Mr. Fergus was quite perplexed and promised to get to the bottom of the problem as soon as possible.

When the call was over Bill asked, "How do you go about changing account codes anyway?"

"It's really done electronically," Shane replied. "The account owner is prompted to different options once he logs in. Changing a pass code is one of them."

"You know, I'm a bit of a computer guy at times myself. I noticed yesterday you left the room for a minute and came back to tell me the pass code had been changed. Do you keep a master file of these types of things somewhere?"

"The Bank keeps a log of this type of activity in its confidential files. Computer files of course," he added.

Asked Bill, "Can I trouble you sir to check those files one more time?"

"Happy to," he replied.

This time, as Shane left the cubicle, Bill rose and watched him as he walked across a large lobby area where a handful of tellers were helping customers with their deposits. As Shane walked, Bill followed him as closely as possible without being noticed. Shane entered a code on a key pad to the side of a door located behind one of the tellers. He pulled and the door opened. Bill made a quick mental note of the entry code The first part of his logistic complete, Bill quickly returned to the cubicle, sat down at Shane's desk and typed in a few commands. He estimated he had three minutes before the small, friendly banker returned. As it turned out he only needed two. He was denied access to Sammy's account for lack of the pass code, but Bill understood the system the Bank used. It was two generations removed from the most sophisticated systems currently in use, but one he knew well. Once he got behind the door to the bank's computer, he could get them everything they needed.

Again, Shane returned with a perplexed look and said to Bill, "I'm afraid it's still a no go, Mr. Palmer. But I've asked the head of our information systems department to check into it. Can I call you somewhere later today?"

"Yes, although I have accounts to review at another bank today. I'd like to come back tomorrow, say at 10:00 a.m. and see you."

"That'll be fine. I'm sure we'll have this figured out by then."

Bill left the bank and began preparing for Johnny and Maria's arrival. He visited a couple of thrift stores and a costume rental shop. At his third stop he found what he was looking for: a uniform that would be worn by a bank security officer. Maria would bring what she needed for her part of the plan.

....

The report forwarded to Alex Franklin contained information which he was expecting. The lights in Johnny and Maria's house had been seen going on and off at different times of the night and before dawn, for most of the last week. To Alex, this meant they were either making calls to, or receiving phone calls from, a time zone outside of the United States. He was pretty sure they had some help and the report confirmed it. The gamble for Alex was whether Johnny and Maria's associate could handle all the field work alone, or whether one of them would be joining him. He could confront them at home and force the information from them, or wait and hope for a road trip to the source. The problem with confronting them at home was that he had no way of knowing if, or when, the full details regarding Brad's banking regime would be forthcoming. If he jumped in too soon, he might never get what he was after. No, he told himself, he needed to be patient. Past experience proved the former auditor and his resourceful wife would be too hands on not to finish the job. When they moved out, he would be ready.

....

They made reservations to fly together, but not sit together. Maria would leave alone, early enough to get to the airport well before the flight took off. She would wear business clothes and carry her lap top in a brief case. Johnny would leave later, and dress in old clothes and a baseball cap with sun glasses. They would not speak at the airport and Maria would sit in the front portion of the plane and Johnny in the rear. Espionage was not their strong suit, but it was their best attempt for Johnny to see if Maria was being followed.

Their flights from Chicago to New York to Dublin to Douglas went without incident and, if Maria was followed, Johnny certainly couldn't tell. They arrived at the hotel at 6:00 a.m. with just enough time for a couple of hours of sleep, their meeting with Bill scheduled for nine, in the lobby. The three of them had breakfast as Bill led them through the details of the plan to leave the Isle of Man with everything they needed to crack the case.

At 10:00 a.m. sharp, Bill entered the Wilshire Trust for his meeting with Mr. Fergus and the Bank's IT officer. He was lead to the cubicle where the three men started to go over the mechanics of how the bank's system processed various requests from remote locations. The IT officer was pleased that Bill was so curious about the whole system and was more than willing to answer his questions.

At 10:10 a.m., Maria reprised her role as Gina Polarski Smith, looking quite pregnant as she entered Wilshire Trust to open a bank account. The receptionist summoned a matronly looking personal banker to assist her. She was walking to the woman's office, following a couple of steps behind her, when she fainted dead away in the lobby. The same lobby where the tellers were waiting on their customers. Maria had brought a piece of leather with her to hold in her hand so, when she hit the floor, she smacked the leather down hard for effect. Upon hearing the cracking sound, the personal banker turned and shrieked in horror as she saw Maria lying on the floor, convulsing. The banks customers, the tellers and everyone in the lobby all rushed toward Maria. The commotion was heard throughout the entire bank and Shane, the IT officer and Bill joined the crowd.

Just then, a security officer entered the lobby and walked to the door of the room where the computer equipment was located. He pressed Shane's code and opened the door. Inside were four people seated behind their desks, looking confused. They heard the noise in the lobby, but didn't know if they should stay at their desks or try and find out what was going on outside. The security officer told them he had been instructed to clear the area for security purposes and asked them to walk out to the lobby. He assured them he would guard the IT system. When everyone left the computer room, Johnny motioned to Bill, who slipped away from the fracas and into the area the IT people had just abandoned. Working quickly, Bill slipped a disk into the portable drive and began typing away on the keyboard.

Meantime, out in the lobby, Maria was having trouble breathing. With Bill in place, Johnny reneged on his promise to guard the computer equipment and left the area to help revive the pregnant woman in the lobby. The rescue procedure would take as long as Bill needed to download the files they sought. Seeing the security officer approach, the crowd parted to let him through. He began to administer mouth to mouth resuscitation to Maria, who had already turned beet red. He breathed into her mouth while pinching her nostrils with his thumb and forefinger. He then placed his hands on her chest and gently forced air out of her lungs. He repeated the process as he worked into a rhythm. After a couple of minutes, Maria started to breathe more easily and her color began to return to normal.

Johnny was in no great hurry to stop the mouth to mouth. It wasn't everyday you got to play kissy face with your wife while pulling a bank job. Strangely, he found himself having fun with it. The crowd seemed to relax a little as they saw Maria's condition gradually improve. The security officer was a hero as the people realized they were watching a potential tragedy turn into a happy ending.

Bill's work was done in about ten minutes. When Johnny saw him rejoin the crowd, he asked Maria if she wanted to sit up. He gradually helped her, first to a sitting position on the floor, then to a chair. Bill told Mr. Fergus and the IT officer he needed a break after what they had just witnessed and he would like to get some air outside. They understood and made arrangements to meet again later that day. One of the tellers brought Maria some water, which she sipped slowly while still seated. After a few minutes, Johnny helped Maria to her feet. Several of the people in the bank asked Maria if she would like to go to the hospital emergency room for observation, but Johnny assured them he would take her there himself. By 10:50 a.m. Bill, Johnny and Maria were on their way back to the hotel.

As soon as they returned, they went straight to Bill's room to download the disk. Within a couple of minutes, they watched as detailed bank account information flashed on the screen of his lap top computer. Because the information was taken from the bank's computer, no pass codes were necessary to access any files, although they were now available if needed. They easily found the accounts listed under

Cayman Enterprises Bank. There were a total of three different Cayman accounts and the number for one of them matched the account number on the Oak Bank statement Maria had found in her lock box at Sea First Bank. A second account was the one Brad had opened for Sammy with twenty million dollars on deposit. The third had a large volume of activity with money being deposited and withdrawn on a regular basis. Most of the deposits and withdrawals in that account came from, or went to, the Grand Cayman Bank in George Town, Cayman Islands. For each item posted, the corresponding bank account number at Grand Cayman was listed, as well as the account owner's name. The names weren't individuals, but different corporations.

After their initial elation, they stopped to assess what they really had. First, did they have enough information to go to the authorities? After discussing it, they came to the conclusion that it was a matter of how deep a case they wanted to present. There was little doubt the money going into and out of the Oak Bank account could be traced to funds from the Cayman Islands. It would certainly absolve Maria, her father and Johnny from the insider trading accusations. But Johnny and Maria had to ask themselves if they wanted to turn the tables on Mr. Worshaw. After what they had been through, would it be enough for them to simply walk away unscathed? Or, did they need to make sure Worshaw was nailed for whatever insider trading he participated in? If they took that route, it meant they had one more step to complete. They would have to determine the individual ownership behind the corporate accounts at the Grand Cayman Bank and be sure, in some way, they were linked to Bradley Worshaw.

Johnny told Maria he was almost certain Worshaw knew what they were up to. He described Worshaw's mood change of the last few days. He also told her he hadn't seen Alex for about a week and he could be anywhere. If they decided to make the trip to George Town to check the ownership records for the various Grand Cayman accounts, the level of risk increased exponentially. Bill told them he could arrange to have private security waiting for them in George Town. After some back and forth, Johnny and Maria decided they had come too far not to take the final step. Bill would stay on the Isle of Man in case they had further business with Wilshire. He now had the pass codes to all the accounts if he needed to access them.

Johnny and Maria booked a flight to George Town through London. They were tired, still a little scared, but ready to put the final pieces in place. Despite being way beyond their comfort zone, they would now be the aggressors. Defense had given way to offense as the game moved to the final stages.

Thirty Eight

THE FLIGHT ARRANGEMENTS WERE the same, with Johnny in the rear of the plane, Maria in the front. When they landed in Georgetown, Johnny walked off the runway ramp into the terminal and did not immediately see Maria. He thought she might have gone to the rest room, but when she didn't appear after a few minutes, he started to get panicky. He wanted to ask a police officer or female airport worker to check the woman's restroom, but seeing none, he went in himself. He got some strange looks, but after a quick inspection, it was apparent his wife was missing.

Johnny called Bill Palmer's cell phone. When Bill answered, Johnny said, "Bill, its Johnny. Maria's missing."

"Where are you, Johnny?" He asked.

"I'm at the airport in George Town. Where are the security guys?"

Bill responded, "They're waiting for you in front of the main terminal. They're in a white Ford."

"OK, Stay on the phone for a second while I go look." Fortunately, for Johnny the line to pass through immigration was short so he was out on the street in a couple of minutes. He saw the white Ford with two black men in it and motioned to the driver as he hung up with Bill.

He introduced himself to the driver and said, "my wife's been kidnapped. Did you see anyone who looks like this leaving the terminal?" as he flashed a wallet sized photo for the men to see.

The driver, whose name was Sumner said, "I just saw the lady walk out of the terminal next to a tall man. They were picked up in small blue car by a driver who sped off rather quickly."

"OK, lets go after 'em," Johnny said.

Johnny got in the car and Sumner hit the gas pedal. As they moved quickly out of the airport complex, he realized they had been followed all the way from Chicago. Whoever grabbed Maria at the George Town airport knew she'd be getting off the plane before Johnny and would be vulnerable for a few minutes. For whatever it was worth, when they left the Isle of Man, Johnny had taken the disk with all the bank account information Bill Palmer made for them. He did not want Maria carrying it. Now, it might be his best hope of finding her unharmed.

Grand Cayman is not a large island and there is only one main road which runs up the West Coast, where most of the tourist hotels are located. There is a small road leading out of the airport which creates a bottleneck for traffic coming in and out. Once that road merges into island traffic, the bottleneck ends. If they were lucky, the blue car would be held up in traffic and they would be able to spot it. From the front passenger seat, Sumner's partner, Peter was on his cell phone talking in an island dialect Johnny couldn't follow. When there were breaks in the conversation, Peter told Johnny he had called some other security people on the island and they would be on the lookout for the blue car. While all this was going on, Johnny called Maria's cell phone, but was connected directly to her voice message.

They reached the main road to the island without seeing the blue car. They turned left and proceeded North along the road to Seven Mile Beach with Peter working his phone as they went. Sumner drove slowly enough so they could look at the parking areas in front of the hotels as they passed by. Peter explained the people he was on the phone with would drive South and they would meet in the middle. If the blue car was on the main road, they would find it. After about a half hour, they met the other security group. No one had seen the blue car.

Both security details would now patrol the hotel parking lots and secondary streets. Johnny stayed with Sumner and Peter as they turned back to the South. They went through one hotel parking lot after another. They went back into the downtown area of George Town. Peter was on and off the phone the whole time. By just after 9:00 p.m. it was dark and they had found nothing. Maria was gone.

Johnny was exhausted and sick to his stomach. They had pushed it too far this time. He had no business allowing Maria to come with him to George Town. He would never forgive himself if something happened to her.

He talked to Sumner and Peter about going to the Cayman police. They had some reservations about that. They explained, politely, that the police might not have enough resources to put on the case immediately, but nevertheless might order Sumner and Peter not to pursue it further until they could investigate. This would mean no one would be actively working on it. Sumner suggested they wait until morning and look again for the blue car.

Johnny was driven to his hotel and dropped off by Sumner and Peter who arranged to pick him up at 8:00 a.m. the next morning. In the meantime, one security patrol would stay on the streets looking for the blue car, while the other watched the hotel where Johnny was staying.

Johnny couldn't eat and he couldn't sleep. He was numb with fear and his brain wasn't functioning well at all. If Brad and Alex wanted to stop them from going to the FBI, why didn't they just wait until Johnny and Maria were both together and make sure they disappeared in a boating accident or something. It would be much easier and cleaner than doing it one at a time. Of course if Johnny and Maria were together, there was always the chance that they could put up a fight. But if they grabbed Maria first, they knew without a doubt, they could get to Johnny whenever they were ready. So now he was on their time.

It was a little before 1:00 a.m. in the morning when his cell phone rang. The screen flashed a 312 area code, so he knew it was them. "Yes," Johnny answered the phone.

"Johnny," the voice on the other end spoke. "You know who this is." It was really not a question as he recognized Alex voice.

"Yes," again.

"We need the disk."

"OK," he responded.

"I'll give you the address. Come in a cab and make sure your body guards don't follow you, if you want to see Maria again."

"Can I talk to her please?" He asked.

He could hear the phone being passed and then her voice, "Johnny, I'm OK."

Alex took the phone back and said, "All we want is the disk. Once we have that there won't be any reason to harm you. We'll have everything we need."

He gave Johnny an address and told him the house he would be coming to had an entry gate. He should get out of the cab and wait. Once the cab was gone, he would be escorted into the house. He told Johnny again, to be sure he wasn't followed.

Thirty Nine

He wore the old clothes, baseball cap and sun glasses which had become his traveling uniform. Fitting for the occasion, he thought.

He waited for the cab to pull in front of the hotel and ducked quickly into the back seat without being spotted by the men in the white Ford. As they drove away, he looked out the back window and they did not follow.

The cab wound its way North on the beach road and after about five miles turned a couple of times and stopped. He got out, paid the driver and as the cab drove off he turned to see a large house set about fifty yards behind a six foot high gate with metal pickets. From out of nowhere a slightly built man appeared behind the gate and opened it. Johnny entered and followed the man into the house. They walked through a side door, down a half flight of stairs and into a large, poorly lit room. On the far side of the room, Maria sat in front of a sophisticated looking set of computer equipment, with Brad Worshaw to her side. Alex Franklin was stationed about ten feet behind them with a gun pointed at Maria.

"Over here Johnny," Alex said as he turned the gun on Johnny. He motioned for Johnny to walk toward him. As Johnny approached, Alex took out a set of handcuffs and handed them to the man who Johnny had followed into the house. Johnny was told to place his hands behind his back and the handcuffs were closed around each of his wrists. He was then escorted to a chair about six feet from Alex and told to sit.

"Did you bring the disk?" Alex asked.

"Yes, its in my side pocket," Johnny responded.

Alex walked over, reached into the pocket on the right side of Johnny's jacket and extracted the disk. He took it over to Brad who spoke for the first time. "I'm sorry it came to this Johnny. Maria is going through all the files on her lap top now, so we can be sure none of the bank records are there. As soon as she's done, we'll download the disk and erase everything except the cash deposits from the joint trades with her dad shown on the Oak Bank account. That way, Alex and I can keep the disk with our thanks to you for nailing the insider trading case against you. We can hold that for the FBI or SEC, if you two decide you want to make mention of this meeting. Since you'll have no other evidence to support any charges you might want to bring against us, we won't need to hold you."

With that, Brad turned toward Maria and told her to continue what she was doing. Alex turned the gun back on Maria, but glanced back and forth between where she was working on her lap top and where Johnny was sitting.

Johnny made a quick assessment of the situation. Brad did not appear to be armed and he was concentrating, watching the screen on Maria's lap top to see what files popped up. He would be occupied with that. Alex was splitting his attention between Maria and Johnny, mostly watching her screen. The chair Johnny sat in was about six feet from Alex' side. If he made a move toward Alex, Johnny was sure Alex would have plenty of time to turn the gun on him and fire. Even if Johnny could move fast enough to avoid being shot, his hands were cuffed behind him, so he couldn't put up a fight.

From what Johnny could tell, the smallish man who lead him into the house had gone back upstairs and didn't pose an immediate threat.

He had to come up with something. There was no way he was going to test Brad's promise to let them go. And Alex certainly hadn't made the same commitment, now that the disk was in their possession. So what could he do?

Well, for one thing, he could move his hands from side to side. He tried this as Alex looked away and found he could move his hands far enough to the side to touch his cell phone, resting in the case clipped to his belt. He certainly couldn't dial any numbers with his hands in cuffs. But wait a minute! Hadn't the last call he received been from Alex' cell phone? If he could simply press the right keys to redial, Alex' phone would ring, temporarily diverting his attention. This would give Johnny time to lunge at Alex and try to knock the gun out of his hand. From that point on he would have to fight with his legs, and hope Maria could handle the aging Brad Worshaw. She was small, but in great shape. He gave her the odds.

He had to try and remember which keys to press. He was sure it was one key to pull up the number of the last call received and then the green key to dial it. If he was right, he should press the first key now so he could be one key away when the right time came. He had no way to actually look at the phone, so he took his best shot at pressing the first key in the sequence. He wouldn't know if he got it right until he went for the second key.

It took several minutes until Maria was done going through all the files on her lap top. When she was done, Worshaw took the disk and placed in the portable drive. He told Maria to start pulling up the files on the disk so he could see them on the screen. Alex was now paying exclusive attention to what they were doing. Brad told Maria to start erasing the files and Alex said, "Not so fast, Brad." He pointed the gun at Maria and said to her, "You can stop now Ms. Brandt, or is it Ms. Blake?"

Brad turned to Alex with a truly puzzled look on his face and said, "what are you talking about?"

Alex, looking at Maria now said "take the disk out and bring it here." Then he looked back to Brad and said, "Frankly, Brad, I have two customers who'll pay me a lot of money for the information on this disk and you're not one of them."

Brad looked at Alex in disbelief as Maria popped the disk out of the drive. She obeyed Alex and brought the disk to him. He took it from her and reached into his jacket pocket, producing another set of hand cuffs. He told Maria to place the cuffs on Brad, after he put his hands behind his back. While this was going on, Brad said to Alex, "C'mon man, we've been through a lot together. If you need a bigger pay check, we can work it out."

"I already have," was Alex' answer. "I just needed Mr. and Mrs. America here to do the grunt work. The rest is easy."

With Brad handcuffed, Alex had narrowed the field down. Johnny decided it was now or never. He moved his hands slowly to his right side and placed his thumb against what he hoped was the green key. He pressed and waited for what seemed to be an eternity. When Alex' phone rang, he instinctively looked down at it. Johnny drove forward with his head down and caught Alex flush in the mid section. He could hear the wind come out of Alex' mouth as the gun and Alex dropped separately to the ground. With Alex on the ground, Johnny swung his right leg back and then forward with all his might, aiming at Alex right side.

The ex marine still had his battle instincts, and although wounded, moved quickly enough to avoid the kick. He rolled to his side and grabbed the gun, while Johnny, trying to regain his balance from the missed kick, went to his knees. Alex slowly got to his feet while he raised the gun and pointed it at Johnny. With rage in his eyes, Johnny could see him start to pull his finger backward on the trigger.

The first bullet zipped over Johnny's head from behind and caught Alex in the left shoulder, knocking him back, but not down. From out of the corner of his eye, Johnny could see two people dressed fully in black, with black knit caps pulled down tightly over their heads, run into the room. They quickly took positions behind furniture on opposite sides of room. Each carried a hand gun. Alex quickly fired in the direction of one of them, but missed. The other rose up from behind a large leather chair and fired the bullet that killed Alex.

For several seconds after Alex went down, no one moved. Johnny could see Maria was in shock, but otherwise unharmed. Brad much the same. The two in black moved slowly from where they were and looked cautiously around the room. When they were sure no one else posed a threat to them, the smaller of the two removed the black knit cap. As she did so, her long blonde hair fell down around her shoulders. She turned to face Johnny and he could see it was Ellen Caulfield.

Johnny wasn't sure if it was the exhaustion, the shock of witnessing his first gun battle from close range, or the adrenalin rush leaving his body, but he could not get his mouth to say a word. Ellen walked over to him and helped him to his feet, while the other person in black, a man with dark hair, began to talk to Maria.

Johnny ended up back in the chair he had just bolted out of as Ellen searched Alex' pockets for the key to the handcuffs. She found it and released him.

Johnny stammered, "There's another one of them upstairs."

"I know, "said Ellen. "He won't be a problem. We have people right behind us who'll be here to remove the bodies."

"Johnny," she said, "I have a lot to tell you about what happened here. I'll understand if you don't want to hear it now."

"I do," he said, "but let me see Maria first."

He got up, walked over to his wife and held her very tightly for a long time. She sobbed in his arms, almost uncontrollably at first, then she worked herself out of it. When she had gained control, Johnny turned her over to Ellen's partner who said he would take her outside.

Ellen and Johnny moved to a corner of the room while Brad was led away by one of the second group of FBI agents to arrive at the house.

When they were alone she said, "We've been watching Jonathan Blanchard and Brad Worshaw for a long time. Everything I told you was true. I did graduate from law school and I did work for the SEC. After my second year there, I was recruited by the FBI to go under cover at Blanchard and Stone. Blanchard was looking for an associate with SEC experience and that plus my legs got me in the door. No pun intended. They realized without someone on the inside, it might be very difficult to penetrate his shield. He's a very clever man."

She went on, "I don't know if you're aware, but Worshaw worked for Blanchard right after they sold Worshaw's company in 1995. They actually started Investech together as co-owners, with Worshaw at the helm. The deal was they'd throw each other business, inside and out. Since they're both crooks, it was only a matter of time until the double crossing started. We think Blanchard went first when he helped Frank Bishop at Frontier cook up the phony audit scheme. It was easy since Blanchard already had a bunch of dummy companies set up for just such an occasion. Meanwhile, Worshaw had already decided to branch out by taking on some investors on the side. He passed along his insider knowledge for a piece of the action. Since Blanchard didn't tell Worshaw he rigged the Frontier price, Worshaw went ahead and had his investors buy into Frontier right before the merger. Imagine how pissed they were when the Westpac stock they got in the merger started to tank right after the deal closed.

The one thing Worshaw and Blanchard agreed on was the insider stock trading set up involving you and your wife's family. Worshaw created the paper trail and Blanchard was to take care of the legalities. They both saw it as a way to be sure they made additional profits from a settlement with BCC. As it turned out, Warshaw was going to need the settlement money to cover his ass with his investors. That, plus profits on the deals he was counting on you to bring in."

Johnny now spoke, "So you knew this the whole time we were working on the Burgess deal?"

"I knew bits and pieces. It was, and has been a moving target. But, obviously I knew you were set up the whole time.

And I want to tell you, nothing really happened that night in Denver. You fell asleep on me. If you hadn't, I'm really not sure what I would have done. You're a terrific guy and I wasn't necessarily prepared to stop," her eyes averted his as she finished the last sentence.

This time from Johnny, "how does Alex fit into all this?"

"He's been Brad's under cover guy for years and he got tired of seeing Brad sit on a fortune. For the past few months, he's been talking to Blanchard and Worshaw's investors about selling them the keys to Worshaw's castle, as soon as he had the whole banking empire figured out. He just needed someone with the tech skills to package it for him. That little disk you and Maria made is worth a lot to everyone involved in this case. For all we know, he might have decided to kill Worshaw and keep the money himself."

Johnny took in everything she had to say and then countered, "Ellen, I don't want to be accusatory here since you just saved my life, but knowing all this, didn't you let me and Maria get way out on a limb to help you solve this case?"

"Johnny, you were going there anyway. The truth is we were always a step behind you. But, thank God we caught up tonight. The FBI could learn a few tricks from both of you."

The debriefing was over for the night. In fact, it was already daybreak by the time they started to clear the crime scene. One of the FBI agents offered to drive Johnny and Maria back to their hotel. The island vacation Johnny and Maria had hoped for was about to start.

Forty

THE NEXT THREE DAYS were a mixture of work and play. Johnny and Maria met with the FBI for a few hours each day and had the rest of the time for themselves. As soon as they could, they called her father and gave him a condensed version of the story. He was greatly relieved to hear from them. The FBI had offered to take over the surveillance of his house, so the private security detail was released. The FBI would stay on until they were sure the threat to them was over.

Johnny also called Charlie and told him as much as the FBI would allow him to say. He assured Charlie that he and Maria were fine and that the threatened suit against BCC was about to be dropped. He couldn't go into any more details on the phone, but BCC wouldn't be hearing from Jonathan Blanchard again.

After the third day, it was all play for five more days. Johnny and Maria made good on all their plans for the vacation. For the better part of a week they helped each other with stress reduction, sometimes more than once a day. At the end of their time on Grand Cayman, a radiant and relaxed Maria looked at Johnny and said, "promise me our crime solving days are over."

On the last day before they flew back, the Wall Street Journal broke the story on the front page under the headline, "Westpac/Frontier Insider Trading Scandal Revealed". The article was the first in a series of five that ran for a week. Because the relationship between Blanchard and Worshaw involved so many other mergers, the scope of the story went way beyond that one transaction. Although the Journal said the final tally wasn't in, they estimated that, over the years, at least ten other mergers involved some form of insider trading. They had each amassed a fortune. The amount of money went well into the billions.

The Journal article mentioned Johnny and Maria by name and gave some background on their association with BCC and the case in general. It went as far as to say they were able to help the FBI, "by providing crucial evidence obtained in very creative ways." The writers also were kind to BCC by not mentioning details of the Frontier audit. Because the story was so high profile, it was carried in several other publications including local newspapers. When Johnny and Maria got home, they were deluged with calls. They were the couple of the hour.

The Today show called from New York and wanted to fly them in to be interviewed by its anchor, Stan Tower. Mary Pruitt wanted an interview on her show as well. Johnny and Maria could fly to New York, do both interviews and be back in three days, so they decided to go. But before they left, Johnny called Todd Pulaski at Burgess Systems to catch up with him. Todd, of course, had read the Wall Street Journal accounts and praised Johnny for what he had done. He told Johnny that Scott Borden was doing a great job in Johnny's absence and would complete the merger with

Jack Miller and the rest of the Investech team. If the FBI decided to shut Investech down, Scott and Jack would be able to bring their team intact to another investment banking firm. Either way Burgess would be in good hands. Todd was sorry that Johnny wouldn't be around for the finale, but reminded him they had a skiing date that winter.

In New York, the Today show put Johnny and Maria up at the Four Seasons hotel. The staff of the show prepared them both for the interview. Stan would ask Johnny about his work history with BCC, how he first learned that he was accused of insider trading and why he decided to work with Investech. He would ask Maria about the "creative methods" she used to uncover evidence in the case. Maria told the staff that the FBI had asked her to keep a lot of that confidential, so there wouldn't be too much to reveal. But, she could say she now knew more about the advantages off shore banking than she ever expected.

Being invited to the Mary Pruitt show was a big treat for Maria, as she watched the show whenever she could. Their three days in New York was a whirlwind of excitement, but left them tired and ready to be home.

When they returned this time, the number of calls and requests for interviews had started to subside. Charlie left a message indicating he really wanted to see Johnny and there were calls from two other accounting firms as well. After a couple of days, Johnny went down to the Gateway building to meet with Charlie, Bill and Andy. They greeted him warmly and listened attentively as he filled them in on all the details of the events on the Isle of Man and the Cayman Islands. When he was done, they told him they would be honored if he would return to work at BCC. He promised them he would consider their offer and call them the next week.

The two other accounting firms who called were well known in the industry. One of the firms wanted Johnny to consider working with them in their technology consulting division. The other was a forensic accounting firm who wanted to talk to both Johnny and Maria about working with them as a team.

By the week after they returned from New York, things had settled down and they both had time to think about the future. Although Johnny appreciated the offer from BCC, he realized basically nothing would be different for him at his old job. He knew Charlie would do everything he could to get Johnny back in the groove, but it would never be the same. His days at BCC were over, no matter what.

The offer from the firm that wanted both Johnny and Maria as a team started them thinking. They had found that, under pressure, they could work quite well together and it might be fun to give it a try. For profit, this time. But the job would involve a lot of out of town travel for both of them. Maria, after their recent experience, was opposed to that and, to some extent, Johnny was as well. But they could start their own consulting firm and choose their assignments. There might be some travel at first, but eventually they could hire a staff to work with them. This idea had the most appeal for them.

The Investech, Westpac, Frontier matter had drained some of their finances and left them with no regular income. The big money opportunity for Johnny at Investech was gone, even though it was only a mirage anyway. After the intense pressure they had been under, the shocking conclusion of the case in Grand Cayman and the excitement in New York, facing reality was more difficult than Johnny or Maria had expected. They were mentally unable to make any firm business plans and their money would only last so long.

On the third Friday after they returned from New York, Johnny was home working on the lawn, while Maria was out with the kids. A Fedex truck stopped in front of the house and delivered a package addressed to Johnny and Maria Brandt. The sender was William Palmer of the Palmer Consulting Group in Kansas City. Johnny took the package and went inside to the kitchen table. He opened the package and inside were two envelopes. He opened the smaller one first. It was a letter addressed to both of them. It read:

> Dear Johnny and Maria:
>
> I hope this correspondence finds you well and returning to your normal lives after the commotion of the past few months.
>
> Johnny, you will recall when we met last in Kansas City, I indicated to you I would accept the assignment of working with you and Maria, advancing my own expenses, in exchange for fifty percent of whatever I could recover. You were entirely focused on resolving the charges against you and your family and, I think, did not respond to my proposal. Nevertheless, I proceeded on that basis. I took the risk of coming up empty handed because I owe Maria so much.
>
> After you left the Isle of Man, I checked out of the hotel we were staying at and moved to a more out of the way location. I assume Alex Franklin would have come looking for me after he finished with you two. When I received Johnny's desperate call from the Grand Cayman airport, I immediately called the FBI in New York. Obviously, none too soon. About a day after they came to your aid, I was joined by agent Ellen Caulfield in Douglas. We

spent the last three weeks sorting through the bank accounts we uncovered and, I'm happy to report, she is overseeing the process of returning money to everyone who was scammed by Brad Worshaw and Jonathan Blanchard.

Along the way, we discovered a few bank accounts that had deposits not related to any illegal activities. In fact, it appears that Worshaw actually knew how to make money without breaking the law. Agent Caulfield decided Worshaw would have no use for this money, where he is going. She was genuinely appreciative of the effort we expended on behalf of the FBI. She also spoke highly of her work with you, Johnny, on the Burgess merger. Accordingly, she had no problem with me deleting those accounts from the list we supplied to the FBI.

I have enclosed, separately, a schedule of those accounts together with a list of my expenses. Please be sure to dispose of this information after you are done with it. I trust you will find everything is in order and that you will recall the proposal I'm referring to above. I, of course, meant that I would retain fifty percent of any recoveries and forward the balance to you.

I have enjoyed working with and knowing you both, and hope that you will call on me if I can be of service in the future.

Sincerely,
Bill Palmer

Johnny opened the second envelope. Inside was a set of ledger sheets with the names of various bank accounts and a list of Bill Palmer's expenses. The last expense was an item labeled 'referral fee to Gus' in the amount of One Hundred Thousand Dollars. The bottom line on the last schedule was labeled Net Recovery in the total amount of Eight Million Three Hundred Fifty Seven Thousand Dollars. Attached to the schedule was a certified check made payable to Johnny and Maria Brandt for Four Million One Hundred Seventy Eight Thousand, Five Hundred Dollars.

The End